CC

Suddenly, th

rear seat with a sound like a battering ram striking sheet metal.

Several things happened almost simultaneously then. First and foremost, I veered wildly from side to side, the jarring impact on the roof causing me to momentarily lose control of the vehicle. On its part, the car seemed to drop ominously towards the ground, the suspension audibly strained by the jolt it had received, and I was shocked that the undercarriage didn't scrape the ground. As it was, the car started making a number of weird noises, and I got the distinct impression that something internal had broken or come loose.

That said, I immediately understood what had happened: our pursuer hadn't lost track of us. Instead, he had made an incredible leap that not only covered the distance between us but also timed it perfectly.

I heard Stacy trying to tell me something, but the sudden screech of tearing metal drew my attention. Taking my eyes off the road for a second, I looked up and saw a portion of the roof being torn away above the center section of the front seat. It was our erstwhile passenger, of course, ripping open the roof like he was opening a giant can of sardines.

He eyed me for a second through the hole he'd made, and I saw something akin to a malicious gleam in his eye. Under normal circumstances, I probably would have teleported him a zillion miles away, but then Stacy, who had been yelling nonstop in my brain, somehow got through to me.

<Don't use your powers!> she ordered.

<You talk like I have a choice!> I countered as the muscleman on the roof suddenly reached into the car.

CONJURATION

Kid Sensation Series
Sensation: A Superhero Novel
Mutation (A Kid Sensation Novel)
Infiltration (A Kid Sensation Novel)
Revelation (A Kid Sensation Novel)
Coronation (A Kid Sensation Novel)
Replication (A Kid Sensation Novel)
Incarnation (A Kid Sensation Novel)
Isolation (A Kid Sensation Novel)
Conjuration (A Kid Sensation Novel)

Kid Sensation Companion Series
Amped
Mouse's Tale (An Alpha League Supers Novel)

The Warden Series
Warden (Book 1: Wendigo Fever)
Warden (Book 2: Lure of the Lamia)
Warden (Book 3: Attack of the Aswang)

The Fringe Worlds
Terminus (Fringe Worlds #1)
Efferus (Fringe Worlds #2)
Ignotus (Fringe Worlds #3)

Boxed Sets
The Kid Sensation Series (Books 1–3)
The Warden Series (Books 1–3)
Worlds of Wonder

Short Stories
Extraction: A Kid Sensation Story

CONJURATION
A Kid Sensation Novel

By

Kevin Hardman

CONJURATION

Cover Design by Isikol

Edited by Faith Williams, The Atwater Group

This book is published by I&H Recherche Publishing.

ISBN: 978-1-937666-56-9

Printed in the U.S.A.

CONJURATION

ACKNOWLEDGMENTS

I would like to thank the following for their help with this book: GOD first and foremost, since all the blessings in my life come from Him; my family, who continue to love and support me through good times and bad; and my readers, who are the best fans on the planet!

CONJURATION

Thank you for purchasing this book! If, after reading, you find that you enjoyed it, please feel free to leave a review on the site from which it was purchased.

Also, if you would like to be notified when I release new books, please subscribe to my mailing list via the following link: http://eepurl.com/C5a45

Finally, for those who may be interested in following me, I have included my website and social media info:

Website: http://www.kevinhardmanauthor.com/

BookBub: https://www.bookbub.com/authors/kevin-hardman?follow=true

Amazon Author Page: https://www.amazon.com/Kevin-Hardman/e/B00CLTY3YM

Facebook: www.facebook.com/kevin.hardman.967

Twitter: https://twitter.com/kevindhardman

Goodreads: https://www.goodreads.com/author/show/7075077.Kevin_Hardman

And if you like my work, please consider supporting me on Patreon: https://www.patreon.com/kevinhardman

Chapter 1

<I don't like this,> I said telepathically.

<You know what I don't like?> asked Stacy rhetorically. <Getting paired with super-powered teens who are untested in the field. Get used to it; we all have our crosses to bear.>

<Hey!> I shot back. <I'm not untested! I've done plenty, including —>

<Yeah, yeah, yeah. I read your file. You saved the planet a couple of times. Big whoop. We do that on our lunch break around here.>

<Great. Then what do you need me for?>

<Because you're expendable. Now get moving.>

Mentally, I groaned. Stacy was the agent I was paired with on this, my first official assignment for Gray, the enigmatic head of a secret government agency. Like me, she was telepathic — or maybe it was a he. Stacy's voice was completely androgynous, so I honestly couldn't tell (although mentally I had dubbed my erstwhile partner a "she"). Moreover, Stacy was geographically located at some unknown spot, so I couldn't use my empathic senses to get a read on her emotionally (which might have helped me determine her gender).

<So, there's a dossier on me?> I asked as I started moving.

<If you're smart enough to be on the team, you already know the answer to that.>

<So why didn't I get one on you?>

<We operate on a need-to-know basis. And guess what? You don't need to know.>

<Well, people like to know who they're working with. Helps them bond and function better as a unit.>

<It's overrated. I know all about you, and it's not helping our work relationship.>

<Come on, we're in each other's heads, to a certain extent.>

<Look, Kid. There's a reason they keep a wall between us, so to speak. If somebody stepped up to me right now and blew my brains out, you'd still be able to finish the mission. You don't know me, so there'd be no grief, anguish, or anything like that slowing you down.>

<Then why'd they give you a dossier on me?>

Radio silence.

<Come on — give me *some*thing.>

<Fine, what do you want to know — middle name? Hobbies? Who I'm dating?>

<That's a start.>

<Fine. Middle name is Pat. My significant other is named Courtney. For a hobby, I like movies — romances and sci-fi. Now get back to work.>

Telepathically, I rolled my eyes, but continued moving, walking down a sidewalk in a major city of what was formerly an Eastern Bloc country. How I'd come to be here was something of a story in itself.

****

Basically, maybe four hours earlier, I'd been at home when I finally received the call I'd been dreading, but which I knew was inevitable: Gray reaching out to tell me it was time to earn my keep.

"How quickly can you get to Paris?" he'd asked.

CONJURATION

"About two seconds if I drag my feet," I'd replied, wondering why he'd even bothered with the question since he knew that — as a teleporter — I could get almost anywhere instantly.

"Great," Gray had stated, then spent maybe a minute giving me instructions that I immediately sensed were subpar before hanging up.

Afterwards, despite being a teleporter, it had actually taken me two minutes to get to the City of Lights. (The delay had been caused by me reaching out to my mentor, Mouse, to let him know that Gray was finally collecting his pound of flesh.)

I'd popped up in Gay Paree at the Eiffel Tower. Once there — in accordance with the instructions from Gray — I'd waited on a street corner at the foot of the tower until a nondescript black car pulled up. Two of Gray's agents — the proverbial Men in Black — had gotten out and approached me; a few minutes later, I found myself in the back seat of their car, being whisked towards a private airfield.

At that juncture, I'd been hustled aboard a jet and then endured a roughly two-hour flight to some Eastern European nation, the name of which I never really caught. There were only two people on the flight with me: a thirty-something Woman in Black, and a slack-jawed middle-aged man with a slight build, who   from what I could tell — had either been drugged or knocked unconscious. (I suppose there was a pilot and co-pilot as well, but he or they stayed barricaded in the cockpit for the duration of the flight.)

En route to our destination, my female companion instructed me to take on the appearance of our unconscious fellow passenger. Her directive indicated that she knew something about me — that I was a shapeshifter at the very least, but not necessarily that I was the much-heralded Kid Sensation. However, given who she worked for, she likely knew everything about me, including what I'd had for breakfast that morning.

It had only taken me a minute to do as instructed, using a small mirror that the woman had handy in order to double-check my shapeshifting efforts. When I was done, the woman had given me a once-over. Seemingly satisfied, she had then tossed me a trench coat, which I put on. Following this, she'd handed me two items: a passport and a wallet. The former contained a picture of the man whose identity I had just assumed. (Apparently he went by the name Pawel Sobczak.) The wallet held the usual items: Mr. Sobczak's driver's license, a little cash, some bank cards, etcetera.

"Shouldn't I put on his clothes?" I'd asked at one point, gesturing towards Sobczak. "I mean, if I'm supposed to be him —"

"That's the purpose of the trench coat," the woman had interjected. "You could be dressed like a punk rocker underneath and no one would notice."

"Well, what about his voice?" I'd countered. "I still don't know what he sounds like."

"Not important."

I'd given her a surprised look. "You don't think it's important that I be able to mimic this guy's voice?"

"You won't be speaking."

I'd frowned, trying to figure out how to interpret that comment. "So he's mute?"

"No, but he's not a native English speaker, and you don't know his mother tongue."

CONJURATION

"But if I heard him speak English, I could mimic the accent."

The woman let out a frustrated sigh. "Let's try this another way: when the time comes, just don't speak."

"And when, exactly, will that time arrive?"

"At present, it's while you're on my watch."

Following this statement, we'd spent the rest of the flight in silence (which was how the woman seemed to prefer it). I still didn't know exactly what I was supposed to be doing, but figured someone would tell me soon enough — and it turned out I was right.

Upon landing at what appeared to be another private airfield, I had disembarked to find a small compact car waiting for me, while not too far away I could make out a cityscape. At that point, the woman from the plane had tossed me a keyring. There were about fifteen keys on it, one of which was actually a key fob for a vehicle. Using it, I unlocked the car and got inside. However, I'd barely closed the door before I received a call from Gray, at which point he finally told me what all the skullduggery was about.

"We need you to retrieve a package," he'd said.

"A package?" I'd repeated, not bothering to hide my disdain. "Really? Don't you have, like, a billion guys over here who could handle that for you? Instead, you had to make me cross an entire ocean, fly across a conti—"

"I'd love to hear your list of complaints, but we're on a timetable," he'd stated, cutting me off.

He had then told me that there was a GPS device in the car with a preprogrammed destination, and I was to follow the route indicated. Lastly, he'd told me that another agent would reach out shortly and would be serving as my primary contact for the remainder of the assignment. He had then hung up without giving me a chance to ask any questions. Seconds later, Stacy began telepathically tapping on my mental shields.

****

Ultimately, the GPS directions had landed me in the city I'd seen — specifically, in a residential area of town where Sobczak lived. Once there, I had — at Stacy's insistence — parked on the street. Judging by the number of cars lining the road in both directions, this was common practice. However, it was at that point — before I'd even exited the vehicle — that I started getting the bad vibes that I was complaining to Stacy about. Basically, someone had recognized "me" and waved. On my part, I had simply waved back and fiddled around in the car like I was doing something until they moved on, but the interaction had highlighted a problem.

Basically, I was in Sobczak's neighborhood, which meant that people here knew him. Friends, neighbors, colleagues — they were likely to be abundant in this area. Although it was night and there wasn't much foot traffic, there was enough of it that I'd probably bump into someone who knew the person I was pretending to be.

Normally, for a shapeshifter, that wouldn't be a problem. The whole point of pretending to be someone else was generally to fool people, so some type of interaction wasn't entirely unexpected. In this instance, however, failing to have heard Sobczak's voice, among other things, put me at a distinct disadvantage (not to mention the fact that I didn't speak the language). Undeterred, Stacy had merely stressed that I get out of the car, keep my head down, and move quickly towards the apartment building where, per the GPS, Sobczak resided. (Truth be told, however, I had actually parked on the street behind his apartment complex, meaning I'd have to circle the block to get to the front entrance.)

<I *really* don't like this,> I reiterated as I walked along the sidewalk, returning a friendly wave from a passing couple.

<You can safely assume that I heard you the first jillion times you said that,> Stacy replied. <If it'll get you to shut up about it, I'll state that your reservations are formally noted on the record.>

I almost laughed. It didn't take a genius to figure out that pretty much everything that had happened since I'd arrived in Paris was pretty much *off* the record.

<Where are you?> Stacy asked, cutting into my thoughts.

<Just passed the back of Sobczak's building,> I answered. <Any particular reason I can't use the rear door?>

<That area's mostly used as a loading dock — usually for carting furniture back and forth when people are moving in or out. Plus, it's typically locked at night.>

<So it'll look suspicious if I try to go in that way,> I surmised.

<Well, look at that,> Stacy droned sardonically. <No flies on *you*.>

Ignoring her comment, I trudged on. Fortunately, although I passed two other people as I circled the block, they didn't seem to know Sobczak (or else they weren't on speaking terms with him). Shortly thereafter, I found myself approaching the stoop that led up to the building's front entrance. Near the door were three guys who, empathically, gave off menacing vibes. They eyed me warily as I walked up the steps.

<Hmmm,> I droned mentally. <Got some thugs hanging out around the front door.>

<Good,> Stacy commented. <That means the package is probably inside.>

<Wonderful,> I shot back sarcastically as I reached the door. Although the trio outside kept watching me, none of them seemed intent on stopping me from entering as I reached into my pocket for the keys I'd been given earlier. At that moment, however, a young woman exited the building.

Acting on instinct, I grabbed the door and held it for the woman as she came outside. Apparently a neighbor of Sobczak, she smiled and said something to me that I took as some kind of greeting. Putting a hand to my mouth, I coughed a couple of times like I was having some kind of attack and slipped inside, giving her a wave with my other hand as the door swung closed behind me.

<I'm in the lobby,> I announced to Stacy.

<All right, there should be a set of elevators located near the center of the building,> Stacy noted. <Head there and—>

<I'm taking the stairs,> I blurted out, interrupting her as I began walking towards a stairway located off to one side.

<The elevator would be quicker.>

<Right now, I'm more interested in the lay of the land,> I declared as I went up the stairs. <I'm here without backup, I don't speak the language, and — to be honest — I'm not even sure what country I'm in. But I'm at least going to know where the stairs are in this place and the

layout of this building to some extent, just in case I have to make a dash or teleport at some point.>

<I wouldn't do too much of that,> Stacy advised. <You may be fairly anonymous in your private life, but Kid Sensation is a known quantity. You start showcasing a bunch of your powers — like teleporting, turning invisible, and so on — and people are going to figure out who you are.>

<I'm aware of the fact that I need to keep a low profile, but there's nothing suspicious about taking the stairs.>

<There's nothing suspicious about it when you know where you're going. Do you even know what floor Sobczak lives on?>

<Third floor, Apartment D,> I answered. <It was on his driver's license.>

Stacy didn't immediately comment, but I got the feeling that she was impressed. (Of course, this was guesswork to an extent on my part. I couldn't read the language on Sobczak's license, but addresses are pretty formulaic and recognizing basic numbers and letters is elementary.)

Continuing to plod up the stairs, I reached the second floor. Unlike an enclosed stairwell, I was on a stairway that simply opened up on each level of the building, giving me a pretty good view of the layout. More importantly, glancing at a couple of apartment doors, I got an idea of where Apartment D should be on each floor.

<You might want to step on it,> Stacy suggested as I continued up the stairway. <The package could be moved at any time.>

<I'm supposed to be a middle-aged man with a slight, unathletic build,> I reminded her. <I can't go

bounding up the steps three at a time. Besides, I'm here now.>

I stepped out onto the third floor as I finished my statement — and immediately spotted trouble in the form of two men kind of idling in the hallway.

One was huge — a hulking, dark-haired brute about seven feet tall and made of corded muscle. The other was slender, pale, about my height (so roughly six feet tall), and hairless. And by hairless, I didn't mean that he was bald; he actually appeared to be completely hair-free: no five o'clock shadow, no eyebrows, no eyelashes, nothing...

I swiftly conveyed all this to Stacy, including the fact that these two also had the same minacious air about them as the trio on the front stoop.

<Okay, they're probably supers,> she opined.

<Ya think?> I shot back sarcastically as I walked towards the two men, who were between me and Sobczak's apartment.

<Just remember, this is where you live. You're simply heading to *your*—>

Stacy abruptly stopped speaking, apparently picking up on the same thing I myself had noted a second earlier: a mental probe. There was a telepath somewhere nearby.

Stacy immediately retreated, drawing back from my mind to avoid detection. Based on my interaction with her, she was obviously a top-notch telepath and probably could have avoided detection, but discretion is the better part of valor, as they say.

On my part, I obviously couldn't go anywhere mentally, but — being a telepath myself — I'd been trained for this type of thing. Basically, I always kept a running sequence of innocuous thoughts on the surface of my mind. Being a typical teenager, this usually consisted of pretty girls, sports, and video games (and was normally enough to fool anyone trying to take a peek at my thoughts).

As Sobczak, I actually didn't have to stray too far from my usual hunting grounds, as my surface thoughts currently consisted primarily of him dancing with a beautiful young woman. My telepathic visitor saw it as well; however, rather than being satisfied, he (at least mentally, it felt like a male) decided to probe a little deeper.

To the best of my knowledge, Sobczak wasn't telepathic, which meant that my mental visitor wouldn't be expecting strong resistance. In other words, I had to let him in, to a certain extent, or he'd become extremely suspicious. (And it was a sure bet that he was paired with the two in the hallway, who watched me closely as I walked by them.)

Swiftly but carefully, I lowered my mental shields and gave my telepathic visitor something similar to what he'd seen on the surface of my mind: Sobczak canoodling with the same young woman. Apparently satisfied that Sobczak only had one thing on his mind, the telepath withdrew, and I mentally let out a sigh of relief while putting my shields back in place. At the same time, I empathically felt the two men in the hallway relax, apparently having been informed by my telepathic visitor that I wasn't a threat.

At that juncture, I was past them and at Sobczak's door, at which point I felt Stacy reconnect.

<Any problems?> she asked.

<Judging by your timing,> I replied, <you were obviously paying attention and already know the answer to that.>

11

<Just wanted you to feel good about yourself,> Stacy said.

<Whatever,> I muttered telepathically, pulling Sobczak's keys from my pocket. Then I frowned as I realized that I actually *did* have a problem: I didn't know which key would unlock Sobczak's door.

To be frank, the door actually had two locks — a key-entry knob and a deadbolt. Glancing at the keyring, there were at least a half-dozen keys there which might fit either lock. Mentally, I groaned.

<What is it?> Stacy queried. I swiftly brought her up to speed, at which point she said, <Well, don't just stand there. Start trying keys!>

<What do you think I'm doing?"> I grumbled, as the first key I tried to insert failed in both locks. As I selected a second one to try, I cast a surreptitious glance at the two men in the hallway, who I now realized were basically standing guard outside the apartment next door. The pale one glanced in my direction, and I saw a frown starting to form on his face.

<This isn't good,> I noted, as the second key failed to work.

<Just stay calm and take your time,> Stacy advised.

<This isn't a matter of nerves getting the best of me,> I stated defensively. <I don't know which — if any — of these keys will open this door, and people don't spend this much time trying to figure out how to get into their own apartment.>

As if in support of this, I suddenly sensed something akin to suspicion starting to arise in the pale man, who was now staring at me.

<Drop the keys,> Stacy said.

<Huh?> I muttered in confusion.

<Drop the keys!> she repeated. <It'll buy you some time.>

I did as ordered, pretending to let the keyring slip from my hand and then bending down to pick it up. Under normal circumstances, my antics would probably have been enough to buy me one more shot at unlocking the door with one of the keys, but Pale Man wasn't having it. With my peripheral vision, I saw him starting to meander in my direction.

<No time to try another key,> I informed Stacy. <I'm going to have to do something drastic.>

Without giving her a chance to respond, I phased the doorframe on the side where the locks were located, making it insubstantial. I then grabbed the knob and pretended to turn it while at the same time pushing in. The door swung open (albeit with the deadbolt sticking out.)

I swiftly stepped inside, immediately noting that the interior of the apartment was dark. Rather than waste time fumbling for a light switch, I cycled my vision through the light spectrum until I could see almost as well as during the day. At the same time, I began closing the door behind me, turning the deadbolt so that it slid back into its housing while also making the doorframe solid again. Once the door closed, I again turned the deadbolt, locking it once more. However, I didn't relax until, empathically, I felt Pale Man's chariness start to recede. (Apparently, having seen me enter Sobczak's apartment, he was now convinced that all was well.)

I let out a deep breath. <That was close.>

<Don't go patting yourself on the back just yet,> Stacy admonished. <You're not done.>

<I know,> I stated, then took a moment to glance around Sobczak's apartment.

CONJURATION

It appeared to be modest-sized, with a living room and kitchen immediately in view. A set of glass doors opened onto a small balcony, and a door set in a nearby wall led to what I presumed was the bedroom.

<So where's this package I'm supposed to retrieve?> I asked.

<What — with a couple of goons guarding the apartment next door, you think it's in *here*?> Stacy asked acerbically.

<So much for making me feel good about myself, huh?>

Stacy ignored me. <Go to the bedroom.>

<Aren't you going to buy me dinner first?> I quipped as I began walking.

Telepathically, Stacy let out an exasperated sigh. <Just let me know when you're there.>

<Just stepped inside,> I reported, noting that the room contained little more than a full-sized bed and a nightstand with a lamp on it.

<The wall directly across from the door,> Stacy said. <Go through it and you should be in the apartment next door.>

Phasing the wall in question, I walked through it and found myself in a bedroom similar to Sobczak's in terms of size and configuration. However, there happened to be somebody present: a boy, perhaps five years old.

He was sitting on the floor in front of a television, holding a game controller and playing a popular RPG involving magic and monsters. He glanced in my direction, and I immediately raised a forefinger to my lips, in essence telling him to be quiet; he merely nodded his head affirmatively.

<Are you there yet?> Stacy asked.

<Yeah, I'm here,> I answered.

<What do you see?>

Assuming the package I was after was somewhere nearby, I looked around. The place wasn't as bare-bones as Sobczak's bedroom, but I didn't see anything that jumped out at me as being the item I was after. No box all taped up. No envelope sealed shut. Nothing.

<What do you see?>Stacy asked again, obviously impatient.

<Nothing, really,> I replied. <Just some kid playing video games.>

<Okay, grab him.>

<What?> I asked, somewhat shocked.

<The kid's the package. Grab him and get out of there.>

CONJURATION

Chapter 2

I simply stood there in shock for a second.

<No way,> I stressed a moment later. <This is not what I signed up for.>

<Agreed,> Stacy said. <Like the rest of us, you signed up with a huge blank in the job description area, to be filled in later. Well, guess what? This is where you fill in the blank.>

<I'm not doing it.>

<All right, listen. In case you forgot, there are not only a couple of supers in the hallway, but a telepath nearby who's keeping an eye on people mentally. Assuming he's any good, pretty soon he's going to pick up on the fact that you're a lot closer to this kid than you should be with a wall between you.>

<I understand that, but kidnapping a kid? That's not —>

<Okay, stop,> Stacy interjected. <You know the kind of man Gray is, and you knew exactly what you were signing up for when you came on board: anything and everything. So if you're told to eat worms, you eat worms. If you're told to blow up a bridge, you blow up a bridge. And if you're told to snatch a kid — surprise! You snatch a kid. Now stop whining and do your damn job!>

I frowned in anger, but the truth of the matter was that Stacy was right. I knew that signing on with Gray would mean compromising my principles — committing myself to doing things I wouldn't approve of morally or ethically — and I sold my soul anyway. Backing out now wasn't an option.

Still upset, I reached out telepathically to the kid, who had never stopped looking at me.

<Hey,> I said, trying to sound friendly. <I'm here to take you for a ride. Do you want to pause the game for a second and come with me?>

Much to my surprise, the kid nodded eagerly. (Apparently no one had given him the talk yet about accepting candy — or rides — from strangers.) Setting the controller aside, he quickly scrambled towards me and, to my surprise, took my hand.

<Okay, I've got him,> I reported to Stacy.

<Great,> she intoned. <Now get out of there.>

With the boy in tow, I stepped towards the bedroom window. It faced out towards the rear of the apartment complex.

<Remember, no showcasing your power set,> Stacy reminded me.

<It's not showcasing if nobody sees me,> I argued, then spent a moment scanning the area. There were people near the car, so I couldn't teleport us directly to it without possibly being seen. I could, however, get us pretty close.

I teleported us to the ground outside, making us pop up on the sidewalk. Empathically, I didn't sense anyone expressing shock or awe at our sudden appearance, so presumably no one had noticed us seemingly come out of nowhere.

"Come on," I said to the kid as I began swiftly striding towards the car. Somewhat to my surprise, he kept up without issue.

We were almost there when I heard an attention-getting shout ring through the night air. I glanced back towards the apartment building and saw the big guy from the hallway with his head sticking out of a window — presumably the one in the bedroom where I'd found the kid. Looking directly at us, he angrily yelled again. I didn't understand the words, but didn't have any trouble picking up on his meaning.

<They know the kid's gone,> I reported to Stacy as I dashed the last few steps to the car, still holding the boy's hand. Swiftly opening the door, I practically tossed him inside and told him to buckle up.

<Okay, that's not anything we didn't expect,> Stacy assured me as I ran around to the driver's door. <Just get out of there. Follow the GPS.>

Not bothering to respond, I had just opened the car door when I heard a booming clatter come from behind us. The sound was akin to a wrecking ball smashing into the side of a building and had come from the apartment complex.

Glancing back in that direction, I saw a ragged, gaping hole where the big guy had been looking out the window. As pieces of the exterior wall dropped precipitously to the ground, I realized that my assessment hadn't been far off the mark. However, instead of something slamming *into* the building, something had broken *out*. (And in this instance, I realized the "something" was seven feet of angry, super-strong muscle.)

I jumped into the car, shutting the door and starting the engine. Fortunately, having a ton of construction materials hit the ground had caused a number of car alarms to go off, and their blaring appeared to mask the sound of the car starting.

I gave Stacy a quick update, finishing with the announcement that we were about to take off.

<Drive normally,> she advised, <and kill the headlights.>

CONJURATION

I could have kicked myself, as I had actually been on the verge of turning the lights on. (Not that I needed illumination, with my vision still cycled to another part of the spectrum. However, having the lights on would help pedestrians and other cars see *us*.) Instead, I kept the headlights off and eased into the street.

<What's happening?> Stacy asked.

<I'm driving, lights out,> I informed her. <People are starting to come out and gather, trying to figure out what's going on.>

<Any sign of your friends?> she asked.

I cut my eyes to the rearview mirror, noticing a big guy who had just run out into the street.

<Yeah,> I replied. <The circus strongman is in the middle of the road, but I don't think he's spotted us.>

<Good,> she said. <Now whatever you do, don't tap your brakes.>

I drew in a harsh breath, as — acting on instinct — I had just done exactly what Stacy had told me *not* to do while in the process of making a turn. Taking a brief look in the direction we'd just come from, I saw the big guy freeze for a moment, and then he took off in our direction. With our cover effectively blown, I turned on the lights and slammed on the gas, the car nearly peeling rubber as we suddenly zoomed away.

<What's wrong?> Stacy inquired, apparently picking up on something. I gave her a quick rundown of what had just happened, causing her to grumble, <I specifically told you not to tap the brakes!>

<Well, your warning came a second too late,> I declared defensively. <I was following the GPS, and hit the brakes out of habit.>

CONJURATION

I leaned on the horn, swerving around a car that had just pulled away from the curb and into traffic. Looking into the rearview mirror, I saw our muscular pursuer just coming around the corner and into view.

At that moment, another driver gave me a taste of my own medicine, honking madly as I ran through a traffic light.

<What's going on?> asked Stacy. <Are you still being chased?>

<Yeah,> I responded, taking another peek in the rearview mirror. <He's right —>

I stopped abruptly as I realized that the hulkish brute was no longer behind us. Had we given him the slip? Seemed unlikely, as we'd been directly in his line of sight and hadn't turned. Frowning, I pondered the situation for a moment — and then got my answer when the roof of the car caved in above the rear seat with a sound like a battering ram striking sheet metal.

Several things happened almost simultaneously then. First and foremost, I veered wildly from side to side, the jarring impact on the roof causing me to momentarily lose control of the vehicle. On its part, the car seemed to drop ominously towards the ground, the suspension audibly strained by the jolt it had received, and I was shocked that the undercarriage didn't scrape the ground. As it was, the car started making a number of weird noises, and I got the distinct impression that something internal had broken or come loose.

That said, I immediately understood what had happened: our pursuer hadn't lost track of us. Instead, he had made an incredible leap that not only covered the distance between us but also timed it perfectly.

CONJURATION

I heard Stacy trying to tell me something, but the sudden screech of tearing metal drew my attention. Taking my eyes off the road for a second, I looked up and saw a portion of the roof being torn away above the center section of the front seat. It was our erstwhile passenger, of course, ripping open the roof like he was opening a giant can of sardines.

He eyed me for a second through the hole he'd made, and I saw something akin to a malicious gleam in his eye. Under normal circumstances, I probably would have teleported him a zillion miles away, but then Stacy, who had been yelling nonstop in my brain, somehow got through to me.

<Don't use your powers!> she ordered.

<You talk like I have a choice!> I countered as the muscleman on the roof suddenly reached into the car.

Of course, I understood the logic behind Stacy's position on using my powers, but I knew that if this guy got a chance, he was going to squeeze my head like an overripe tomato. Bearing that in mind, I phased his arm from the elbow down as it came into the car.

His forearm swung wildly around the interior as our passenger, reaching in every direction, desperately tried to find something to grab. It was almost comical. In fact, the kid in the front passenger seat actually laughed at his antics. (Truth be told, I'd almost forgotten about my "package," other than checking to make sure his seat belt was buckled when I first got in.)

After a few seconds, the guy on the roof obviously realized that something was amiss. He pulled his arm out, with me making the limb substantial again as he did so. I glanced up through the hole and saw him staring at his arm and flexing his fingers for a moment, clearly trying to figure

21

out what had happened. Obviously confused, he peered back through the hole — seemingly in an effort to make sure his quarry was still there — then growled when he saw me watching him.

He drew back his arm, clearly intent on having another go at me, but I didn't give him the chance. Telekinetically, I walloped him hard on the crown of his head. The man grunted as the blow struck and went tumbling off the roof. Taking a quick peek in the rearview mirror, I saw him slam into a mid-sized SUV that was behind us, smashing the windshield before his momentum took him rolling up and over the rest of the vehicle.

<All right, I got rid of him,> I told Stacy as I turned my attention back to the road. <But I had to use telekinesis.>

She let out a groan of frustration. <Did you hear nothing I said about flaunting a bunch of powers?>

<There was no flaunting. He was looking down into the car, and I whacked him on top of his head. He doesn't know what hit him — a baseball, a low bridge, a meteorite...>

<Whatever,> she muttered dismissively. <Just follow the GPS — and hurry.>

<I'm going as fast as I can,> I informed her as I made a sharp turn onto a busy thoroughfare. <Where's this thing taking me, anyway? Back to the airfield?>

<No — the subway.>

I frowned. I had just assumed the GPS was taking me back to the plane I'd arrived on via some circuitous route. I hadn't even considered the subway — didn't even know this city had one.

Now curious, I was about to ask what was so important about the subway when something like a miniature bolt of lightning struck the hood of the car. At the same time, all the gauges on the dashboard — the speedometer, the tachometer, everything — appeared to rev up for a second, and then fall to zero. The car immediately began to slow down; it was unresponsive when I stepped on the gas, and I quickly discovered that we'd also lost power steering. We were still moving forward by virtue of our momentum, but our vehicle was apparently dying on us.

On top of everything else, the weird bolt of lightning was still on the hood of the car, almost like it was transfixed. I then realized that it was, in a way. One end of it seemed to pierce the hood, while the other led off to the side of us. Although still doing my best to drive the car, I looked to where the bolt of lightning led to, trying to identify its source — and then drew in a harsh breath.

<We got trouble,> I told Stacy.

<What is it?> she asked.

<The Hairless Wonder from the hallway outside Sobczak's apartment. He's flying next to us.>

<Flying?> she asked.

<Yeah,> I confirmed, nodding as I watched the man pacing us as he zoomed along beside the car. <He's also glowing — he's got some kind of electrical superpower, I think. He's sucking the juice out of the engine.>

The hairless guy was, of course, the source of the lightning bolt. It came from a hand that the man kept extended in our direction. For a moment, I wondered why he was bothering to siphon the energy from the car's battery (which was what I assumed he was doing), instead of just frying me. Then I remembered: I had the kid with me. If he had roasted me in my seat, I was likely to have wrecked the car and the boy might have gotten hurt. That said, it was a sure bet that once the car slowed down enough, there would be nothing to stop him from sending a few gigawatts my way.

We were going maybe fifty at that juncture, and as the car continued to slow, other drivers began to agitatedly blow their horns. A couple of them went around us, honking in anger. One couple, however — a guy in a station wagon with a woman in the passenger seat — decided to voice their irritation. Passing on the driver's side of my car, their vehicle slowed as the woman rolled her window down and started yelling at me.

I didn't understand a word she said, but obscenities in any language rarely need interpretation. (She also made some gestures that I really didn't grasp, although I garnered the impression they were unladylike.) She only paused long enough to catch her breath and take a sip of something she had in a large plastic to-go cup that she held.

On my part, I was more surprised that anyone took note of me rather than gaping at the human lightning bug next to us. It was as if they couldn't see him. And then I realized the truth: they *couldn't*.

<Stacy,> I mentally blurted out, <do you remember that telepath back at the apartment complex?>

<I more than remember him,> she declared, sounding a little winded.

<Well, I think he's blocking people around me from seeing the pale man from the hallway.>

<That's not all he's doing,> she stated. <He's also trying to claw his way into your mind.>

<What?!> I mentally screeched. Her words were a shock to me, because I should have felt *some*thing if another

telepath was trying to get into my head. <I haven't sensed anything!>

<Because I've been blocking him — telepathically tussling with him so you could concentrate on the problem at hand. Now handle it.>

<On it,> I assured her, just as the woman in the station wagon started up with her invective again. Glancing in her direction, I saw that she was practically leaning out of the car, with her cup resting on the upper part of the door panel.

Seized with a sudden inspiration, I telekinetically grabbed her cup and flung it at the guy draining our battery. "Flung," however, is probably a misnomer; I actually ushered it straight towards him like a guided missile.

I'm not sure if he thought he could avoid the cup or simply didn't notice it until it was too late, but he ended up getting the contents — some sort of red juice or soda — splashed directly in his face. He closed his eyes instinctively, and put a hand to his face to wipe away the liquid. I took the opportunity to give him a telekinetic shove to the side; a second later, he smashed into a road sign, and then basically face-planted on the ground.

I didn't think our hairless friend was permanently injured, but he'd hit hard enough to surely have the fight knocked out of him. In fact, from what I could see in the rearview mirror, he didn't seem to be moving.

<How we doin'?> Stacy asked.

<I'll let you know in a sec,> I replied as I switched the car into neutral and turned the ignition off.

We continued moving forward, and after a few seconds, I turned the ignition on. The engine sputtered, but didn't start. I turned the ignition off, and tried again, only to get the same result. I turned the car off, sent up a quick prayer, and tried once more.

Third time, however, turned out to be the charm; the car finally started. I wanted to shout with glee as the dials on the dashboard came back to life, but settled for a quick fist-pump.

<Okay, we're good,> I told Stacy.

<How far are you from the subway station?> she asked.

I took a moment to eye the GPS's details. <About a mile.>

<Good. You're practically home free.>

<And the telepath?>

<He's still at it,> she reported. <He's good, but lucky for you, I'm better.>

<Whatever,> I muttered, then turned my attention back to the road as I noticed a motorcycle in the side view mirror approaching at high speed.

I made a mental note to keep an eye on the cycle. People in general were always in a rush to get where they were going, but motorcyclists in particular always seemed like they were trying to set a new land speed record, and this one was no different. Within seconds he had caught up to us, and I fully expected him to go zipping by. Much to my surprise, he slowed down when he came abreast of us. Almost out of curiosity, I looked over at the rider — and almost did a double-take.

<We're not out of the woods yet,> I hurriedly told Stacy. <Our muscular friend is back — next to us on a motorcycle.>

<Huh?> she murmured. <Where'd he get a motorcycle?>

<Well, I assume after we threw him off, he asked someone politely if he could borrow theirs and they obliged,> I stated flippantly, noting that the musclebound guy was now yelling at me — presumably telling me to pull over.

<I get it,> Stacy intoned. <He snatched some poor schmuck off his bike and took it.>

<But we left him miles back and blocks away. How'd he even find us?>

<I assume they've got some way to track that package you took. Any idea what that might be?>

I frowned at her statement, at the same time veering sharply as the muscular guy sidled close and reached for us. (Apparently he'd picked up on the fact that I had no attention of stopping.) Focusing on what Stacy had said, I glanced at the boy — who gave me a big smile — and then the truth hit me.

<The kid's bugged?> I blurted out. <Where is it — in his clothes?>

<You wish it was that easy,> Stacy countered. <It's *inside* him.>

<Of course it is,> I muttered, shaking my head in disdain. <Can't have it somewhere easily accessible, like a pocket.>

<Hey, it's not like *we're* the ones who bugged him,> Stacy admonished.

I was about to make a wiseacre response when I realized that I'd made a critical error. Chatting with Stacy had distracted me, allowing our pursuer to get close enough to get a hand on my door up near the window. More to the point, I heard the metal skin on the exterior groan as the man tightened his grip.

CONJURATION

Almost in a panic, I phased the frame around the door, making it insubstantial. At the same time, I cut the wheel sharply to the right. As a result, the door basically came off in the big guy's hand.

He stared at it dumbly for a second, seemingly confused about what had happened. Even better, his befuddlement caused him to check his speed, allowing our car to move ahead (although I used the mirrors to keep an eye on him). After a few moments, however, he seemed to just accept the fact that he had ripped the door off. He tossed it down angrily, and it immediately began kicking up sparks as it skidded along the road, causing other motorists to swerve wildly and slam on their brakes.

Leaning heavily on the gas, our pursuer began gaining on us again. On my part, I had no intention of letting him get as close as he did last time. Thus, I kept the car zigzagging back and forth across the road in an effort to keep the big guy behind us. It wasn't a permanent solution — we'd have to stop and get out soon — but we'd cross that bridge when we came to it. As it happened, however, that bridge never even came into view.

Despite my best attempts, I only managed to hold our muscular stalker at bay for five or ten seconds. Eventually, he managed to slip around and started coming up on the driver's side again. Noting that he was about even with the rear door, I cut the wheel in his direction, hoping to force him to fall back. Unfortunately, our adversary was having none of it.

Instead of giving way, he swatted at us, landing a fierce, uppercut-like backhand on the rear door. The next thing I knew, we were airborne, rolling longitudinally through the air like a plane doing aerobatic maneuvers.

CONJURATION

I shifted into super speed, and the world slowed almost to a halt. I then phased and — noting that we were upside down at the time — flew "up" through the floor of the vehicle and into the open.

From what I could tell, we were probably a good thirty feet aloft. A couple of people on the road were staring in our direction in disbelief. Surprisingly, one of them was our friend on the motorcycle. I wasn't sure why he'd look surprised, then it hit me: he probably hadn't intended to send us soaring into the wild blue yonder. Striking us had been reactionary, and he probably realized now that he'd put the kid in danger.

Now that he'd come to mind, I flew close to the passenger side window and checked on the boy. He was fine for the moment (although I noticed that neither his nor my airbag had deployed). With that established, I took another gander at our surroundings.

Not far away, I spotted what looked like the opening to an underground tunnel. It was roughly in the direction the GPS had been leading us, so I assumed it to be the subway entrance.

With an idea now of which way to go, I turned back to the kid and teleported him out; holding him up telekinetically, I turned us both invisible. Following this, I made sure we were out of the path of the car, then switched back to normal speed.

Almost immediately, I heard Stacy jabbering in my head, but I shushed her as the car we'd been in continued on its previous trajectory. I kept us in close proximity to it, basically tracking its path until it hit the ground in what looked like a park. It struck like a meteor and continued tumbling, plowing up grass and dirt like an out-of-control excavator.

CONJURATION

There were more people in the park than I would have anticipated at that hour, and they went scrambling and screaming as the car continued its gymnastic floor routine. Eventually, it came to a rest, oddly enough, on the passenger side of the vehicle, with the undercarriage facing the roadway we'd been on.

I'd kept us close enough so that, to anyone tracking the boy, it probably looked like he'd been in the vehicle. I set us down by the roof of the car, where we couldn't be seen from the road, then made us visible, not worrying about whether anyone had noticed our sudden appearance.

I picked up the boy and began hustling — at regular speed — towards the tunnel entrance I'd seen earlier. The park was fairly well-lit, but I made it a point to keep to the shadows.

<Okay,> I said to Stacy as I ran. <What were you trying to say before?>

<Just that you need to get to the subway asap,> she replied.

<Well, I'm trying!> I shot back. <But we got into a little fender bender.>

<Are you kidding?> Stacy blurted out, almost in shock.

<Don't worry — the kid's fine,> I assured her before giving an overview of what had happened.

<Did anyone see you use your powers?> she asked.

<I don't think so, but there are more people around than I would have expected.>

<It's a popular area of town,> Stacy explained. <Lots of restaurants, bars, clubs.>

CONJURATION

<Great,> I grumbled sarcastically. <Send me to a place with a bunch of witnesses when you don't want anyone seeing me use my powers.>

Stacy muttered something, but I didn't catch it. Instead, my attention was suddenly drawn to an angry grunting to our rear, which was accompanied by something akin to the sound of a car compactor in full operation. I didn't need to turn around to know that it was our pursuer, angry that we were gone and taking his frustration out on our vehicle.

At that point, we had stopped beneath a large tree with overhanging branches. I had done a pretty good job of staying out of the light, and I was certain that the big guy pursuing us didn't have any kind of special vision. (If such had been the case, he wouldn't have needed my brake lights to tip him off earlier.)

I put the boy down and spent a moment sizing up our options. With the kid being bugged, we obviously couldn't stay where we were — not for long, anyway. Thankfully, we were pretty close to the subway entrance, but to get there we'd have to cross a well-lit intersection. It would leave us pretty exposed — especially if I wasn't supposed to be using my powers. Basically, we needed a distraction.

<Hmmm,> I droned mentally, noting a fair number of people on the street.

<What is it?> Stacy inquired.

<How good are you?> I asked.

<Telepathically, I'm A-Level — an elite,> she declared. <What do you need?>

I quickly explained what I wanted. <Do you think you can swing that?>

<No problem,> she declared, <but I'll need a sec.>

<What about your dance partner — the other telepath?>

<I can do what you need and still fend him off,> she insisted. <Plus, he's preoccupied — trying to give your muscular playmate directions on where you are, but it's not working. Seems like wherever he is, the kid is at the fringe of his tracking ability. He knows you're in the vicinity but can't pinpoint where.>

I simply nodded, as it explained why the big guy hadn't made a beeline for us. That said, it would only buy us a little time.

<And you were able to get all of that from him?> I asked, suddenly curious.

<He's a strong telepath, but not that great at multi-tasking,> she explained. <In short, stuff's leaking through. Now get ready.>

Picking the boy up again, I stayed quiet and merely watched.

For a moment, nothing noteworthy occurred; folks continued going about their business — heading to dinner, out for drinks and so on. And then it happened. Almost everyone around essentially came to a complete halt and went silent. Even those in cars stopped driving, bringing their vehicles to a stop. It was as if the entire city had suddenly decided to participate in some Mannequin Challenge.

The silence was incredibly eerie. It was unnatural to have that many people being quiet for no apparent reason (although, if one looked closely, they all seemed to be listening to something). And then, in a flash, it was over. Without warning, everyone suddenly and simultaneously went into motion, screaming and yelling in panicky voices while making a mad dash for the subway entrance.

Recognizing that as my cue — and still holding the boy — I joined the throngs racing for the subway from all directions. I was, of course, taking a risk of being seen by our muscular pursuer, but I had a few things working in my favor.

First of all, it was pure pandemonium at the moment. People were running like a giant monster was attacking the city, and I soon found myself hemmed in by bodies on all sides. In addition, I wasn't the only person carrying a kid; apparently there had been families on the street, and many parents had protectively scooped their children up in their arms.

<How'd I do?> Stacy asked.

<Fine — it's complete bedlam here,> I told her as I used my telekinesis to keep the boy and me from getting banged around too much. <What did you say to them?>

<Just what you told me,> she responded. <That there was a bomb about to go off and everyone should seek shelter immediately — preferably indoors and below ground.>

<I only offered that as an example,> I stressed, recognizing that Stacy had made the telepathic equivalent of a PA announcement. <I just needed something that would make them all rush to the subway.>

<And did they?>

<Yes,> I confirmed as we reached the subway entrance and began running down a descending escalator, along with everyone else. <You managed to send everyone into a frenzied state of panic.>

Stacy didn't reply, but I sensed smug satisfaction on her part as we reached the bottom of the escalator and raced out onto the subway platform.

<I'm in the subway,> I announced hurriedly. <Now what?>

<Head to the tunnel,> Stacy ordered.

<There's no train there right now,> I reported, noting that the tracks were empty.

<Good, because you're not taking a ride anywhere,> she stated. <Go left into the tunnel.>

I was about to state that she had to be joking, but found my thoughts cut off by angry shouts coming from behind me. Acting out of instinct, I turned and saw our pursuer forcefully shoving his way through the crowd, agitating and inflaming those around him. From all appearances, he hadn't seen us yet, although he assiduously scanned the platform while essentially ignoring the outrage of those around him.

I turned and pushed forward as fast as I could without soliciting the same level of scrutiny and irritation as the big guy behind us. Moments later, I reached the edge of the platform and — still holding the boy — jumped down onto the tracks. It was a mistake.

All of a sudden, people were yelling and pointing at us, obviously urging us to get back up on the platform. It was the equivalent of pointing a bright red arrow at me and the kid — something I knew the guy chasing us wouldn't miss.

Still holding the boy, I raced for the tunnel opening to the left, as Stacy had instructed.

<We're here!> I exclaimed as we stepped into the shadow of the tunnel, the darkness presumably making it difficult for anyone to see us.

<Okay, you can use your powers now,> Stacy informed me.

As she spoke, I heard something like a boulder strike the ground behind us. I turned myself and the boy invisible as I spun around. As I suspected, the big guy was now down on the subway tracks, apparently having made one of his impressive leaps in order to quickly get there from the subway platform. Thankfully, he had been mindful of the tracks themselves and seemingly avoided landing on or crushing them as he'd done to the roof of the car.

He stared in our direction for a moment, then started running towards the tunnel entrance where we were located. I phased myself and the boy, then flew us up to the top of the tunnel, which was maybe twenty feet in height.

Oddly enough, our pursuer stopped almost directly below us. He stood there, silent and unmoving, and a moment later I realized that he was listening. Of course — the tunnel was almost completely dark, so he probably couldn't have seen us even if we were visible. He was clearly hoping we'd make some telltale sound to give away our location.

I almost laughed. Even if either me or the boy had made any noise, I wasn't sure he'd be able to hear us. In essence, the people back on the platform were seemingly going bananas, as there were now three people — including a small child — not just on the tracks but in one of the tunnels. Adding fuel to the fire, a single beam of light suddenly lit up the tunnel. It was the headlight of an approaching subway train.

The big guy seemed to hesitate for a moment, unsure of what to do. He clearly didn't want to abandon the chase, but he plainly didn't care to be in the tunnel with the subway train approaching. (Frankly speaking, given what I'd seen of his strength, I wasn't sure the train would hurt him if it came to that, but any kind of collision between them would obviously be a disaster.)

With the train drawing closer, our muscular playmate finally made a decision. Letting out a grunt of frustration, he turned and ran, essentially retracing his steps and then hopping back up onto the subway platform.

Scant seconds later, the train arrived, passing harmlessly through the phased forms of me and the kid.

CONJURATION

Chapter 3

Following the train's arrival (and in accordance with instructions from Stacy), I dashed down the tunnel with the boy for about half a mile until I came to what looked like the entrance to some sort of side chamber. I'd been in a subway tunnel before, and knew that they generally contained rooms that performed support functions: HVAC, communications, and so on. This particular door sat on a raised walkway on one side of the tunnel. There was writing on it (which, of course, I couldn't read), but the door appeared almost rusted solid, like it hadn't been opened in ages. Still phased and invisible, the kid and I went through it.

We found ourselves in what appeared to be some kind of maintenance room. Covered in dust and cobwebs, it obviously hadn't been used in a long time.

Now that we were no longer being chased, I made us visible again and took a moment to look over my charge. Physically, he seemed none the worse for wear, despite everything we'd been through. During the course of our exploits, I'd tried to get a bead on him emotionally but could never quite read him for some reason. That said, I garnered the impression that he'd had the time of his life during our little misadventure.

Satisfied that the boy was okay, I continued taking us through the maintenance area, which turned out to be a suite of connecting rooms (none of which looked like they'd had recent use.) Eventually, we came to a dead end in what I took to be some type of storage space, as there were boxes and bins all around.

At that point, following directions from Stacy, I flew straight up, holding the boy. Phased, we passed through the ceiling of the room and then through maybe twenty feet of earth before emerging into what looked like some kind of expansive underground bunker.

The first thing I noted was that there were half-a-dozen people standing around — two women and four men. There was also a dark SUV with tinted windows parked nearby.

Two of the men were dressed in black and stood at what appeared to be defensive positions near the walls. From their attire and demeanor, they were presumably agents of Gray. Still, I kept my guard up while I reached out to Stacy.

<We're in a subterranean blockhouse of some sort,> I relayed to her. <Six people present.>

<Okay, they're friendlies,> she assured me. <You can stand down now. Mission accomplished.> With that, she broke the telepathic connection between us.

Around the same time, the other people in the bunker started to notice me and my charge. I made us substantial again and put the boy down. At that juncture, one of the women seemed to gasp slightly and grasp the arm of a man standing next to her. I got the impression that they were both civilians (that is, not employed by Gray) and also a couple. A moment later, they were racing towards us. Or rather, racing towards the boy.

Realizing that I wasn't the focus of anyone's attention, I took a few steps back. As soon as she was close enough, the woman who had gasped scooped the boy up in her arms, while the man who was with her put his arms around them both. The three of them then began making some sort of buzzing sound. It wasn't irritating — like an insect droning around your ear — just unusual.

CONJURATION

The two Men in Black didn't move, but the remaining man and woman — a middle-aged fellow with horn-rimmed glasses and a thirty-something blonde with her hair in a bun — hurried towards the boy, almost on the heels of the couple (whom I took to be the boy's parents). Then, while the family trio hugged, the man with the glasses waved some kind of metallic wand around the boy. Nothing seemed to happen initially, but then, as it was brought over the boy's left upper arm, the wand beeped.

The guy with the wand nodded towards the blonde, who stepped close to the boy. At that point, I noticed that she was carrying what looked like an injector gun equipped with a large needle. She pushed it up against the kid's arm — in the area where the wand had beeped — and then squeezed the trigger. She held it there for maybe ten seconds, and then slowly pulled it back. I saw what I expected: the needle coming out of the boy's arm. However, as it cleared the skin, I noticed that a small metallic object, like a miniature bullet with a flashing diode, was attached to the end of it. The bug that the kid had been carrying.

The blonde took the tracking device and handed it to the guy with the glasses. He, in turn, placed it in a small metal case he had produced from somewhere and then closed the lid. Turning my attention back to the boy, I was surprised not to see even a speck of blood on his arm where the needle had gone in. In fact, he hadn't even seemed to notice the man and woman extracting the bug. He had simply continued making the buzzing noise with his parents.

I found myself breathing a sigh of relief. I hadn't realized how much I'd been on edge. However, it shouldn't have been a surprise, because this had been far from an ideal first assignment. With that thought in mind, I looked at the SUV and felt myself getting angry.

I teleported, popping up next to the rear door of the vehicle. I tried the handle and found it locked. I waited a few seconds — enough time for anyone inside to unlock the door — then tried to open it again. No luck. Undaunted, I phased the door and slipped inside, then made it substantial again.

Sitting in the back seat was an elderly man with iron-gray hair who was dressed in a gray suit. He appeared to be in his sixties, but didn't give the impression of being feeble or infirm. It was my new boss, Gray.

"There's an issue with your lock," I said, gesturing towards the door. "You might want to get that looked at."

Gray let out a sigh. "Something I can help you with?"

"For starters, you can explain to me why I had to kidnap a kid."

"Does that look like a kidnapping to you?" Gray asked, pointing to where the boy and his parents were still hugging. "All you did was facilitate a family reunion."

I stared at the trio for a second, then asked, "What's with that buzzing noise they're making?"

"It's one of the ways they communicate."

I turned back to Gray and merely stared at him for a moment. "They're not human."

"No," Gray confirmed, his answer reminding me that he had authority over extraterrestrials on Earth. "A certain faction took the kid in an effort to force the parents to do some things that wouldn't have been good for the planet as a whole."

"And now that we've brought them back together, what — they owe us?"

Gray shook his head. "I wouldn't put it that way. I prefer to think that they simply feel a certain amount of gratitude for what we've done."

I gave him a disdainful look. "You know, it would have been great if I'd known all this going in."

"Except we didn't *want* you to know."

I frowned. "What's that supposed to mean?"

Gray seemed to consider for a moment before responding. "Look, with your power set, you're easily one of the preeminent supers on the planet — even as a teen. But for all your abilities, your biggest asset is what's up *here*." As he spoke, he tapped his temple with a forefinger.

"We don't just need people who can do amazing things," he continued. "We need folks who can think on their feet, who can tackle issues with brains as easily as they can with some first-rate power like teleportation or telekinesis."

"So you wanted to see how I'd handle things with almost no intel and minimal use of my powers," I surmised.

"We needed to assess you."

"In other words, this was my probationary period," I concluded. "So if I had simply failed, I'd be out?"

"You wish," Gray muttered, chuckling. "It would have just meant you needed more training. But apparently that won't be necessary. Stacy said you did fine."

I raised an eyebrow. "She did?"

"Well, it was a preliminary report, but that was Stacy's general opinion."

"Did she say anything else?"

"Stacy likes to keep things simple, so no."

"Will I be working with her again?"

Gray shrugged. "Although Stacy said you did well, I'm not sure you make a great team."

"Okay," I droned, "but did she —"

"Stop," Gray interjected, holding a hand up, palm out, in my direction. "Just stop. I know what you're trying to do."

"Huh?" I murmured, giving him a confused look.

"You keep asking all these questions about Stacy — 'Did she...,' 'Will she...,' 'Was she...' You're trying to get me to drop a hint about Stacy's gender."

"No," I insisted, shaking my head. "All my questions were sincere and..." I trailed off as I noticed Gray giving me a skeptical look. Realizing he was on to me, I sighed and said, "Okay, fine — I was trying to get you to either confirm she was female or correct me and say she was male."

"Well, you'll have to live with not knowing," Gray stated flatly. "Also, mission's over, so you're free to switch back to your own face now."

"Excuse me?" I uttered in a perplexed tone, then realized what he was talking about: I was still mimicking Sobczak. I immediately shifted back to my own semblance and also switched my vision back to normal. As I did, another question occurred to me.

"So, what will happen to him?" I asked. "The *real* Sobczak."

"I suppose the folks who originally had the boy will want to chat with him," Gray noted. "He'll probably find himself having to answer some very uncomfortable questions soon."

I stared at him in stunned silence for a moment, then finally asked, "And we're just going to leave him to their tender mercies?"

"Sure," Gray replied nonchalantly. "Why not?"

"Because we basically set him up. *I* set him up."

Gray took a moment to clear his throat before speaking. "Ahem. This is one of those areas where we kept information from you, but Sobczak is actually one of our agents. Turns out, however, he was more of a *double* agent."

"Oh," I murmured. "So setting him up was essentially punishment for being a turncoat."

"That's one way to look at it."

"So what now?"

"Now nothing," Gray stated. "As I said, mission's over, so you can take off now. Vamoose. Skedaddle. Go home."

"Works for me," I said. "I'm glad to be done."

"Until next time," Gray smugly declared, his words a stinging reminder that I was indebted to him. Forever.

Feeling myself getting angry, I gave Gray a smoldering look and then teleported.

CONJURATION

Chapter 4

I popped up in my bedroom back home, sans the trench coat and Sobczak's personal items (all of which I'd left in the SUV with Gray). Once there, I spent a moment mentally kicking myself for ever getting involved with him. I had never liked the notion of working for Gray, and this first assignment had confirmed my initial intuition that he'd have me doing things I loathed. That said, I was glad to be home now that it was over.

At this point in my life, "home" was a three-story mansion — technically the ambassadorial residence and embassy of the envoy from the planet Caeles. Originally, my alien grandmother had served as ambassador, but more recently the role had been foisted onto me. Truth be told, it wasn't a title I was entirely comfortable with, and that was *before* my mother and grandparents had left the planet. Now that they were gone, the position occasionally felt like a weight, even though I didn't really have any official duties.

With them having come to mind, I reflected momentarily on my family. My maternal grandmother was a Caelesian princess, who — after coming to Earth, marrying, and giving birth to my mother — had been called back to her homeworld. Leaving my grandfather to raise their infant daughter alone, it was decades before she returned. (I'd had a little something to do with her being able to come back, although there had been a price to pay.) At present, the three of them were on something of a vacation, traveling through space and truly bonding for the first time.

Their absence, of course, left me on my own to a certain extent. That said, my father was still around and

44

kept regular tabs on me. Plus, I also had a couple of housemates.

Speaking of which…, I said to myself, then reached out empathically. A few seconds later, after pinpointing the location of everyone else in the mansion, I teleported to the breakfast area.

There were three people present when I appeared: my best friend Smokescreen, my ex-girlfriend Electra, and Myshtal, a Caelesian princess who — technically — was my fiancée. All three were sitting at the breakfast table chatting, but then seemed to notice my appearance simultaneously.

"There you are," said Smokescreen. "Where have you been?"

"Don't ask," I replied, sidestepping the question. My friends didn't really know about Gray, and I preferred to keep it that way.

Electra gave me a disapproving look. "Did you forget I was coming over?"

"No," I assured her, "but something came up."

She frowned. "So, are you free now, or…"

"I'm free," I confirmed as Electra trailed off, at which point she gave me a quick smile.

Basically, I was going off the next day to visit some friends, so Electra and I had made plans to hang out. We weren't a couple anymore, but had recently decided that we missed each other's company. Thus, we had been testing the waters lately in terms of spending more time together.

"Well, you basically disappeared without any warning," Smokey admonished. "We were all thinking that maybe you left early."

"No, I would have left word," I insisted.

CONJURATION

"That's what I told them," said Myshtal, earning her a sharp look from Electra.

Mentally, I sighed. Myshtal's great-great-grandmother was the queen of Caeles and ruled an interstellar empire. Although I had saved the queen's life during a visit to the planet, becoming engaged to Myshtal had been the price of a ticket home for both me and my grandmother. That said, it was more of a business arrangement than anything else.

Needless to say, Electra hadn't seen it that way and had subsequently broken up with me. However, she had made an effort to be friendly with Myshtal (who really knew almost no one on Earth), although there were obviously times when the princess rubbed my ex the wrong way.

"Well, I'm starving," I announced, hoping to change the subject. "I'm gonna see what's in the fridge."

Despite my ulterior motive in making the statement, I actually *was* hungry. I hadn't eaten since well before heading to Paris earlier. During my mission for Gray, I had tweaked my internal systems to keep any hunger pangs at bay, but since arriving home I'd gone back to normal and found myself famished.

"As luck would have it, we've ordered pizza," Smokey said as I was about to head to the kitchen. "It should be here any minute."

"Works for me," I declared. A moment later, the doorbell rang.

"Wow — perfect timing," Electra noted with a smile.

I, on the other hand, frowned.

The grounds of the mansion were actually surrounded by a wall and had a gated entrance. Anyone coming to visit typically had to use an intercom located at the gate to call the embassy and get buzzed in.

I turned to my trio of friends. "Did you guys let someone in before I showed up?"

"No," Myshtal said, shaking her head.

Brow knitted in concern, I simply nodded. "Okay, I'll check it out."

Without giving anyone a chance to respond, I then teleported to the front door. Once there, I reached out empathically. I immediately picked up on emotions that were familiar but found myself unable to ascribe them to anyone in particular — much like recognizing a face but being unable to place it.

Not exactly sure what to expect, I opened the door. Standing outside was a tall, attractive girl with short, dark hair. More importantly, I recognized her, although it was probably fair to say that she was someone I probably never expected to see again. Thus, I simply stood there, dumbfounded, for a moment.

My visitor, however, gave me almost no time to get over my surprise.

"Congratulations," she said after a few seconds. "It's a girl."

CONJURATION

Chapter 5

Her voice seemed to snap me out of my stupor.

"Ursula?" I muttered almost in surprise. "What are you doing here?"

Ursula gave me a pained look. "Nice to see you, too," she blurted out, then pushed past me into the mansion.

I shook my head almost in disbelief as I shut the door. Ursula was someone I'd met in a place called Permovren, which — frankly speaking — existed outside of space and time. That being the case, I hadn't really expected our paths to cross again.

"So this is where you hang your hat," she observed, giving my home a once-over. "Nice."

"Thanks," I replied. It was indeed a nice place and exponentially larger than the average home. That said, the castle in Permovren where I'd met Ursula had seemed infinite in size. In other words, she was probably just being kind, and I was about to comment to that effect when Smokey, Electra, and Myshtal came into the room.

"Hey," Smokey said, his eyes darting from me to Ursula and back again. "Everything okay?"

"Yeah," I assured him with a nod. "Uh, everybody, this is Ursula. Ursula, this is Smokescreen, Electra, and Myshtal."

There was a general round of how-do-you-dos, and then Ursula spent a moment scrutinizing both Electra and Myshtal.

"Let me guess," she said a few seconds later. "This one" — she hooked a thumb at Myshtal — "is the ex."

Internally, I winced. Electra had only just really reached the point where she had stopped viewing my nominal fiancée as a rival. The last thing I needed was someone intimating that Myshtal and I made a better couple. (It also didn't help that Myshtal was a gorgeous redhead with the innate ability to charm almost everyone she met.)

"Uh," I muttered, "that would actually be Electra."

"My mistake," Ursula admitted. "Regardless, it's nice to know who the competition is."

As she spoke, Ursula gave Electra an emulous look. Electra, in turn, glanced at me with a *who-is-this-girl?* expression. On my part, it was all I could do not to groan aloud and wipe my face with my hand.

Ursula was actually nothing more than a big flirt, with no romantic interest in me whatsoever. More to the point, she loved playing these coquettish games (and obviously didn't care about the fallout).

"Anyway," Ursula continued, "I'm in town for a bit and I was hoping you could put me up."

"Uh, sure," I declared with a nod. "That's not a problem."

As I spoke, I felt more than saw Electra's unfettered surprise, as well as similar emotions coming from Smokey and Myshtal (although not as intense).

"But just so you know," I went on, "Myshtal and Smokey live here as well."

"The more the merrier," Ursula stated. "Now why don't you show me where I can crash."

CONJURATION

Chapter 6

"Will this do?" I asked.

As I spoke, I made an expansive gesture towards the room Ursula and I had just entered, which contained a queen-sized bed, a dresser-and-mirror, and an entertainment center with a flatscreen television. It was surely modest in comparison to what she was used to, but Ursula didn't seem to care.

"It's perfect," she practically squealed, then raced to the bed, falling back onto it with her arms outstretched, giggling.

We had left the others a few minutes earlier — right after Ursula had asked about staying. The mansion, of course, had plenty of room, so I had just randomly picked a bedroom for her.

I simply watched Ursula for a moment, then noticed something that gave me pause.

Frowning, I asked, "What happened to you?"

Ursula sat up, a confused expression on her face. "What do you mean?"

"I just realized that you look different," I explained. "When we first met, you looked like you were in your twenties, but now you look younger — like a teenage girl."

"Oh *that*," she droned dismissively. "I had Endow make me look more like my actual age."

I nodded in understanding. Endow was an Incarnate — an immensely powerful being who could actually warp reality. Ursula served her in a capacity that was similar to a personal assistant. However, because she had wanted to be taken more seriously, she'd had Endow make her look older. Until now, that is.

"So what prompted the change?" I inquired.

"Well, you teased me before about how I looked when you found out my real age," she said.

"I don't think I teased you," I insisted. "I was just curious."

"Regardless, I figured I'd avoid it when I saw you *this* time."

"And that segues nicely into my prior question: why are you here?"

Ursula sighed. "It's actually Endow's idea. She thinks I could benefit from spending time with other teens."

I raised an eyebrow. "Really?"

"Yeah," Ursula confirmed with a nod. "When you came to Permovren, it really highlighted the fact that I'd never really spent time around people my own age."

"So Endow sent you here to expand your horizons."

"Something like that," Ursula acknowledged.

"Well, you're welcome to stay here, like I said, but I'm actually taking off tomorrow."

"Oh?" she muttered curiously.

"Yeah, a friend of mine is having a get-together of sorts. I'll be gone a couple of days, but Smokey and Myshtal will be here. They'll show you around."

"Well, maybe I'll just tag along with you," she suggested.

"I don't know if it's permitted," I said truthfully. "My friend Kane is participating in some kind of formal ceremony, and he's only allowed a limited number of guests."

"But you're Kid Sensation," she said in a flattering tone. "Surely you can snag an extra ticket."

"Again, it's not my event, so I don't control the guest list. Besides, I'm sure you'll want to just kick back and relax, so why don't you just unpack and..."

I trailed off and my brow crinkled as something suddenly dawned on me.

"So, just how long are you planning to stay for?" I asked.

Ursula shrugged. "It's kind of up in the air. Why — is there a time limit on your hospitality?"

"No," I assured her, shaking my head. "But I just realized that you don't have any luggage. No overnight bag, no carry-on...not even a purse."

"All that stuff's overrated and unnecessary."

I looked at her askance. "So you're just going to wear the same thing every day while you're here?"

"No," she insisted, shaking her head. "My clothes are already unpacked."

As she spoke, she gestured towards the dresser. Not sure that I believed her, I walked over to it and opened a drawer. Sure enough, it was full of clothes — women's apparel, to be precise.

"I've got some things in the closet, too," Ursula stated with a smile.

"Of course you do," I noted flatly as I closed the drawer. Ursula somehow managing to bring in a wardrobe undetected was a stark reminder that — as factotum to a nigh-omnipotent being — she had been granted the power to do some pretty amazing things herself. And that, in turn, brought to mind something else.

When I'd been in Permovren, some strange and unusual things had happened to me. I'd been brought there by Rune — another Incarnate I was acquainted with —

and before I left, he and Endow had revealed something startling. They had told me that I was an Incarnate as well.

Since then, however, Rune had reassessed. He was no longer convinced that I was an Incarnate, but he was certain that I was "something else," although he wasn't sure what that was. He was supposed to do more research and get back to me, but I hadn't seen or heard from him since.

As all of this flitted through my mind, I wondered how much Ursula knew in regard to my suspected Incarnate status. I was tempted to ask — at least inquire as to whether she'd seen Rune lately — but ultimately decided to simply trust that Rune would reach out whenever he had news.

"Anyway," I droned, "feel free to tone down the flirting while you're here. The last thing I need is Electra thinking you honestly have feelings for me."

"Oh, please — I did you a favor," Ursula declared. "Anyone with half a brain would realize inside of two seconds that she's got all the power in your relationship. All I did was show her that she can't take your feelings for granted."

"She doesn't and never has."

"Well, showing her that other females might be interested is a good thing. It won't put you on even footing in terms of who's running the relationship, but it'll help the pendulum swing a little more your way."

"So you fired a shot over her bow for my benefit," I noted sarcastically. "How kind of you."

"It's the kind of thing I do for my friends," she noted with a wink. "Besides, it's not like that redhead is giving her a run for her money."

CONJURATION

I blinked in surprise. The "redhead," of course, was Myshtal, and although our engagement really was a business arrangement, she had admitted to actually having feelings for me. However, she hadn't mentioned it to anyone else.

"There's no way you just guessed at Myshtal and Electra being romantic rivals," I noted. "Not after being around them for little more than a minute."

"Okay, fine," Ursula capitulated. "I may have had a peek at some things in the Cosmos Corridor before I came here."

I nodded. "That certainly explains some things."

The Cosmos Corridor was a room in Castle Permovren that allowed Incarnates to see the entire universe. It was under Endow's authority, so it would have been nothing for Ursula to use it to see what was happening on Earth.

"Just to be clear," Ursula continued, "I wasn't using it to spy on people. I was just trying to get a feel for the place before I came here."

"It's okay," I assured her. "Come on — let's go see what the others are up to."

CONJURATION

Chapter 7

We found the others in the breakfast area eating the previously-mentioned pizza, which apparently was delivered while I was showing Ursula to her room.

"Help yourselves," Smokey uttered between bites, pointing to a couple of pizza boxes in the middle of the breakfast table.

"Thanks," Ursula said, then reached for the top box. A moment later, she pulled out what looked like a slice of cheese pizza and took a bite.

"Mmmm," she droned, making a yummy sound as she chewed. "This is delicious. Jim, you have to try it."

"Yeah," I replied with a nod. "I was planning to do just —"

My words were cut off as Ursula, showing her impulsive nature, shoved the piece of pizza she was holding into my mouth. With little choice, I took a bite.

"Good, huh?" she asked as I chewed.

With food in my mouth, I merely gave an affirmative nod and droned, "Mm-hmm."

"Oh, wait," Ursula chirped, reaching towards my face. I felt her wipe the corner of my mouth with her thumb, which she then put in her mouth and then popped out with a slight sucking sound.

Frankly speaking, I wasn't sure there had even been anything there for her to wipe away, but I immediately sensed Electra seething.

"Jim," she said with a hard edge to her voice, "can I talk to you for a second?"

"Uh, sure," I answered, but found myself saying it to Electra's back, as she was already marching away. I quickly followed in her wake, glancing back once at Ursula with a *thanks-for-nothing* expression on my face. In return, she surreptitiously winked and gave me a thumbs-up, overtly indicating that she had intentionally ruffled Electra's feathers.

Turning once more to Electra, I continued trailing her as she practically stomped her way through the mansion like a famished T-Rex looking for a meal. Of course, I already knew where she was going: the sliding glass door at the rear of the embassy.

It didn't take us long to reach it, and for a second it looked like Electra wasn't planning to stop — that she was going to march straight through the glass. Fortunately, she took a moment to unlock the door (although she seemed to fling it open with more force than necessary) before stepping outside, with me right behind her.

We found ourselves on an expansive loggia and pool area. A little farther out, the grounds opened up, revealing — among other things — a parterre garden and a gazebo.

I took a moment to close the door, and had barely done so before Electra demanded, "Okay, who's that girl, Jim?"

"Well, uh, her name's Ursula," I began. "And —"

"I got her name," Electra interjected, crossing her arms as she cut me off. "What I'm really interested in is how you know her."

It wasn't a completely unfair question. Smokey, Electra, and I were members of the teen affiliate of the Alpha League, the world's greatest team of superheroes. Prior to joining them, I hadn't been much of a social butterfly and didn't regularly hang out with people. Things had obviously changed since then, but — because I essentially lacked a social life before — my friends in the

League were pretty much familiar with everyone I knew. Having an unknown acquaintance like Ursula just pop up out of the blue was surprising, to say the least.

"I met her on that last little jaunt I took with Rune," I stated after a few seconds. I didn't explain in any further detail, as no one knew exactly where Rune and I had gone.

"So that was what — maybe a month-and-a-half ago?" she asked.

I nodded. "Sounds about right."

"So you've known her less than two months and you're letting her move in?"

"She's not moving in," I corrected. "She's just staying for a few days."

Electra gave me a skeptical look. "You sure about that?"

"What's that supposed to mean?" I asked, plainly confused.

"From the way she's behaving, I'm sure she'll stay as long as you let her."

"That's all an act," I explained. "Ursula's just a big flirt. She's got no romantic designs on me. Trust me, I'd know."

"Even if that's true, having her stay here is probably a bad idea."

I gave her a perplexed look. "Why's that?"

"Because it's gone from just you and Myshtal to Smokey and now this new girl."

"I thought you'd be happy that Myshtal and I weren't staying here by ourselves."

"That was before this place started morphing into something else. It's practically a frat house now. All you need is a toga party and a live cow to complete the image."

"Live cow?" I repeated, chuckling.

"I saw it in a movie," she said, trying not to grin. "Anyway, won't Ursula's friends and family be worried about her staying with some guy she's known less than two months?"

"I doubt it," I answered.

"How can you be sure?" Electra asked.

"Because she doesn't really know anybody else."

Electra frowned. "What's that supposed to mean?"

"It means that literally I'm one of the few people she's ever met in person."

"Not to nitpick, but you can't actually mean that *literally*. She must know *someone* else."

I let out a sigh. "You know something? You're right; she *does* know other people. As of maybe half an hour ago, she also knows you, Myshtal, and Smokey."

Electra looked at me with a confused expression on her face.

"It's complicated," I stated.

CONJURATION

Chapter 8

Electra and I returned to the breakfast area after our chat. Thankfully, she didn't ask any more questions about Ursula, preferring instead to simply accept my statement that the situation was complex.

We found the others seated around the breakfast table, laughing at something Ursula had just said. Once Electra and I rejoined the group, we all spent a few minutes brainstorming on what to do.

Basically, since I was leaving the next day, the plan had just been to hang out, with no specific agenda. That said, since this was probably Ursula's first time really interacting with people her own age, I wanted to make sure she had a good time. Thus, although we debated things like getting into the pool or going out to catch a movie, we ultimately ended up playing video games.

The mansion had a theater room with a one-hundred-twenty-inch projector screen, which was where the game system was located. Historically, I had played on a somewhat regular basis with my grandfather, but after joining the Alpha League, I simply didn't have as much time. However, after my grandmother returned to Earth, we had occasionally played together as a family — usually something with a multi-player option that would allow me, my mother, and grandparents to play simultaneously. As a result, we had several game controllers and a decent variety of games.

Since Ursula was our guest, so to speak, we let her make the selection. After considering the options, she settled on a warfare game where the five of us would compose a special ops team trying to complete various missions.

CONJURATION

It turned out to be a blast. It became evident almost immediately that Smokey was the most competent player, so we made him team leader. He was incredibly effective in the role, guiding us to success after success. The gameplay itself was awesome, and it was great fun trying to complete each mission. But more entertaining than anything else was the ongoing commentary between us as we played.

"Can you shoot the bad guy and not me?"

"You wanna toss that grenade before it blows us up?"

"I vote for going *around* the minefield this time."

It was so much fun that none of us really wanted it to end. Needless to say, however, as the hour grew late, we eventually had to shut things down. Thus, it was with great reluctance that we ended the game, but with a promise to resume as soon as possible.

With four of our little group staying at the mansion, Electra was the only person who actually had to leave. After giving her a moment to say goodbye to the others, I offered to teleport her home but she turned me down.

"In case you didn't know," she said, "I actually drove here today."

"Sorry," I intoned. "I don't think I realized that."

"Well, you can still be a gentleman and see me home."

"Huh?" I muttered, not sure what she was saying.

"Ride with me," she explained. "It'll give us a chance to talk some more."

I smiled. "Works for me."

****

"So," Electra droned, "how long will you be gone?"

"It's not exactly clear," I replied, "but no more than a couple of days."

Electra merely nodded. We were currently in her car — with Electra behind the wheel and me in the front passenger seat — and had just gone through the embassy gate and onto the street.

"What exactly is this thing again?" she asked.

"Some kind of sorcerous ceremony," I explained. "From what I can gather, it's sort of a rite of passage for people like Kane — folks who can wield magic. They don't usually allow outsiders, but Kane was able to finagle an invite for me."

"Well, aren't you special?" she teased, smiling.

I chuckled. "I think he just had an extra ticket and didn't know who else to give it to." We both laughed at that, and I spent a moment reflecting on how my upcoming trip had come about.

My friend Kane was a sorcerous teen about our age. He and his girlfriend Gossamer (whom I tended to think of as an elfin warrior-maiden) had already come to visit me several times since we became acquainted. More importantly, they had also helped save the planet on a couple of occasions. Long story short, I owed them a visit (if not more) and had already been looking for an opportunity to go see them before this ceremony thing had come up.

"What's the plan for your little buddy while you're gone?" Electra asked, cutting in on my thoughts.

"Who, Ursula?" I said. "I reached out telepathically to Smokey earlier and asked him to keep an eye on her. He said it wouldn't be a problem."

"That's nice of him," she noted.

I nodded in agreement. I had reached out to Smokey right before we started playing the video game. It was practically a given that he'd help me out, but I hadn't wanted to take anything for granted.

"You know, you could have asked me," Electra continued. "I'd have been happy to show her around."

"Ha!" I barked. "After your reaction earlier? Didn't seem like a good idea."

"But if she really doesn't know anybody, she might have an easier time acclimating if she's with another female."

"Thanks, but I think she'll be okay with Smokey."

Electra gave me a sideways glance and then let out a sigh. "Why do you make everything so hard?"

I frowned, not quite sure what she was talking about — then picked up on feelings of contrition and regret coming from her. It took me a moment to get a grasp on the emotions and interpret what I was sensing from her, but then I understood: she was trying to make up for her earlier behavior.

"On second thought, you actually make a good point," I noted after a few seconds. "If you've got some time, I'd be grateful if you'd help Smokey keep Ursula entertained."

Electra turned to me with a smile. "Sure — my pleasure."

CONJURATION

Chapter 9

Electra and I engaged in general chitchat for the remainder of the drive to her house. Once there, I walked her to the door. A goodnight kiss was obviously too much to hope for given the fact that we were no longer a couple, but I did manage to get a peck on the cheek. It wasn't much, but was well in excess of anything I could have gotten just a few weeks earlier. After wrangling a promise from me to call her before I left the next day, Electra went inside. I waited until the door closed, and then teleported home.

I popped up in my bedroom, suddenly feeling both mentally and physically exhausted from the day's exertions. However, it occurred to me at that moment that I had never contacted Mouse to let him know that I was back from the mission for Gray. (I had been so upset with Gray upon my return that it had completely slipped my mind.)

Pulling out my cell phone, I flopped down on the bed and sent Mouse a quick text stating that I was back and everything was fine. (I also added that I'd drop by in the morning so we could chat before I left.) I then tossed the phone onto the nightstand and stretched out on the bed. Moments later, I was fast asleep.

****

I ended up sleeping in the next day, waking up around mid-morning. Shifting into super speed, I hurriedly showered and went through my morning routine before getting dressed. Afterwards, I spent a few minutes throwing some clothes, toiletries and such into an overnight bag, which I then tossed onto the bed before heading downstairs.

When I reached the breakfast area, I found Myshtal, Smokey, and Ursula already present. There was also a smorgasbord laid out in the center of the table and on a nearby counter: waffles, scrambled eggs, bacon, croissants, fresh fruit, and more.

"What's all this?" I asked, gesturing towards the food.

"That's Ursula's doing," Smokey explained as he bit a piece of bacon. "Apparently she woke up early and went to town in terms of cooking."

"Really," I droned, trying to keep the sarcasm out of my voice as I turned my attention to our newest houseguest.

"Just wanted to earn my keep," Ursula stated. "I figured cooking breakfast was as good a way as any."

<What cooking?> I asked, opening a telepathic channel with her. <You conjured all this stuff.>

<Yeah,> she admitted, <but I still had to put some thought into it.>

Mentally shaking my head in disdain, I broke the connection. I really didn't want Ursula doing a bunch of stuff that would result in my friends asking questions that I preferred not to answer. Nevertheless, I grabbed a plate and helped myself to a generous portion of the food on display.

Conjured or not, I had to admit that everything was delicious. I even went back for seconds (as did everyone else).

"That was awesome," Smokey commented when we were done.

"Agreed," added Myshtal.

"Thanks," Ursula said with a smile. "I'm glad the two of you enjoyed it." She then looked pointedly at me.

"I think you did a great job of whipping up breakfast for us," I admitted. "Now if you'll excuse me, I need to run some errands before I leave."

"Oh?" Ursula intoned, raising an eyebrow. "Where are you off to?"

"I have a mentor who I usually stay in close contact with," I explained. "Since I'm taking off later today, I wanted to touch base with him before I departed."

"Cool," Ursula chirped. "Mind if I tag along?"

"Actually, we've got some confidential things we need to discuss," I explained. "But I'll be back before you know it."

Without waiting for additional commentary, I then teleported.

CONJURATION

Chapter 10

I popped up in Mouse's lab, an expansive chamber at Alpha League HQ that contained highly sophisticated computer equipment, various large worktables, and monitors displaying a continuous stream of data. It was the place where my league mentor, Mouse, could usually be found, and today was no exception.

When I appeared, Mouse was at one of the worktables, typing on a keyboard that was connected to a nearby monitor. Despite his nickname, he was actually a big guy — around six-three with a well-muscled frame. Standing next to him and looking over his shoulder was an attractive blonde; apparently sensing my presence, she glanced in my direction.

"Hey, Jim," she said, waving.

I returned the gesture as I began walking in their direction, saying, "Good to see you, BT."

The blonde gave a short nod in reply before turning her attention back to Mouse. Contrary to appearances, BT (which was short for "Braintrust") wasn't a person, per se. Instead, the blonde was actually part of a cluster of clones that shared a single hive mind.

I stopped when I was a few feet from Mouse and BT, at which point I heard my mentor say, "Take over." He then stepped aside, allowing BT to move in front of the keyboard and start typing. He watched her for a moment, and then — apparently satisfied — finally looked in my direction.

"So," he began as he walked towards me. "How'd it go yesterday?"

"Okay, I guess," I answered with a shrug, then gave him a complete rundown of what had happened on my

66

mission for Gray. "All in all, I suppose it turned out okay, despite the fact that I was working for the devil."

"At least it's the devil you know," Mouse quipped, chuckling. "Regardless, it sounds like you passed whatever test he had with flying colors."

"I'm not sure that's a good thing. With Gray, it just means the next assignment will be that much harder."

"And you'll do just as well then," Mouse insisted. "Anyway, this trip you've got coming up — how long will you be gone?"

"Couple of days at the most," I stated. "Why? Do you need me for something?"

Mouse shook his head. "No. Just curious."

"Actually," BT chimed in unexpectedly, "he wants to know when he should start getting worried if you don't come back."

"First, that's a bit of an exaggeration," Mouse shot back. "And second, why are you eavesdropping?"

"What eavesdropping?" BT practically demanded. "You guys are well within earshot."

"But if you were focused on the task at hand," Mouse countered, "you'd be tuning us out."

BT merely grunted in response, but didn't offer further comment, at which point Mouse turned back to me.

"So," I droned, "does that mean you were getting worried about me yesterday?"

Mouse frowned. "Huh?"

"My mission for Gray. I didn't give you a heads-up when it was over or that I was okay."

"Oh, that," Mouse muttered. "To be honest, I didn't give it much thought."

"Thanks for being concerned," I said sarcastically.

"Look, there's a big difference between you taking some leisure time and going off on a mission. For the former, there's generally a defined length for the trip and an expected return date. For the latter, the length of time to complete the task isn't always defined and quite often you're expected to be incommunicado."

I rubbed my chin in thought for a second. "So basically, you'll worry if I take a few extra days for a vacation, but you won't sweat it if I go radio silent while on a dangerous mission."

"In essence," Mouse stated with a grin.

"Somehow, that just strikes me as being completely backwards," I declared, causing Mouse to laugh.

"Well," he chortled, "this is the worldview that allows me to sleep at night. If you ever find yourself in charge of this place, feel free to rearrange the priorities."

"Trust me, I will," I promised, causing Mouse to chuckle again.

CONJURATION

Chapter 11

I spent perhaps another half-hour chatting with Mouse and BT. Then, after promising to let Mouse know when I returned from my trip, I teleported home.

I popped up in the living room. No one was in the immediate vicinity, so I reached out empathically and promptly located Ursula in the breakfast area. I headed in that direction, noting when I entered the room that the breakfast buffet was now gone. Ursula, who hadn't yet noticed me, was sitting at the table with a fork and spoon in front of her.

At first glance, it appeared that she had balanced the utensils so that they stood upright on the tabletop. Moreover, they appeared to be twirling around, like she had somehow managed to spin them in an odd fashion. And then I did a double-take.

The fork and spoon weren't just spinning. They were *dancing*.

Hardly believing my eyes, I now noticed that both utensils had somehow sprouted metallic limbs — miniature arms and legs that were on full display as they waltzed around the tabletop. I didn't hear any music, but fork and spoon seemingly moved in perfect sync with each other.

Needless to say, I was too stunned to speak and merely watched the cutlery dance in silence. After a few seconds, however, Ursula — who hadn't noticed me come in — suddenly seemed to become aware of my presence.

"Hey!" she effused. "You're back." As she spoke, the spoon and fork suddenly fell to the table with a mild degree of clatter, seemingly normal once more.

"Yeah," I muttered, then gestured at the utensils. "What exactly was going on here?"

"Oh, that," Ursula said dismissively. "I guess I was kind of bored."

"Bored?" I repeated quizzically.

"Yeah," she confirmed with a nod. "After you left, your friends offered to help me put the food away and clean up. I suddenly realized that, with them present, I'd have to do everything by hand. I mean, based on our little telepathic conversation earlier, I got the feeling you didn't want them to know about me — what I can do, that is."

"It's more like I didn't want to answer a bunch of questions," I clarified.

"Anyway," she went on, "the idea of having to physically do all that stuff — clear the table, load the dishwasher, etcetera — didn't have a lot of appeal to me."

"I can imagine," I said, chuckling. Ursula probably had as much experience doing household chores as I had drinking gasoline. "So what happened?"

"I finally convinced them that it was something I wanted to do myself to pull my weight around here."

"Let me guess," I uttered. "The minute they left the room, you snapped your fingers and the place was clean."

"Something like that," Ursula confirmed with a grin. "But I couldn't just turn around two seconds later and say I was finished, so…"

She trailed off, but it was easy to pick up where she'd left off. "So you had to stay here, pretending to clean up when it was actually already done. But that raises the question: where are Smokey and Myshtal now?"

"Oh, I think they went back to playing the video game again — along with that new kid."

I frowned. "What new kid?"

CONJURATION

Chapter 12

We found the others — Smokey, Myshtal, and Kane — in the theater room. Obviously the person whom Ursula had referred to as the "new kid," Kane had apparently showed up shortly after I left to go meet with Mouse.

He was a teen roughly sixteen years old, and currently dressed in jeans and a dark T-shirt. The most notable thing about him was the assortment of rings that he always wore — one on every finger (including his thumbs).

Sparing us a quick glance as Ursula and I came into the room, Kane greeted me with a short "Hey," before turning his attention back to the game.

"Sorry, man," I muttered. "I must have gotten confused about the time. I thought you were coming a little later."

"You're good," Kane assured me without taking his eyes from the screen. "I'm actually early — had some time to kill, so I figured I'd see what you guys were up to."

"Well, I'm glad you found a way to stay occupied," I stated.

"Hey, I appreciate the fact that you two are getting caught up," Smokey suddenly chimed in. "But it would be great, Jim, if you didn't distract one of my guys in the middle of a mission. Even better, why don't you and Ursula join in?"

Neither of us needed to be asked twice, and within minutes we had happily joined Smokey's squadron once again.

****

CONJURATION

We played for maybe half an hour — just long enough to complete a particularly thorny mission. Truth be told, however, we probably would have played longer if not for an unanticipated interruption: Electra showed up.

Basically, the doorbell rang, sounding on a special device designed specifically for the theater room (which was built to be as soundproof as possible). Reaching out empathically, I recognized the emotional vibe of my ex almost immediately.

"I'll get it," I stated, pausing the game. Then, without waiting for comment, I teleported to the front door and swiftly opened it.

As expected, Electra was standing outside. Much like Ursula the day before, she hadn't bothered with calling from the intercom at the gate in order to get buzzed in. (In Electra's case, however, it was because her power over electricity allowed her to override the gate's lock.)

"Great — you're still here," she noted as she walked inside. "I was afraid I'd missed you."

"You didn't have to make a special trip," I assured her. "I was going to call you before I left, as promised."

"I know," Electra replied with a smile. "But I figured I'd surprise you. Still, I had to do a fair amount of chores at home before Dad and Aunt Esper let me out on parole."

"All for *moi*?" I muttered, placing a hand on my chest in false modesty.

"Don't let it go to your head," she said in a playfully snarky tone. "By the way, my dad and aunt said to tell you 'Hello' and to have a safe trip."

"Tell them I said 'Thanks,'" I stated sincerely. Electra lived with her father and maternal aunt, who were

— respectively — a former and current member of the Alpha League.

"So, where is everybody?" she asked.

"Theater room," I answered. "Playing the game again."

"Without *me?*" Electra blurted out, feigning distress.

"Sort of," I chuckled. "We've got Kane subbing for you. He doesn't have your talent for stepping on land mines or causing friendly fire incidents, but — ow!"

I rubbed my arm where Electra had playfully punched me, probably a little harder than necessary.

"My gameplay is epic," she declared. "And don't you forget it."

"If you say so," I remarked in tongue-in-cheek fashion, causing her to giggle.

"Come on," she said. "Let's go join the others."

CONJURATION

Chapter 13

Unfortunately, when we got to the theater room, we found the others shutting the game system off.

"You're quitting?" Electra asked, sounding disappointed.

"I can't speak for anyone else, but I'm done," Kane declared. "If I play any more, Jim and I will never get out of here."

We all chuckled at that, with me adding, "Agreed. The game's addictive."

"And I was hoping to get my fix," Electra attested, causing another round of laughter.

"Sorry, but you'll have to wait until next time," Smokey declared.

"Be sure to send me an invite," Kane chimed in. "I can always join remotely."

"Works for me," Smokey assured him, with the rest of us agreeing.

"So," Myshtal droned, looking at me and Kane, "when exactly are you two leaving?"

"As soon as Jim's ready," Kane replied, then glanced at me expectantly.

"I'm already packed," I responded. "I just need to grab my bag."

"I'll give you a hand," Electra remarked unexpectedly.

"Uh, okay," I murmured, caught slightly off guard by her offer. Truth be told, I had simply planned to teleport to my room and scoop up my bag. Instead, I found myself once again trudging behind my ex as she turned and left the room.

CONJURATION

We walked silently through the mansion; I sensed that Electra had something she wanted to say, but was comfortable waiting until she was ready to talk about it. A minute or so later, we reached my bedroom. Once inside, Electra turned, and then shut the door after I entered.

"You know," I began in a jovial tone, "I only have the one bag. I can probably manage it without any help."

She merely stared at me for a moment, then stated flatly, "You're not funny."

"Just trying to lighten the mood," I said, "since you obviously have something serious on your mind."

"No, not really serious," she clarified. "I just want to know if this is what it's going to be like."

"Huh?" I muttered, frowning. "I'm not sure what you mean."

"Well, we were supposed to hang out yesterday — you and I," she stated. "But you took off unexpectedly, and around the time you came back, your little friend showed up. Then we all wound up doing something as a group."

"I was hoping there'd be an opportunity to make up for it today," she continued, "but it looks like bad timing again, thanks to my chores. Even if I'd gotten here earlier, though, it looks like we would have had another group activity."

"I'm sorry," I declared sincerely. "I hadn't really thought about it from that angle."

Electra sighed. "I like our friends — I really do. I'm just trying to figure out if us hanging out really means us and other people."

I nodded in understanding. We were supposed to be trying to figure out if, given our history, we could still spend time together as friends. From that point of view, she was right; it was really hard to work on the Jim-and-

Electra dynamic if there was always a bunch of other people around.

"Okay, you have a point," I conceded as I walked to the bed and grabbed my overnight bag. "How about this? When I get back, we do whatever you want — dinner, a movie, whatever — just the two of us."

She smiled. "I think I like that idea."

CONJURATION

Chapter 14

The others were still in the theater room when Electra and I made it back.

Kane gave me a quick once-over as I walked in and then asked, "You ready?"

I nodded. "I think so. Bag's all packed."

"And no cell phone, right?"

"No cell phone," I confirmed, remembering that we'd agreed to make this an "unplugged" visit.

"Ahem," Ursula muttered unexpectedly, clearing her throat and drawing everyone's attention. "Now seems a good time to mention that I was hoping to tag along with Jim on this little jaunt."

Much as when Ursula had asked about staying at the mansion, I immediately felt surprise — and a number of other emotions — spike in Electra. (Needless to say, her statement caught everyone else, including me, a little flatfooted as well.) Fortunately, Kane never missed a beat.

"Honestly," he began, "I wish I could accommodate, but it's kind of a private event and the guest list is really restricted."

"But aren't you, like, the guest of honor?" Ursula asked him. "Doesn't that merit special consideration?"

"It's a lot like graduating from high school," Kane explained. "Other people tell you when and where to show up for the ceremony, and in this case they also give you a limited number of invites."

"Look, it's just a couple of days," I chimed in. "I'll be back before you know it, and in the meantime, Electra, Smokey, and Myshtal will keep you company."

"Well, if that's the way it has to be," Ursula muttered reluctantly. "Although I'd still rather go with you guys."

"Believe me, I've got no objection to you coming with us," Kane assured her. "But the people in charge? They're sticklers when it comes to rules — especially regarding things like outside attendees."

"So you don't think I could change their minds?" Ursula asked.

"You could make your case to them," Kane replied, "but your argument would probably fall on deaf ears."

"I guess that settles it then," Ursula acknowledged, looking dejected.

"Sorry," Kane remarked in a sympathetic tone, then turned to me. "Shall we?"

"Sure," I answered, then hurriedly said goodbye to my friends, getting hugs from both Electra and Myshtal.

Saving Ursula for last, I gave her a quick hug and said, "It's okay. I'll be back before you know it. You won't even notice I'm gone."

"If you say so," she murmured.

Happy that she'd finally accepted the fact that she couldn't come with us, I turned to Kane and gave him a subtle nod. Taking that as his cue, Kane raised his right hand and balled it into a fist. A moment later, his hand began to glow with a crimson light.

The illumination quickly expanded in size until it encompassed the two of us. It also grew in intensity, becoming bright enough to obscure our surroundings, but not harsh enough to hurt our eyes.

That said, I wasn't too keen on not being able to see my environs. Thus, I was on the verge of cycling my vision through the light spectrum in an attempt to obtain some degree of sight when the red light suddenly faded.

I blinked. Although I'd known what to expect, I was still a little surprised. The crimson glow, of course, had been a manifestation of Kane's magic, and now that it was gone I found myself in a new environment — what appeared to be a spacious, elongated hallway in a large building. Kane had transported us.

"About time you two showed up," said a feminine voice, capturing my attention before I even had a chance to look around.

Standing a few feet away from us was a willowy blonde girl with pointed ears, sporting a pair of ceremonial daggers at her waist. Despite a wicked-looking scar across her right eye — a memento from a clash with a supervillain — she was strikingly beautiful. This was Gossamer, an elf who was also Kane's girlfriend.

"Hey," I said in greeting, stepping forward to give her a quick hug. "Great to see you."

"You, too," she replied. "Kane's super-excited about you being here for this."

"Uh, I think I said I was excited about the *ceremony*," Kane corrected, "and glad Jim could be here for it."

Gossamer gave him a quick peck on the lips, then turned to me, saying, "He's trying to downplay it, but it means a lot to him that you could make it."

"Again, not quite how I expressed it," Kane insisted.

I chuckled. "Well, he can't be half as ecstatic as I am to be here. I really appreciate the invite."

"In that case, I guess we're *all* elated about this thing," Gossamer concluded with a slight snicker. A moment later, she frowned. "Hmmm. I guess I misunderstood. I thought only Jim was coming."

"Huh?" Kane muttered, giving her a confused look. "What are you talking about?"

Gossamer, who was still in front of us, pointed to our rear with her chin. Simultaneously, Kane and I both looked over our respective shoulders, and a moment later I had to fight to keep my mouth from dropping open.

Standing roughly ten feet behind us was Ursula.

CONJURATION

Chapter 15

"Hello," Ursula said with a cheeky grin, at the same time wiggling her fingers at us in greeting.

Kane stared at her in disbelief (as did I). "How…? How did you get here?"

"I hitched a ride with you guys, of course," she answered matter-of-factly.

"Hitched a ride?" Kane repeated, frowning.

"I kind of latched on to that translocation thing you did," she explained. "Basically, it's like you guys were taking off in a motorboat, and I attached a rope and started waterskiing behind you."

"That's not possible," Kane uttered, shaking his head.

"Anything's possible when you know how," Ursula countered, winking.

"But I shield against stuff like that," Kane insisted.

"Then I guess I'm shield-proof," Ursula offered, "because nothing prevented me from tagging along with you two. I hope that's okay."

"No, it's absolutely *not* okay," I interjected, finally finding my tongue. "You aren't supposed to be here."

"Well, thankfully, it's not your event," Ursula noted. "You're a guest, Jim — not the host — so you don't get a say in that regard." She then looked expectantly at Kane.

"I'm sorry," Kane muttered, "but like I told you before, it's a restricted guest list. I have to send you back."

"Really?" Ursula whined. "After all the trouble I went through to get here?"

"I'm afraid so," Kane stated.

CONJURATION

Ursula sighed in resignation. "Go ahead then, if you have to."

Kane raised his hand, again curling it into a fist. This time, however, there was no crimson glow. In fact, nothing happened at all.

After a few moments, Kane frowned, confusion plainly evident on his face. He lowered his hand, then spent a few seconds clenching and unclenching his fist, as if working out a cramp. Afterwards, brow creased in concentration, he raised his fist once more into the air. However, as before, nothing happened: no ruby-red glow, no growth of illumination, and no Ursula magically disappearing. Clearly perplexed, Kane lowered his hand and just stared at it like he'd never seen it before.

"Problem?" Ursula inquired, almost jocosely.

Rather than answer directly, Kane, still frowning, said, "Come with me."

CONJURATION

Chapter 16

Kane strode purposely through the building we were in, clearly a man on a mission, his brow furrowed in thought. Recognizing that he had something important on his mind (and knowing what it was), I walked beside him in silence.

Behind us were Ursula and Gossamer, whom I had quickly introduced after Kane stated that we should follow him. Ursula was her usual, garrulous self and talked incessantly. Gossamer, on the other hand — picking up on Kane's mood — seemed more reserved. If Ursula noticed, however, it wasn't reflected in her demeanor, as she continued chatting up a storm about nothing in particular: asking Gossamer how long we'd all known each other, how we'd met, etcetera.

It went without saying, of course, that I was incredibly irritated with Ursula. If she hadn't been prattling nonstop, I would have been telepathically giving her an earful. As it was, however, I decided to wait until we were alone and then give her a serious dressing-down. At the moment, however, with nothing more pressing to do, I kept myself preoccupied by studiously observing our surroundings.

As previously noted, the area where Kane and I had initially appeared was part of a broad, lengthy hallway. As we walked through it, I quickly realized that it was actually the central corridor of the building we were in, which — as we traversed its length — revealed itself to be an immense structure that was reminiscent of a palace in terms of size and a cathedral with respect to solemnity. In essence, as we traipsed along, I sensed an atmosphere about the place that seemed to demand reverence.

CONJURATION

Of course, it could have been the fact that — other than Ursula's chatter — the place felt unusually quiet. Even though we passed several groups of people (and a number of them said a brief "Hello" to Kane), none of them appeared to speak above a whisper. In addition, there was a fair amount of what appeared to be recherché artwork on display: paintings, sculptures, and so on. All in all, it gave the place a museum-quality feel — a look-but-don't-touch aura of veneration.

On that note, however, there actually was a fair amount to look at, mostly because sortilege was actively taking place all around us. For instance, at one point as we walked down the hall, a door suddenly appeared on one wall, and a moment later a young woman walked through it. At another juncture, I saw what appeared to be a painting of a soldier in uniform; however, as we passed it, I noticed our reflections in the "painting" and suddenly realized that it was a mirror. (On his part, the soldier frowned and took a step back as our reflections in the mirror passed in front of him.) Also, at the intersection of the main corridor and another hallway, I witnessed the stone sculpture of a nymph turn its head in our direction. In short, there was a notable amount of enchantment on display throughout the building — a reminder that Kane was part of a magic-wielding cadre of warlocks, witches, and sorcerers.

After a few minutes, Kane led us up a winding staircase, taking us up several floors until we emerged onto a circular landing. At that juncture, I noticed three hallways branching off from our position: one to either side and another that went straight ahead. Kane took the corridor heading left and the rest of us followed. Less than a minute later, he brought our group to a stop in front of a set of baroque double doors.

Kane rapped lightly on one of the doors. So faintly, in fact, that I barely heard the sound. That being the case, I was almost certain that no one on the other side had detected it. However, I was swiftly proved wrong in that regard as the two doors, rather than open, simply vanished altogether. One moment they were there, and the next, they were gone.

Taking this as an invitation, Kane walked inside. Naturally, the rest of us followed and found ourselves in what appeared to be a good-sized study that was perhaps five hundred square feet in size. Three of the walls — including the one around the doorway we'd come through — had built-in, floor-to-ceiling bookshelves that were all seemingly filled with thick, antiquated tomes. (I also noted that the double doors had reappeared.) The fourth wall was actually a broad picture window offering an eye-catching view of a well-manicured garden and an adjoining pond with a fountain in the center.

Near the center of the room was a cozy sitting area, consisting of a sofa, coffee table, and a couple of armchairs. At the far side of the study was a desk, and standing near it were a man and woman — the only occupants of the room. Upon entering, Kane began walking in their direction; the rest of us followed, although I — assuming it was okay — took the liberty of placing my bag in one of the armchairs as we went by. Then, as we drew close, I took a good look at the individuals Kane was leading us to.

The man was about medium height and a bit on the chubby side, with a youthful-looking face that suggested he was in his mid- to late twenties. However, male pattern baldness had taken hold with fierce intensity, leaving him with a thinning ring of hair that seemingly went in a semi-circle around the sides and back of his head.

The woman was older — in her late sixties, I guessed — with dark-gray hair. She was about five-eight in height and had a stately appearance and bearing. Finally, she was dressed in some type of layered maroon dress that seemed to be boho-chic in terms of style, and wore a simple but elegant necklace of wooden beads around her neck.

We were about ten feet away from the man and woman when Kane brought our group to a halt.

"Praecantator," he said in greeting, nodding slightly at the woman.

"Ugh," the woman groaned, rolling her eyes. "What's with the titles and formality? Come here and give an old lady a hug."

She smiled and spread her arms. Kane, grinning back at her, stepped forward and embraced her as instructed.

"Now," said the woman as Kane stepped back, "who's this with you?"

Turning towards us, Kane stated, "You already know Gossamer. That's Jim — who I told you about — and his friend Ursula. Everyone, this is Praecantator Razi."

"Nice to meet you," the woman declared sincerely, speaking more to me and Ursula since she was already acquainted with Gossamer. "But I hate my title, so please just call me Razi."

I murmured a soft "Yes, ma'am," as did Ursula.

"Now that introductions are out of the way," Razi went on, "why don't you—"

CONJURATION

Razi was interrupted by the balding man clearing his throat with a conspicuous, "Ahem."

"Sorry," Kane muttered apologetically. "Everyone, this is my cousin Lamont. Lamont, this is—"

"I got the names before," Lamont interjected, at which point we went through a quick round of how-do-you-dos.

"Well, now that *everyone's* been introduced," Razi declared, "why don't you tell me why you're here."

Kane then stepped in front of Razi, obscuring her somewhat from view. Based on what I could see, he appeared to be speaking to her (presumably explaining Ursula's unexpected presence), but — despite the fact that they were fairly close to us — I couldn't hear a word. In fact, I couldn't even pick up on anything that I would have interpreted as whispering. It was as if, with respect to their conversation, someone had pressed a mute button, and I spent a moment reflecting on whether it was something magically induced.

Not surprisingly, the notion of magic brought Ursula to mind, and since we had a few moments while Kane and Razi conferenced, I reached out to her telepathically.

<What exactly do you think you're doing?> I asked. <You know you aren't supposed to be here.>

<But Kane said it was okay,> Ursula shot back.

<Huh?> I muttered in confusion. <What are you talking about? Kane never said that.>

<Well, his exact words were that he had no objection to me coming.>

I reflected on what she was saying for a moment before responding. <That was in the context of him being in charge, which he isn't. Other people are running the

show and they've restricted the guest list, as you've been told.>

<True, but I was also told that I could present my case to them.>

Mentally, I blinked. <What?>

<Kane said that they probably wouldn't listen, but I could make my argument to the folks in charge,> Ursula stated.

<I don't think there was ever any expectation that you'd pursue that option.>

<Well, reality and expectations don't always converge,> Ursula declared. <In this instance, I'm just going off what I was told. Basically, when you put it all together, there was no objection to me coming, and I get a shot at convincing the bigwigs around here to let me stay. That's almost verbatim what your buddy Kane said.>

The soundness of her logic took me a little by surprise, but I stuck to my guns, saying, <You baited him into making those statements — tricked him into creating a loophole you could exploit to tag along with us.>

Mentally, Ursula giggled. <I didn't bait anybody. I asked simple questions and worked with the answers I was given. If your friend meant something other than what he said, how's that my fault?>

I was on the verge of replying when Razi and Kane seemingly ended their discussion. At that point, Razi stepped forward, walking directly towards Ursula. The older woman stopped a few feet away and appeared to scrutinize Ursula intensely for a few moments.

"Well, she certainly doesn't *seem* evil," Razi announced to no one in particular.

Ursula's mouth almost dropped open, and she turned to Kane with a stunned expression on her face. "You told her I was evil?!"

"No!" Kane blurted out defensively, shaking his head. "I—"

"Perhaps I should explain," Razi stated, cutting him off. "The place where you now find yourself is the Templum Praefator, which loosely translates as 'Wizard's Temple.' Generally, the only way to get inside these walls is by invitation or being transported by someone with access. Those who come here outside of those parameters usually do so with malicious intent."

"Well, I don't have a malicious bone in my body," Ursula assured her. "I was just really intent on hanging out with my friend Jim, and it sort of defeated the purpose of my visit if he took off for parts unknown as soon as I got in town."

"So you simply accompanied Jim when Kane brought him here," Razi concluded.

"Pretty much," Ursula admitted.

"Hmmm," Razi droned, frowning as she fiddled with one of the beads on her necklace. After a few seconds, she said, "Lamont, please tell the Council we need to assemble immediately. If you get pushback, tell them it's an emergency."

"Understood," Lamont replied, and then began marching towards the doors we'd come through.

"Kane," Razi continued, "would you mind taking your friends to the Council's antechamber until everyone is assembled?"

"No problem," Kane said, then turned to me, Ursula, and Gossamer. "You heard the lady — let's go, boys and girls."

Like Lamont, he began heading for the exit, with the rest of us preparing to follow him. As he came abreast of me, I began to turn — intending to fall in step behind him — when Razi's voice caused me to stop short.

"Uh, not you, Jim," Razi declared unexpectedly, causing us all to turn in her direction. "I was hoping to speak to you privately for a moment."

"Oh, um…sure," I murmured, then gave Kane a puzzled *what's-this-about?* expression.

He merely shrugged before turning to Gossamer and Ursula, saying, "Okay, let's roll out."

With that, he continued walking towards the exit with the girls behind him. When they drew near, the double doors vanished as before, then reappeared after my friends were gone.

Now alone with Razi and feeling slightly apprehensive about what she wanted, I looked in her direction. Much to my surprise, she had a warm and welcoming smile on her face.

"So," she stated cheerfully, "you're Nightmare's grandson."

Chapter 17

I stared at her in surprise. "You knew my grandfather?"

"Knew?" she repeated quizzically. "Did he die or something?"

"No," I uttered, shaking my head. "That's not… I mean, I wasn't saying—"

"It's okay," she interjected, grinning. "I was just teasing. But yes, I know your grandfather very well. We were teammates, in fact."

"You were?"

"Yes," she replied, and began meandering towards the picture window. I instinctively understood that she expected me to walk with her, and I complied.

"When was this?" I asked.

"Oh, a long time ago, as you might imagine. I was known as Razzle Dazzle back then."

Razzle Dazzle! I repeated to myself. *Of course!*

Razzle Dazzle — generally known as Razzle — had been a powerful sorceress and a superhero decades ago. My grandfather had mentioned her several times and even shown me pictures of her, but I hadn't immediately made the connection between the young lady I'd seen in his old photographs and the woman in whose company I presently found myself.

"I'm sorry," I muttered. "My grandfather told me about you, but I didn't realize who you were."

"No reason why you should," she said, waving a hand at the picture window as we approached. Much to my surprise, the glass in the window vanished. In addition, a stairway suddenly appeared, leading down to the garden outside. "I'm an old lady now, not the winsome young

91

thing you might have seen in photos or news clips from my heyday."

"So what was my grandfather like back then?" I asked as we began descending the stairs.

"Brave, strong, noble — and quite handsome, to boot," she answered. "More than a few of the female capes had mad crushes on him — me among them."

I wasn't quite sure what to say to this, so I stayed silent. Fortunately, Razi didn't seem to expect a response.

"Your grandmother, however, would brook no competition where John was concerned," she continued, using my grandfather's given name. "Any female daring to show anything more than platonic interest in him was guaranteed to have a bad day."

I glanced at her with a stunned expression. I had trouble imagining my grandmother Indigo — who was an absolute sweetheart, in my opinion — being some ruthless cutthroat when it came to matters of the heart.

After a moment, I muttered, "You're kidding, right?"

"Oh, no," Razi declared as we reached the bottom of the stairs and began walking along an adjoining path through the garden. Meanwhile, a harp on a nearby bench began playing itself, filling the air with soothing, melodic music.

"Don't get me wrong," she continued. "Indigo was a congenial, lovable person and the milk of human kindness in general. But she ran roughshod over anyone she viewed as a romantic rival. From the way she acted, you'd have thought she traveled halfway across the galaxy solely for the purpose of meeting John."

I didn't say anything, but Razi was more right than she knew. Basically, my grandmother had actually told me on one occasion that she'd felt my grandfather's mind calling to her across the void of space and had been compelled to find him.

"Anyway," Razi went on, "your grandparents eventually married, and I became a close friend of the family. Unfortunately, we lost touch after your grandmother left the planet — especially after John hung up his cape. However, I remember them fondly, and really do hate that I was unable to make the soiree they had."

I simply nodded at this. Razi was referring to a small get-together my grandparents had intended to host in honor of my grandmother returning to Earth. Somehow, however, it had ultimately morphed into a giant gala event attended by a who's who of celebrities, supers, heads of state, and so on.

"Speaking on behalf of my grandparents," I said, "they realized that not all of their friends were able to attend, so I know they'd understand if you had a conflict."

"That's good to hear," Razi declared sincerely as a pair of disembodied eyes the size of saucers suddenly appeared a few feet ahead of us. They bobbed in front of us for a few seconds, rapidly changing color in an almost hypnotic fashion, until Razi shooed them away.

The eyes went charging through a cluster of giant roses that lined the current portion of the garden path. The roses, which grew up from the ground like sunflowers on thick stems to a height of about five feet, had flowers the size of a human head. More to the point, the roses appeared to be covered with dew, and as the eyes went bounding through them, the plants sent a cascade of water flying towards us.

Razi made a sharp gesture with her hand, and the water droplets froze in midair before touching us. We continued walking along the path, and — once we were past the roses — I glanced back just in time to see the beads of water resume their journey, watching as they ultimately struck nothing but the ground

Noting my interest in what had happened, Razi said, "I guess all of this must seem strange to you — the things we can do."

"More like different than strange," I admitted.

"Then you're the exception, although I guess I shouldn't be surprised, considering your friendship with my grandson."

I gave her a perplexed look. "Your grandson?"

"Kane," she stated matter-of-factly.

Of course, I thought, mentally smacking myself on the head for not realizing who she was referring to.

"Plus," she went on, "you have a magic-wielder in your lineup, I'm sure. Most superhero squads do, in order to help combat mystical and metaphysical threats. Who's the mage on your team?"

"He goes by Rune," I said, reflecting on the fact that most considered Rune to be just a magician of sorts and had no idea of his status as an Incarnate.

Razi frowned. "Oh, that one. He's an enigma — pretty much came out of nowhere. No one's sure what group he hails from, and none of the established sects have claimed him."

"Sects?" I repeated, plainly nonplussed.

"Like I said, most superhero teams have at least one person on the roster who's familiar with sortilege," she explained. "Those people all come from somewhere, get trained someplace."

"Here?" I guessed.

"Some of them, yes," she acknowledged. "But there are various orders around the globe that offer instruction in the arcane. We, for instance, are the Kroten Venefici, which generally translates as 'Wizards of Kroten.'"

"Kroten?" I repeated, my eyebrows rising in surprise.

"Yes. The term refers to a legendary artifact that purportedly was once in the possession of the founder of our guild. It's supposed to be an ancient and powerful relic, as well as the wellspring for much of our magic."

My brow furrowed in thought as I considered what Razi had just said. I was actually familiar with an ancient relic known as the Kroten Yoso Va. In fact, I had been designated as its Keeper and had it in my possession (although not on my person — it was back at the mansion). At one point, however, it had been in the hands of a supervillain, who had used it to cause catastrophic damage on an epic scale.

"So, where is this Kroten now?" I inquired.

Razi shrugged. "Who knows? Assuming the thing ever actually existed, it allegedly disappeared ages ago. Some say it was lost; some say it was stolen. Others say it was given to one of our founder's protégés for safekeeping." Suddenly, her eyes narrowed. "Why do you ask?"

"Just curious," I replied, which wasn't completely untrue.

"Hmmm," she murmured, in a way that suggested she wasn't sure whether to believe me. "Anyway, as I was saying before, your level of comfort with magic is an exception. Our talents generally tend to make people uncomfortable. All we really do, however, is manipulate forces that most can't perceive or comprehend."

"What do you mean?" I asked.

She seemed to contemplate for a moment, then said, "Think of all the things that people typically consider to be commonplace today. From aircraft that let us fly like birds, to cell phones that let us talk to people on the other side of the world, to something as simple as electric lights. They're all things that one or two centuries ago would have been construed as magic, but today they're part of everyday life."

"So you're saying that one day everyone will be able to do magic," I concluded.

"Not exactly," she stated with a snicker. "That's akin to saying everyone can do brain surgery. The truth, however, is that everyone is *familiar* with brain surgery and it's an accepted practice of medicine, but only a select few have the skill to actually perform it. Likewise, at some point in the future, what we mages can do will be viewed as common, but only the *corps d'elite* will be actual practitioners of the mystical arts."

"Then I suppose it'll be like med school," I offered. "Many will apply, but not everyone will get in."

"Something like that," she agreed with a smile. We walked on in silence for a moment, now passing the pond I'd observed earlier, and I sensed Razi's demeanor growing more somber. "So, this girl Ursula. What can you tell me about her?"

"Hmmm. Kind of a broad question," I noted, realizing that we were now at the meat-and-potatoes of what Razi really wanted to talk to me about.

"You're right," she acknowledged. "Let me rephrase: how well do you know her?"

I shrugged. "Well enough, I guess. I mean, I haven't known her long, but I trust her."

"And her intent in coming here?"

"I don't know that there was any specific intent other than tagging along with me," I admitted. "She's impulsive, and at the moment a bit like a bratty little sister who wants to follow her older brother around."

"I see," Razi remarked. "And her powers?"

I frowned. "I'm not sure what you're asking."

"Well, you may not have realized it because you don't have a basis for comparison, but Kane is actually a prodigy. He has the knowledge, skill, and competence of a mage twice his age. He's likely to become Maximus someday."

There was a sense of pride in her voice as she spoke, but — having no idea what she was talking about — I simply murmured, "Excuse me?"

"I'm sorry," she apologized. "That last part was more me thinking aloud, but I was referring to the leader of the Kroten Venefici. The person holding that position is formally known as the Veneficus Maximus, or just Maximus for short. Ranking just below that level are the Praecantators, like myself, who — along with the Maximus — make up the Kroten Council, which is our ruling body. And beneath the Council, as you might guess, are various levels and grades."

"And you think that Kane will be Maximus one day."

"It's quite likely," she admitted. "But the point I was trying to make is that Kane is advanced enough that he should have been able to send your friend back, but he couldn't. Even I couldn't manage it, and believe me, I tried — back when we were in my study. That implies she has some incredibly potent power or ability. More importantly, because she wasn't formally invited or brought here, it's necessary to determine whether she's a threat."

"Which explains why you wanted to talk to me," I surmised.

"Yes," she admitted. "Kane trusts you, and he's a good judge of character, so I thought it worthwhile to get your opinion of this girl. But I also wanted to ask another question."

"Oh?" I muttered curiously. "What's that?"

"I'm somewhat familiar with your abilities, so I'm curious as to why *you* haven't tried to send her back."

I frowned. "How do you know I haven't?"

"Just a feeling," Razi said, noncommittally.

I contemplated for a moment then shrugged. "I just figured it would be an exercise in futility. Assuming I *could* teleport her, she'd probably just come right back."

"So she *is* powerful," Razi concluded.

"She's more headstrong than anything else," I offered. "But overall, she's a good person."

"Thanks — I'm sure she'd appreciate having your endorsement," Razi noted. "Anyway, we should get back. The Council's about to meet."

As she spoke, a door appeared on the path before us. Frankly speaking, standing upright and unsupported, it looked odd and out of place, to say the least. Razi, however, without hesitation, merely opened the door and stepped through. With no other options available, I followed her.

CONJURATION

Chapter 18

We emerged in what I initially took to be a roomy lounge. There were a couple of sitting areas judiciously spaced around the room — including a trio of easy chairs where I noticed Kane, Gossamer, and Ursula currently sitting. I immediately understood that we were in the antechamber that Razi had previously mentioned.

Now that she had come to mind, I turned in Razi's direction just in time to see her close the door we had come through. The door immediately vanished, with nothing whatsoever to indicate that it had ever been there. However, I didn't have time to comment on it, as I noticed Kane and the others, who had risen from their seats, swiftly approaching us.

Stopping when they were a few feet away, Kane greeted Razi with a curt, "Praecantator."

His grandmother rolled her eyes in mock irritation, murmuring, "Again with the titles…"

Smiling, Kane said, "The Council is assembled — except for you, that is. We can enter and begin whenever you're ready."

As he finished speaking, Kane gestured towards a nearby pair of elegant wooden doors set in a magnificent stone archway. Running flush with the extrados at the top of the arch was a strip of metal roughly a foot wide. Although the metal itself was dark, it was emblazoned with golden emblems that I couldn't even begin to decipher. In fact, the symbols on the metal were so foreign to me that I had no idea whether they were meant to depict some type of script, artwork, or something else altogether.

I studied it for a few moments, then had my attention pulled away as Razi began speaking to Ursula.

99

"Has Kane explained what's supposed to happen here?" she asked.

"Yes," Ursula acknowledged. "Basically, I get to explain to you and the rest of your C-Suite what I'm doing here and why I should get to stay. At the same time, you folks get to look me over and try to figure out if I'm a wicked witch here to destroy you all."

I fought to keep my expression impassive, but cringed internally at what Ursula had just said. She was obviously kidding, but I was tempted to reach out telepathically and tell her not to even joke like that. Much to my surprise, however, Razi burst out laughing.

"Ha-ha!" she chuckled heartily, plainly amused by Ursula's statement. "Well, regardless of anything else, you're definitely going to make an impression."

With that, she headed towards the doors in the archway, with the rest of us following.

CONJURATION

Chapter 19

The doors led into a stately chamber with a high, coffered ceiling and Romanesque columns along the side walls. The extravagantly tiled floor was literally a work of art, containing an exquisitely detailed image of a large, golden dragon (which I thought I saw blink as we walked over it). Directly across from the entry was an elevated bench that resembled an oversized executive desk, behind which — sitting equidistant apart — were six men and two women. Each of them appeared serious and somber (not to mention *senior*, because none struck me as being less than sixty years old, at a minimum).

I didn't see a jury box or a witness stand, but — all in all — the room had the atmospheric quality of a courtroom. (Or, if not a courtroom per se, a place where people got judged, which pretty much coincided with why we were present.)

"Wait here," Razi muttered softly when we were about ten feet away from the bench. The rest of us came to a halt, but she continued walking, heading to the right side of the assembled panel. At that moment, I noticed that the end of the bench on that side had an empty chair. Moments later, Razi appeared to walk up a couple of steps that weren't visible from my position and took a seat.

With her in place, the group at the bench looked very much like a judicial panel: a chief justice in the center flanked by four associate justices on either side. This, then, was presumably the Kroten Council mentioned earlier by Razi. That, in turn, meant that the "chief justice" — an elderly fellow with a neatly trimmed gray goatee — was probably the Veneficus Maximus.

CONJURATION

Dismissing with any pleasantries, the Maximus looked pointedly at Ursula and declared, "I take it you're the reason we're here, young lady?"

"So it would seem," Ursula stated, stepping forward.

"Now, it's my understanding that you somehow managed to 'hitch a ride' with a mage who was coming here."

"Pretty much," Ursula admitted.

"Thank you for your candor," the Maximus said, "but let me be blunt. We have an important but private ceremony coming up. We don't take kindly to gatecrashers at the best of times, but particularly on momentous occasions such as this."

"But I'm *not* a gatecrasher," Ursula insisted.

"So you're arguing that you were invited?" asked another member of the Council — an urbane woman with burgundy hair that was lined with streaks of gray.

"Not specifically, but it's my understanding that I'm welcome here," Ursula insisted.

"And what would give you that impression?" asked a man with a thick white beard and a hawkish countenance.

"That script over your door," she answered, pointing.

Looking where she indicated, I saw the same metalwork over the archway (with the indecipherable symbols) that I'd observed when we were in the antechamber.

"The calligraphy's a little rough," Ursula continued, "but that writing invokes the Powers Incarnate, asking them to stand with the Kroten Venefici as a light against all darkness."

CONJURATION

The Maximus looked at her with something akin to shock. "You…You can read that?"

"Of course," Ursula uttered matter-of-factly. "But more importantly, as a representative of those same Powers Incarnate, my presence here should — at the very least — be tolerated, if not openly accepted."

There was silence for a moment as the members of the Council exchanged knowing glances, their expressions seeming to indicate that they knew something the rest of us didn't.

Finally, the white-bearded man, giving Ursula a skeptical look, said, "Just to be clear, are you saying that you're here on behalf of the Powers Incarnate?"

"As I said, I represent them," Ursula answered.

"Then by your own words, you admit to being here under false pretenses," the man smugly declared.

Ursula frowned. "What do you mean?"

"You get points for originality," the man stated. "We've had obtruders show up here before, but this is the first time one has claimed to appear on behalf of the Powers Incarnate. So, while we applaud your imagination and inventiveness, your argument suffers from one fatal flaw."

"Oh?" Ursula droned. "What's that?"

"Incarnates don't exist," the man declared.

Ursula didn't immediately reply, but I could suddenly sense anger and irritation starting to swell in her.

"Excuse me?" she blurted out between nearly-clenched teeth.

"I said that Incarnates don't exist," the bearded man repeated. "They're a construct, like Greek myths — originally aimed at explaining certain aspects of the world around us. Frankly speaking, however, there's no such thing."

Fists balled, Ursula stared at him and said in a smoldering tone, "Just out of courtesy, I'm going to give you a chance to take that back."

"Or what?" the bearded man chided. "The Incarnates will strike me down?"

For a moment, I got the distinct impression that Ursula was going to accept that challenge. Fortunately, she swiftly allayed my fears.

"Nothing so melodramatic," she assured the bearded fellow. "I'll just nullify your magic."

There followed a few seconds of stunned silence, as the members of the Council merely stared at her.

The quiet was then abruptly shattered by the burgundy-haired woman blurting out, "What did you say?"

"You heard me," Ursula announced sullenly. "As of this moment, none of you can so much as pull a rabbit from a hat or a coin from behind a kid's ear. Give it a try, if you like."

It wasn't immediately clear whether the Council believed her, but I noticed several of them appearing to mutter words under their breath, while a few others made vague hand gestures. (Razi, I noticed, simply toyed absentmindedly with one of the beads on her necklace.) They were obviously making various, sundry attempts at *some*thing — presumably individually, but possibly as a collective. Regardless, after a few seconds, various expressions (which ran the gamut from deep concern to nigh shock) began to settle on most of their faces. Empathically, I also sensed something else that wasn't fully conveyed by their demeanor: resignation.

CONJURATION

The last holdout was the bearded man. Seemingly frustrated that his attempts at sortilege were being negated, he suddenly stood and shouted something I couldn't quite make out, at the same time seeming to gesture towards the floor beneath us.

Ursula looked in the direction indicated and then put a hand up to her mouth, stifling a laugh.

"I'm sorry," she giggled, "but your little guardian is nothing more than ordinary artwork at the moment."

It was plainly obvious that Ursula was referring to the dragon painted on the floor tiles. Looking at it now — although it was still a beautiful piece of art — it didn't seem as sharp and detailed as when I'd first noticed it. In fact, it seemed drab and lackluster in comparison to its initial appearance. (I also realized then that Lamont had slipped into the room — seemingly without anyone noticing — and was standing a few feet away from us.)

"Okay — you win," Razi announced to Ursula, bringing my attention back to the matter at hand. "We apologize for any offense we may have caused the Incarnates."

"And?" Ursula asked expectantly.

"And you are most welcome here," added the Maximus.

"Why, thank you," Ursula said with an exuberant smile. "That's very kind of you. I'm sure I'll enjoy my stay."

"We'll make sure of it," Razi assured her, then turned her attention to Lamont. "Please find our guest appropriate lodging."

"Right away," Lamont responded.

"Can you make sure Jim's close by?" Ursula asked, pointing at me. "He's really the only person I know here."

"That shouldn't be a problem," Razi stated.

"Awesome," Ursula uttered with a grin, before turning and walking towards Lamont.

However, she'd taken no more than a couple of steps before the Maximus cleared his throat with a sonorous, "Ahem."

Understanding this was meant to get her attention, Ursula turned back towards the Council.

"Yes?" she muttered quizzically with a raised eyebrow.

"Our magic?" the Maximus queried.

"Oh, *that*," Ursula intoned. "Don't worry — everything's back the way it was. All of you can once again pull pigeons out of your sleeves and yank an endless stream of scarves out of your pockets."

She then spun back towards Lamont, saying, "Shall we?"

CONJURATION

Chapter 20

"Did you have to do it like that?" I asked.

Ursula gave me a confused look. "What do you mean?"

"The Council," I explained. "Did you have to humiliate them by taking away their powers?"

"That wasn't humiliating," she insisted. "Humbling maybe, but not humiliating. Besides, it's no worse than what they were trying to do to me."

I frowned. "What do you mean?"

"While they were giving me the third degree, a couple of them also tried a few spells on me."

"What?!" I exclaimed. "Are you kidding?"

"It was mostly benign stuff," she explained. "Trying to turn my hair blue, levitate me a few feet in the air, etcetera. Basically, they were just trying to see if any of their powers could work on me."

I mentally chewed on this for a moment while Ursula leaned back on the couch where she was sitting, luxuriating in our current surroundings.

At present, we were in the great room of an extravagant, oversized suite. After leaving the Council chamber, the two of us had been escorted here by Lamont. I had initially thought Kane and Gossamer would be accompanying us. However, as we were leaving the Council chamber, the former had been asked to stay behind for a private discussion with the Council, and Gossamer had insisted on waiting for her boyfriend in the antechamber.

On his part, Lamont had been single-mindedly methodical in carrying out his appointed task. He had seen us to the door of the suite, opened it so we could enter, and then departed without setting foot inside. Left to our own devices, Ursula and I had then made a quick inspection of the premises.

My initial impression upon stepping inside had been that our new lodgings were spacious, and our impromptu inspection confirmed that. There were more rooms than I had anticipated, including an elegant dining room, an area I mentally dubbed a parlor, and at least four capacious bedrooms. (Surprisingly, one of the bedrooms actually contained my overnight bag, which I had practically forgotten about.)

But the suite wasn't just large; it was also lavish. From the furnishings to the décor, the place was incredibly posh and opulent — almost to the point of being garish. These were clearly VIP accommodations. The Council had rolled out the red carpet, but I wasn't foolish enough to think it was for my benefit. It was all for Ursula.

Ultimately, we had ended up in the great room, where I had begun quizzing Ursula about her treatment of the Council. Bearing in mind her last statement, a question suddenly popped into my brain.

"You said *mostly* benign," I noted. "Did the Council actually try to do something harmful to you?"

"I think they were just frustrated," she replied, "but towards the end, that dude with the beard tried to rouse the dragon."

"The dragon?" I repeated. "The one on the floor of the Council's chamber?"

She nodded. "Yeah, it's kind of a magical guard dog. If someone gets out of hand in there, they can sic that little beastie on them."

"And they tried to make it attack you?" I uttered in surprise.

"Well, it was just that one guy — not all of them," she clarified. "And I don't believe having the dragon pounce on me was really the intent. As I said, I think he was frustrated that his magic was on the fritz and was willing to try anything to see if it might work."

"Which harkens back to my earlier question of whether dealing with them like that was really necessary. I mean, I honestly can't imagine Incarnates losing any sleep over the fact that these folks don't think they exist."

"Puh-leeze," Ursula droned, rolling her eyes. "Most people have never even heard of Incarnates. The fact that a secret society of conjurers doesn't believe they're real isn't going to make the Incarnates bat an eye."

"That's what I thought," I stated with a nod. "So if it doesn't bother the Incarnates, why did *you* get worked up about it?"

She seemed to deliberate on this for a moment, then said, "It's kind of like when someone calls your mom fat. Doesn't matter if she weighs five hundred pounds and considers herself a land whale. She's still your mom, and you're not going to let anyone bad-mouth her."

I nodded in understanding. "I get it. The Incarnates are your family. The Council insulted them, and you felt compelled to defend the family name, so to speak."

"Exactly," Ursula agreed.

"Okay, while that's understandable to an extent, let's remember that we're guests here."

She raised an eyebrow. "Meaning?"

"Meaning that you've already shown your superiority, so let's make an extra effort not to appear patronizing or condescending."

"I'm not patronizing!" Ursula strongly insisted. "Or condescending!"

"I didn't say you were. I just want to make sure we give our hosts the respect they deserve."

"By not doing things like taking away their magical talents," she concluded.

"Now you're getting it," I said with a grin.

CONJURATION

Chapter 21

We sat around chatting in the great room for perhaps another ten minutes or so. Most of that time consisted of Ursula expressing a desire to leave our quarters and explore the rest of the Templum. On my part, I continually stressed that we were guests, and as such we didn't have carte blanche to simply wander all over the place. Simply put, I was of the opinion that we needed an escort — namely, Kane.

"I don't necessarily disagree with that position," Ursula said, "but I'm really curious about these people. I mean, they obviously had contact with Incarnates at some point in the past."

"You bring up an interesting point," I noted. "Did you already know about that script over the chamber door before we got here?"

She shook her head. "No. How would I know about that?"

"Because you have access to the Cosmos Corridor, which can let you see anywhere in the universe."

"Well, that's not what I did. It was just a coincidence that they welcome Incarnates — and their representatives — here."

"That's quite the coinky-dink," I stated skeptically.

"Not really," she retorted. "Incarnates have been interacting with folks for thousands of years. This is just an instance where someone actually knew who they were dealing with and noted it."

"Hmmm," I droned, thinking. "Did that script say anything else?"

"The only other noteworthy thing it mentioned was the Kroten Yoso Va," Ursula replied. "At a guess, I'd say that somewhere in the past, someone affiliated with this group was the relic's Keeper."

"The founder of their guild," I stated, remembering what Razi had told me.

Ursula looked as though she wanted to discuss the topic further, but at that moment the door opened.

Turning in that direction, I saw Kane and Gossamer enter the suite.

"Hey," Kane called out as they walked towards us. "Sorry to keep you guys waiting."

"No problem," I responded as Ursula and I came to our feet.

"Also, I want to apologize," Ursula said. "I really wasn't trying to get you in trouble, so I hope the Council didn't come down too hard on you."

"No worries," Kane assured her. Glancing around, he then added, "I should actually be thanking you. These are VIP quarters that I never get to set foot in. Now, thanks to you, I'll be staying here."

"Huh?" Ursula uttered in surprise.

"Officially, you guys are *my* guests," Kane explained. "That being the case, I'm supposed to stick close and make sure you enjoy your time here. As part of that, I get to crash here with you during your stay."

"Me, too," Gossamer added.

"Awesome!" Ursula practically squealed. She then took Gossamer by the hand. "Come on — let me show you the girls' end."

"The girls' end?" Kane echoed, eyebrows raised in curiosity.

"Yeah," Ursula said with a nod. Hooking a thumb over her shoulder, she declared, "We're taking the two bedrooms on *this* side of the suite."

CONJURATION

With that, she turned and continued in the direction indicated, pulling Gossamer along. Her statement, however, brought to mind something I hadn't given much thought to previously: the configuration of our current lodgings.

Basically, two of the bedrooms were located down a short hallway on one side of the suite, while the other two were similarly located at the end of a hallway on the exact opposite side. More to the point, although all four bedrooms could be considered sizable, the two Ursula was claiming for herself and Gossamer were noticeably larger.

I passed this info along to Kane, who merely chuckled as he sat down in the spot Ursula had vacated, saying, "In that case, I guess Gossamer is getting *your* room."

Taking a seat as well, I gave him a confused look. "What do you mean?"

"Well, from what you're saying, it sounds like they put in two master bedrooms."

"Put in?" I repeated. "Are you saying they can change the layout of this place?"

"Of course. What's the benefit of a magical habitation if you can't change rooms around?" he asked rhetorically. "Anyway, Ursula asked them to put you close by, so I'm guessing that's why the two masters are in the same part of the suite."

"I don't think so," I declared, shaking my head. "My bag was already in one of the *other* bedrooms."

"Really?" he muttered in surprise. "That was probably an oversight."

"Not a big deal," I assured him. "So, do you need to follow your girlfriend's example and check out the room you'll be staying in?"

Kane shook his head. "I'll look at it later. Right now, I'm just savoring the fact that I'll be staying here."

"So you've really never been in this suite before?"

"Nope," he answered. "As I said, it's always reserved for VIPs."

"But you're being allowed to stay here *now*," I noted.

"Again, you and Ursula are my guests, so the Council figured I should be close in case you need anything."

"Or to spy on us," I suggested, verbalizing an emotion I'd picked up from Kane.

He merely looked at me for a moment, internally debating how to respond, then sighed. "Look dude, I want you to know this is not how I typically treat my friends."

"I get it," I said. "You're just following the Council's orders."

He nodded. "And to be clear, it's not *you* — it's Ursula. Plus, I'm not spying on her, per se. I'm really just supposed to get a sense of why she's here and whether she poses some kind of danger to us."

"I thought she explained all that. The Council still doesn't believe her?"

"Well, she claims to represent the Incarnates, which is pretty farfetched," Kane stated. "But I guess I should explain. According to the stories, Incarnates are—"

"I know what Incarnates are," I interjected. "For what it's worth, I think Ursula overreacted earlier, and she agrees. The Incarnates themselves probably would have found the whole thing amusing."

"Wait a minute!" Kane blurted out almost in shock. "Incarnates are *real*?! You've seen them?"

"Yeah," I answered flatly.

"What are they like?" he asked excitedly.

I shrugged, not sure how to answer. My initial thought was to say that they were just like regular people, but that wasn't quite true.

"They're unique," I finally said. "They stand out, but you wouldn't necessarily know what they are just by looking at them."

"Did you see them do anything?"

I gave him a confused look. "I'm not sure what you mean."

"Incarnates are supposed to be incredibly powerful and have these amazing abilities."

"Well, I can certainly vouch for that," I said. "But Ursula would be the real expert on them."

"Hmmm," Kane droned, frowning. "That seems to be a sensitive topic for her. Suddenly I'm not that curious about Incarnates anymore."

I laughed at that, and a moment later Kane began snickering as well. We were still chuckling a few seconds later when Ursula and Gossamer made their way back into the room.

"What's so funny?" Gossamer asked.

"Guy stuff," Kane replied, nimbly avoiding giving a direct answer. "Anyway, despite all the excitement thus far, we've still got some time to kill before the ceremony tonight. What would you guys like to do?"

His question was seemingly directed at me and Ursula. Having given little thought to the matter, I asked, "What are our options?"

"Fairly broad," Kane declared. "We could do almost anything you want. Water skiing, go-kart racing, hiking, whatever…"

CONJURATION

I looked at Ursula. "I've got no preferences, so it's really up to you."

She smiled. "Well, there *is* something I've always wanted to do…"

CONJURATION

Chapter 22

It turned out that Ursula wanted to build a snowman. Considering the options, it seemed like a rather meek and unassuming request. In fact, it was so benign that, upon hearing it, Kane gave me an *Is-your-friend-all-there?* look. My response was a shrug.

"We aim to please," Kane said flatly, clearly unimpressed by the activity Ursula had chosen for us. Then, indicating that we should follow him, he led us out of the great room and towards a nearby hallway.

Once in the corridor, he stopped near an expanse of wall where a frosted globe about a foot in diameter sat atop a four-foot-tall pedestal. I had noticed it earlier when Ursula and I had first explored the suite, but had assumed it to be some type of artwork.

Kane placed a hand on the globe, which immediately began to glow with a soft, white light. Moments later, a broad wooden door appeared in the wall. Kane removed his hand from the globe, and the light from it began to fade.

Turning to Ursula, he said, "Per your request." At the same time, he opened the door. The rest of us peeked in, and I found myself staring in amazement.

On the other side of the door was a winter wonderland.

It was a wide, outdoor area completely blanketed by snow. A light flurry was starting to fall, giving a seasonal effect to what we were seeing. There were also fir trees interspersed throughout the vicinity, their branches heavy-laden with snow. All in all, it was practically a Yuletide scene, one which would have been perfect for any postcard.

CONJURATION

"Wow," muttered Ursula, before dashing through the doorway. Grinning widely, she began spinning around, face turned up and arms outstretched. Gossamer, who had been right behind her, began sticking out her tongue, trying to catch snowflakes.

Realizing I was flagging myself as the person most unfamiliar with magic in our group, I looked at Kane and asked, "How did you do this?"

"There's a powerful enchantment on the globe," he explained as he sauntered into the snowy landscape with me beside him. "It responds to the desire of the person touching it, creating pretty much whatever they want on the other side of the door."

"So it can fashion anything you want?"

"Anything within reason," he explained. "I mean, there are safeguards in place, so it's not going to give you a nuclear bomb, an assault rifle, or anything dangerous. It's really just meant to ensure that anyone staying here has a good time."

"Is that type of thing common?"

"I wish," Kane muttered wistfully. "No, it's fairly unique."

"Oh, so it's a VIP privilege."

"Exactly," Kane confirmed.

"But it'll operate as sort of a 'wish room' for anybody staying in the suite?"

"No, there's a key that's required to activate the globe — more of a charm, to be honest. Typically, we'd give it to the guest, but given the Council's view on Ursula…"

He trailed off, but it wasn't hard to guess what he was implying.

"*You* have it," I surmised.

118

Kane responded with a nod before turning his attention to the girls, who were still frolicking in the snow. "Hey — any objection to doing this with coats and gloves?"

As he spoke, Kane made an odd gesture with his right hand. Seconds later, I felt an odd weight settle on my shoulders. It wasn't heavy or burdensome — just unexpected. At the same time, I felt a mild constriction enveloping my fingers and hands. Giving myself a once-over, I suddenly realized that I was now wearing a winter coat with matching gloves.

I immediately understood what had happened. Kane had magically added to my attire, so that I was now dressed for the weather. And not just me — everyone else was also outfitted in winter wear. Or rather, everyone but Ursula.

I saw a frown stamp itself momentarily on Kane's face, and it wasn't difficult to understand why. He had obviously expected his efforts to affect all four of us. Ursula, however, had remained conspicuously *un*affected, making it plainly obvious that whatever measures she had employed earlier to keep the Council's magic at bay was still in effect.

"No worries," Ursula declared, breaking a stony silence I hadn't fully been aware of. "I'll handle my own wardrobe."

I didn't notice Ursula do anything out of the ordinary, but a moment later she, too, was dressed in winter garb.

"All right," Gossamer chimed in. "Let's get this snowman built."

With that, we went to work. Ursula stressed a desire for a snowman with three sections, so while she and

CONJURATION

Gossamer handled the middle portion, Kane and I focused on the base. Thankfully, it just involved putting together a snowball and then rolling it around until it was large enough to suit our purposes.

When it was about two feet in diameter, we stopped for a moment to consider whether it was currently adequate or needed to be larger. We were still debating the matter when something cold and wet struck the back of my head, causing me to wince. Thankfully it wasn't painful. More importantly, having experienced this particular sensation before, I knew exactly what had struck me: a snowball.

Spinning to my rear, I saw Gossamer and Ursula giggling merrily at me from about twenty feet away.

"Funny," I deadpanned, then turned my attention back to the snowman base Kane and I had been working on. Almost immediately, I found myself struck by another snowball.

Turning back to the girls, I found them laughing even more heartily than before.

"Really?" I muttered acerbically, which only seemed to amuse them more (and even caused Kane to start chortling softly).

Shaking my head, I once more put my back to Gossamer and Ursula, intent on trying to finish the snowman. Not unexpectedly, a snowball hit me from behind a third time.

"That's it!" I belted out. "Game on!"

I shifted into super speed, and the world basically froze around me, with even the snowflakes appearing to stop in midair. Wasting no time, I quickly built myself a small pile of about ten snowballs. The initial temptation was to follow up by immediately flinging them at the girls.

Common sense, however, said that my friends wouldn't take kindly to being pounded by globs of snow packing the punch of two-hundred-mile-per-hour fastballs. Thus, I shifted back to normal speed, and then began pelting Ursula and Gossamer with my snowball arsenal.

As one might expect, the girls twisted and squirmed in an effort to avoid being hit, giggling all the while. A couple of throws went wild, but I managed to tag Ursula on the back and leg. Gossamer, however, I nailed point-blank between the eyes, causing Kane to guffaw uproariously.

"What are *you* laughing at?" Gossamer asked rhetorically as she wiped the snow from her face. Then she whipped one of the daggers from its sheath at her waist, pointed it at her boyfriend, and made a twirling motion.

A geyser of snow suddenly erupted beneath Kane's feet, causing him to stagger back as it blew frost and graupel all over him like his own personal blizzard. It only lasted a few seconds, but it was enough to make him look like he'd fallen into a snowdrift.

Kane spent a moment knocking snow off himself before giving Gossamer a faux angry look and stating, "Just remember: you asked for this."

Without warning, the two-foot orb of snow we'd made went flying towards Gossamer. I'm not sure who did what, but when it was about halfway to her, it seemed to explode, blasting all four of us with snow.

There followed a moment of silence, when we all looked at each other mischievously, and then it became a free-for-all snowball fight.

CONJURATION

Chapter 23

In retrospect, it was the strangest snowball fight I'd ever been involved in. The explosion of our snowman's base effectively served as a catalyst, putting everyone on the offensive and causing my friends to deploy their magic.

Gossamer, for instance, conjured up some type of snowcat — a saddled, saber-toothed feline as big as a horse — which she rode like a champion equestrian. Ghostly white in color, the beast had a prehensile tail, which it used to scoop up clumps of snow to both fling at targets, as well as dump into a saddlebag for Gossamer's use.

Not to be outdone, Ursula seemingly brought a ten-foot fir to life. With its trunk split into wooden legs, I expected the tree to do little more than lumber about. However, it turned out to be surprisingly agile, serving as both a sword and shield for Ursula, flinging clumps of snow from its branches at her adversaries while competently blocking almost anything tossed at her.

On his part, Kane fashioned something akin to a machine gun made of hoarfrost. Of course, it fired snowballs instead of bullets, which — despite their speed — only struck with a mild amount of force.

As for me, my innate abilities adequately made up for any lack of magic. For the most part, I spent my time being invisible, which generally allowed me to sneak up on the others and pelt them with snow.

Needless to say, it was incredibly fun and we all had a great time peppering each other with snowballs. Eventually, however, we called a truce, at which point my friends put away their magical accoutrement and I became visible.

"That was awesome!" Ursula exclaimed as we all came together.

"Completely," Gossamer agreed. "Although I hated having to destroy you guys like that."

"Destroy?" Kane echoed in surprise. "What are you talking about? I must have blasted you and your little kitty twice as often as you hit me."

"Ha!" Gossamer belted out contemptuously. "Are we even talking about the same thing? You must be blind if you think—"

"Hey," I interjected. "Any chance we can continue this discussion somewhere inside?"

"Of course," said Kane. "Will this suffice?"

As he spoke, he gestured off to the side with one hand. Looking in the direction indicated, my eyebrows went up in surprise as I noticed that a log cabin had suddenly appeared, essentially out of nowhere.

I stared at the structure for a moment, which was obviously another product of the Wish Room. Like the snowy landscape earlier, it presented an image that was almost straight off a postcard, with a rocking chair on the porch, a snow-covered roof, and a stone chimney that was currently emitting a continuous cloud of smoke.

"Looks good to me," muttered Ursula, who immediately began heading towards the structure. The rest of us quickly fell into step behind her; moments later, we were inside the cabin.

The interior of the place was as cozy as the outside had led us to believe. There were several logs of wood burning brightly in the fireplace, and a couple of couches were strategically placed around the hearth, with a coffee table between them. Looking like warped tennis rackets, a pair of vintage snowshoes were set as decorations on the wall above the fireplace mantel. Finally, the aroma of rich chocolate filled the air; a moment later, I realized that it was coming from four cups of hot cocoa that sat on the coffee table.

We quickly got out of our coats, hanging them on a couple of hooks that were placed near the cabin door. We then flopped down on the couches, with Gossamer and Kane sitting on one while Ursula and I sat on the other. Seconds later, we were enjoying our cocoa.

"This is delicious," declared Ursula after taking a few sips.

"I second that," said Gossamer. "It's a perfect way to end a snowball fight."

"Agreed," said Kane. "But it's too bad we never got around to finishing the snowman."

His last statement was directed at Ursula, who pooh-poohed his concerns with a wave of her hand.

"Don't worry about it," she said. "Besides, I really didn't want to build a snowman anyway."

We all stared at her, plainly surprised.

"Excuse me?" I said. "I thought building a snowman was the entire reason we were here."

"Actually, the snowball fight was what I wanted," Ursula admitted. "I've never been in one before."

"So why didn't you just say that's what you wanted to do?" I asked.

"Because from everything I've seen, snowball fights are much more fun when they're spontaneous," she explained. "Planning one just seemed like it would take some of the joy out of actually doing it."

Mentally, I nodded, agreeing with her point.

"So the snowman was just a ploy," Gossamer concluded.

"Pretty much," Ursula confirmed. "I hope you aren't mad about that."

"No," Kane assured her, shaking his head (as did Gossamer). "But since we still have some time, is there anything else you'd like to do that doesn't require a pretext?"

"As a matter of fact, there is," Ursula admitted.

CONJURATION

Chapter 24

We ended up playing beach volleyball, which was what Ursula had in mind, and it was literally magical how swiftly the environment altered to accommodate us. One second, we could see a snowy landscape outside one of the cabin windows; the next, there was white, sandy beach and ocean tides. Even the cabin changed, morphing into a beach house with a bright interior, hardwood floors, and broad windows on every side that let in lots of sunlight.

It was another testament to how adaptable the Wish Room could be. That said, I was surprised that the modifications didn't require touching the globe in our suite again.

"It's a lot like a TV remote," Kane explained when I asked him about it later. "You have to press the power button to turn the television on, but you don't have to press it every time you want to change channels. Likewise, once the globe is activated, the 'Wish Room,' as you call it, will continue to respond to the person with the key until they leave."

Much like before, we weren't quite dressed for the weather. This time, however, it was Ursula who did the honors; following a brief wave of her hand, we all found ourselves in swimsuits and flip-flops.

We then headed outside, where I noticed a volleyball net set up on the sand, not too far from the beach house. There was also a picnic table nearby, with a large covered basket on it.

Kicking off my shoes, I stepped onto the sand and was happy to find that it was not as hot as I initially suspected. In fact, the temperature of the sand (as well as the beach in general) was perfect: not too hot, not too cold

— a sublime amalgam of summer sun and gentle ocean breeze.

"All right," said Kane, producing a volleyball from thin air. "Let's play."

****

It wasn't quite as much fun as the snowball fight (probably because nobody used any magic or special powers), but we had a great time playing volleyball. I got to team up with everyone at least once, and had the good fortune to win about half the time. Surprisingly, I paired best with Gossamer. Our styles of play simply meshed, with each of us intuitively understanding what the other was going to do in terms of playing the ball.

As with the snowball fight, however, things eventually wound down. At that juncture, somewhat parched, I informed the others that I was going inside the beach house for a drink of water, only to have Kane direct my attention to the basket on the picnic table, which I had practically forgotten about.

"I think I might have you covered," he said.

Following Kane's suggestion, I walked towards the picnic table, followed by the others. The basket turned out to be a garden-variety wicker container with a double-lid. Upon opening it, I saw that the interior was lined with a red-and-white checkered cloth. Unsurprisingly, I also noticed that it was filled with food — sandwiches, to be specific, as well as chips and sodas.

The sight of victuals was an instant reminder that it had been awhile since I'd eaten. Although I had tweaked my bodily systems so that I wouldn't feel hunger pangs, I suddenly felt famished. Apparently I wasn't the only one, because a short time later we were all seated at the picnic table, eating with relish the goodies that had been in the basket.

No one said anything for a few minutes; we just sat there enjoying our food, the sun, and the breeze. It was incredibly relaxing and a moment to be savored, made all the more memorable by the presence of good friends.

Others were seemingly having the same thoughts, because Gossamer unexpectedly spoke up, saying, "It's too bad Li couldn't be here."

I simply nodded, while Kane added, "Yeah, he would have enjoyed this."

"Li?" Ursula repeated, obviously confused.

"He's another friend of ours," I explained. "Kane was initially supposed to invite him instead of me."

"Unfortunately, some of the enchantments here can have an odd effect on non-living things," Kane explained.

Ursula frowned, looking confused. "Wait a minute — your friend's not alive?"

"Li's an AI — artificial intelligence — housed in an android body," I stated in clarification. "*We* consider him to be alive, but I'm not sure he'd fit any scientific definition of the word."

"Wow," Ursula muttered. "That's surprising."

"What, that our friend's an android?" Gossamer inquired.

Ursula shook her head. "No — that the great Kid Sensation was someone's second choice for something."

Noting her smirk, I said, "If only I were the second choice in terms of people tagging along behind me."

Following my comment, Ursula playfully shot daggers at me with her eyes.

"Actually, I powwowed with Li and Jim about the fact that I only had one invite to give," Kane commented. "To their credit, each of them suggested that I take the other. In the end, however, the house rules dictated who got to attend."

"That would be this ban on non-living items," Ursula surmised.

Kane frowned. "I probably didn't explain that very well. It's not really a ban on non-living things. For instance, we have a ton of stuff around that could be called non-living: furniture, books, kitchen utensils, and so on. What we really have are wards against certain contrivances."

Ursula frowned. "Like what?"

Kane seemed to contemplate for a moment before answering. "You probably can't tell because we're such a laid-back group, but occasionally the Kroten Venefici have to take the gloves off. There have been times in the past when we had to put our game face on and go to war. And believe me, magical battles are the last place you want to be."

"No kidding," Gossamer added. "You've got people hurling around lightning bolts, wielding enchanted weapons…not to mention spewing out spells, hexes, and curses on anybody within shouting distance."

"So how does that end up keeping your friend from coming here?" Ursula asked.

"Wizards and warlocks don't always fight their battles in person," Kane responded. "They sometimes do it by proxy. Why risk life and limb when you can have a surrogate take your place? In short, we've been attacked by all sorts of runic creations in the past: golems, magical contraptions, mechanical constructs…"

CONJURATION

"So you put enchantments in place to stop them," Ursula concluded.

Kane nodded. "Anything along those lines will be rendered inert before it even gets close to the Templum."

Ursula nodded in understanding. "And that would happen to your android friend if he came here."

"Don't know," Kane stated with a shrug. "I asked around, and no one — not even the Maximus — could say what would happen to him if Li came here. It certainly wasn't worth risking his life to find out."

"Hmmm," I droned. "What about *this* place — the Wish Room? Could some kind of automaton be fashioned in here?"

Kane shook his head. "Like I said before, the room won't create anything dangerous. So even if it manufactured something like what you're suggesting, the end product would presumably be benign."

"What about Gossamer's snowcat?" I asked. "It looked like it could ruin someone's day."

Kane looked at his girlfriend. "You want to explain?"

"Sure," Gossamer replied, then turned to me. "Actually, all I did was animate some snow and cast a glamour on it to make it *look* like a ferocious feline."

"So there was never really a snowcat," I realized. "That brings up another question: is this an actual place" — I waved an arm to encompass our surroundings — "or a complete fabrication?"

"I'd describe it as a type of augmented reality," Kane replied.

"So, it's fake," I declared, causing everyone else to grin. "But is it actually capable of showing a real place — some location that actually exists?"

Kane frowned. "The enchantment would have to be modified, almost to an extreme degree. It's not something *I* could do. In fact, it's probably outside the skill set of anyone except the Council."

I suddenly sensed an easy confidence, as well as calm assurance and certainty, welling up in Ursula. I knew without a shadow of a doubt what she was about to say, and could practically see the words forming on her lips: *I bet I could do it.*

I telepathically pinged her to get her attention, then gave a subtle shake of my head. She stuck her lip out, plainly pouting, but thankfully remained silent.

"Anyway," Kane continued, "it's getting close to showtime, so we should head back."

With that, we reluctantly brought the picnic to an end.

CONJURATION

Chapter 25

In literally the blink of an eye, Ursula had us back in our regular clothes. Kane then led us out of the Wish Room through a door that seemed to materialize out of nowhere — much like the one that had appeared during my walk with Razi.

Once back in the suite, we huddled together just long enough to agree on meeting in the great room in half an hour. Following that, we all scattered, heading to our individual rooms in order to get ready for the upcoming ceremony.

I, of course, went to the room containing my overnight bag. Once there, I shifted into super speed and quickly unpacked, making use of a nearby dresser, as well as a walk-in closet. Of particular note was the fact that there was a tuxedo already hanging in the closet — a subtle indication of what I was expected to wear to the upcoming function. Satisfied that I'd done an adequate job of unpacking, I then dashed to the bathroom for a quick shower.

****

Ursula was already sitting on the sofa in the great room when I arrived, sporting the tuxedo I'd found in my closet. I had to admit to being surprised. Having showered and gotten dressed at super speed, I had naturally expected to be the first to arrive at our rendezvous point. In fact, I had been so certain of being early that I'd spent a few minutes idling in my room in an effort to kill time. Her presence was a reminder that Ursula could freshen up and get dressed with a simple wave of her hand. (Upon

132

reflection, I was pretty sure that Kane and Gossamer could do the same.)

"Hey," she said as I took a seat in a chair diagonal to her. "Guess we're both a little early."

"Probably preferable to being late," I chided. "I'm sure Kane will appreciate the fact that we're ready to walk out the door when he arrives."

"I like him — he's a nice guy," Ursula stated. "Even if he *is* operating as a watchdog and keeping an eye on me." I gave her an appraising glance, causing her to blurt out, "What — you thought you were the only one who figured that out?"

"No," I admitted, shaking my head. "But in his defense, it's an assignment he really detests."

"It's not a big deal," she assured me. "We all have to occasionally do things we dislike."

As she spoke, I noticed a faraway look in her eyes as she seemed to ruminate on something important. At the same time, I picked up on an emotion that appeared to be a commingling of resolve and regret.

"Anyway," she droned, "you look nice."

"Thanks — so do you," I replied, noting that she was wearing an elegant black keyhole dress.

"What, this old thing?" she said playfully, giving herself a once-over. "Actually, it was hanging in the closet in my room, so I took the hint — especially since it turned out to be a perfect fit."

I simply nodded, as my tux had been an ideal fit as well.

"To be honest, though," Ursula continued, tugging slightly at her dress, "I'm not wild about this."

I looked at her in surprise. "You don't like the dress?"

"It's not that I don't like it. I just prefer something a little more casual."

"Like what?"

Ursula gave a sly grin, and a moment later her dress had vanished, replaced by a blue-and-gray superhero outfit, complete with cape. And if that wasn't enough, my tux had disappeared as well, and I was now wearing a similar uniform (sans cape) that was cobalt in color.

I stared at her in nigh disbelief. "You're kidding, right?"

"Oh, come on," she pleaded. "We look awesome in these outfits, and you know it."

"That's not the point," I stressed. "This is not an event that calls for costume attire, and — even if we do look awesome — I'm not trying to upstage my friend."

"Well, what if a situation arose that *did* require costume attire?"

"Huh?" I muttered, frowning. "What are you talking about?"

"Anything can happen," Ursula replied. "You never know when Kid Sensation might need to spring into action."

As she finished speaking, the room expectedly changed. Actually, "changed" is something of a misnomer; the room essentially vanished, and we were suddenly outside, beneath the night sky with stars twinkling above us. Not far away was an immense cathedral-like building with glittering spires and resplendent domes populating its roof. Based on what I'd seen during my walk with Razi, I took it to be the Templum.

A whooshing sound caught my attention. Trying to pinpoint the source, I looked up and saw what appeared to be some kind of oversized artillery shell rocketing through the sky. In fact, there were dozens of them.

Confused, I glanced at Ursula and saw that she was now floating a few feet off the ground. She was watching the artillery shells streak above us, and I picked up a vibe from her that I would probably equate to some amalgam of hope and glee. I was about to ask what was going on, but before I could get a word out, the artillery shells started exploding.

Oddly enough, the explosions weren't particularly loud, but they *were* bright. They lit up the sky like fireworks, an unexpected but engrossing pyrotechnic display. (There was also no shrapnel, a fact which made it all the more evident that what I was seeing was nothing more than an illusion conjured by Ursula. Still, it was an enjoyable sound-and-light show.)

"Whoa…" murmured someone near me.

I turned in the direction of the voice and saw Kane a few feet away from me, staring up at the exploding shells in unfettered surprise. Outfitted in a tuxedo, he had obviously come to meet us as agreed and wandered into Ursula's illusion.

However, before anyone could make further comment, everything shifted and we were back in the great room. I looked at Ursula and noted that she was once more in her dress, while I was again in my tux.

I turned back to Kane, who was now giving Ursula an odd look. The entire episode of us being "outside" had probably lasted no more than ten or fifteen seconds, but Kane had clearly gotten to experience a few moments of it. Reaching out empathically, I picked up surprise and bewilderment from him (neither of which was unexpected), while from Ursula I detected contrition, self-reproach, and disappointment. Apparently she interpreted Kane's gaze as being judgmental and disapproving.

Reaching out telepathically, I told her, <*It's fine. He's not upset.*>

As if in support of this, Kane simply stated, "I'm going to go see if Gossamer's ready."

He then headed towards the girls' end of the suite, shaking his head in disbelief.

CONJURATION

Chapter 26

After retrieving Gossamer, Kane quickly hustled us out of the suite and began guiding us through the Templum. It wasn't double-time, but we strode through the place at a fairly brisk pace.

"We're not late," Kane assured us as we walked, "but there are a couple of things I probably need to do before the ceremony begins."

After about ten minutes, we arrived at our destination: a spacious, theater-like venue with stadium seating centered around a raised stage. Kane took us up to the balcony area, and — to my surprise — led us to a luxury box with a commanding view of the stage.

The box contained a dozen upscale chairs separated into two equal rows. There were also a number of people present when we arrived. Kane swiftly made introductions, and it turned out that those in attendance were members of his family, including a couple in their late thirties who turned out to be his parents and a girl around six years old who was apparently his sister.

The introductions, of course, were for my and Ursula's benefit; judging from the way they greeted her, Kane's family already knew Gossamer. Moreover, as we met the members of his clan, I felt a minute ball of anxiety and concern in Kane swiftly dissolving. I understood then that rushing us to get here had been for the purpose of acquainting me and Ursula with his relatives.

In essence, he hadn't wanted to simply shove us into a balcony box with a bunch of strangers before taking off. Of course, Gossamer could have made the requisite intros, if necessary, but it obviously wouldn't have been quite the same as Kane doing it himself. (Plus, it probably helped reduce any awkwardness if — as I assumed — his family had heard about Ursula's earlier antics.)

After making sure that we'd met everyone, Kane said a hasty goodbye to us all en masse and then left. It was only then that I noticed that his grandmother Razi wasn't among those in the luxury box with us.

Regardless, Kane's departure served as the cue for everyone to take their seats. Ursula and I sat down next to each other on the second row, while Gossamer was given a seat on the first by her boyfriend's family.

From what I could see, the theater held about a thousand people, and from all indications, it was going to be a full house. Like myself and Ursula, everyone was dressed formally, which helped foster a somewhat stuffy atmosphere and somber mood.

Knowing how spirited she was (and picking up on a restless vibe from her), I worried that Ursula would find the sober ambience stifling. Hoping to keep her engaged in some way, I reached out to her telepathically.

<You okay?> I asked.

<I'm fine,> she stated. <Just ready for things to get underway.>

<Well, I think you're about to get your wish.>

I gave a mental nod in the direction of the stage, where the Maximus had appeared. Like everyone else, he was dressed in formal attire. After a moment, as those in attendance grew aware of his presence, a pensive silence spread throughout the theater.

When all was quiet, the Maximus smiled and said, "Friends, family, honored guests. Thank you for joining us on this momentous occasion."

My eyebrows went up in surprise. I wasn't sure if it was some type of magic or the effect of acoustical design, but it sounded like the Maximus was just a few feet away from me rather than on a faraway stage.

"We come together once again to celebrate a rite of passage for those of our order," he continued. "For those of the Kroten Venefici who have excelled and are ready to advance. And — since I'm quite sure no one came to hear me speak — we'll turn to the business at hand."

As he finished speaking, a line of children came onto the stage. There were eight of them, five girls and three boys, all of whom appeared to be about ten years old. The Maximus turned towards them and stepped to the first in line — a brown-haired girl with long pigtails wearing a white dress.

The Maximus spread his arms wide, then brought them together in front of him. With his back to the audience, I couldn't quite make out what he was doing, although I noticed that there seemed to be a glow in the area of his hands. He then reached towards the girl with the pigtails, and I saw that he now held a medallion on a ribbon, having seemingly conjured it out of thin air.

He placed the medallion around the girl's neck. On her part, she said something inaudible to the Maximus (presumably "Thank you") and then took a few steps forward until everyone in the audience had a clear view of her. She waved her right hand in the air, and a moment later a bouquet of red roses in the shape of a heart appeared in the air above her. Everyone applauded; the girl curtsied, and as she turned to walk back to her place in line, the roses disappeared.

At that juncture, the Maximus moved to the next person in line — a young boy this time. Once again, the Maximus conjured a medallion and placed it around the neck of the boy, who then walked forward. Similar to the girl in pigtails, he made a twirling motion with his index finger and a fiery whirlwind about six feet tall materialized. It bobbed around the stage for a few moments and then disappeared. Again, there was widespread applause as the boy bowed and returned to his original spot.

<That was pretty cool,> I noted, telepathically opening a channel with Ursula.

<Yeah,> she agreed. <This thing might be a bit livelier than I originally thought.>

CONJURATION

Chapter 27

As expected, the process with the remaining kids on stage was the same as with the first two: the Maximus would place a medallion around the neck of a child, who would then perform a feat of magic.

After the pattern had been repeated for the eighth and final child, the Maximus turned to the audience and said, "Ladies and gentlemen, I present to you the Minor Mages."

At that juncture, all of the children on stage bowed, while we in the audience again applauded them. The children then exited the stage, but were immediately replaced by another group of boys and girls who were slightly older — probably twelve years or so in age.

As before, the Maximus stepped towards the kids and began presenting each of them with a medallion.

****

Ultimately, we ended up sitting through about five sets of individuals parading onto the stage and being presented with medallions that presumably represented an advancement to the next level of wizardry (or something along those lines). Each group was generally older than the last, although there were occasionally individuals who seemed to be a few years older or younger than the others in their troop.

Ursula and I spent much of that time in telepathic contact. Initially, we made friendly wagers regarding what magical feats the folks on stage would perform. However, those antics were apparently limited to the younger mages, because as the on-stage groups got older, the magical displays diminished. By the time Kane's group marched out, there was no expectation that any of them would do anything other than simply accept their medallions.

<Why'd they stop the magic show?> Ursula asked. <That was the best part.>

Mentally, I shrugged. <I suppose it relates to the fact that certain actions are more entertaining when performed by youngsters. For instance, people are entranced if a three-year-old can say his ABCs. Not so much if it's a grown man standing around reciting them.>

<Got it,> she attested with a telepathic nod. <Anyway, looks like Kane is finally up.>

I focused on the stage, where my friend was now standing with four other individuals, including Lamont, all positioned a few feet apart. However, Kane stood out by virtue of the fact that he was the youngest in his group by a mile. The nearest person in age to him was Lamont, and there was at least a ten-year age difference between them — maybe more. The other three included a woman whom I pegged as being around thirty, and two men who I assumed were in their late thirties or early forties. Although his grandmother had mentioned him being a prodigy, seeing the others he was advancing with clearly highlighted the fact that Kane was some kind of wunderkind.

Much to my surprise, Razi actually walked out onto the stage a moment later, accompanied by four other people. She took up a position next to her grandson, and those with her followed suit, with each of them choosing to stand beside one of the other individuals in Kane's group.

This was, of course, a slight deviation from the ceremonial pattern that had been observed throughout the evening. This departure from the expected norm continued when the Maximus, rather than present medallions to Kane's group, simply gave a subtle nod to those on stage.

At that juncture, Razi stepped in front of her grandson, and I suddenly noticed that she held a medallion in her hand. Unsurprisingly, she placed it around Kane's neck, while those who had come on stage with her did the same with respect to Kane's fellows.

Based on Razi's presence, I assumed that those bestowing the medallions were probably related to the recipients. It suggested that the ceremony — at least this part of it — was not just momentous, as the Maximus had indicated, but significant and meaningful in a way I hadn't fully appreciated (although I should have, given the initial reaction to Ursula).

As soon as the last person had received their medallion, the entire theater erupted in thunderous applause, with just about everyone coming to their feet. Ursula and I rose as well, and I noticed the Maximus attempting to say something but his words were drowned out by the sounds of hands clapping loudly, earsplitting whistles, and deafening cheers.

Kane's group took a deep bow and then swiftly left the stage, followed by the Maximus, Razi, and the others.

CONJURATION

Chapter 28

The formal ceremony was followed by a reception in a nearby banquet hall. Once there, Ursula, Gossamer, and I found a table to huddle around while waiting for Kane to join us.

"He's taking his sweet time," Gossamer noted glumly, watching her boyfriend — who had entered through a side door — work his way across the room.

In Kane's defense, he was getting congratulated every few steps. Ergo, even though he had quickly spied us after entering the banquet hall, getting to us was proving to be no easy feat. Eventually, however, he made his way to our table, at which point I sensed Gossamer's mood lighten considerably.

"Congrats, babe," she cooed, giving Kane a hug. "I'm so happy for you."

She then planted a loving, lingering kiss on him. In truth, it only lasted a few seconds, but was of such intensity that it seemed longer. When they separated, Kane looked like he was on cloud nine.

"Uh," I droned, "I'm just going to limit my warm wishes to 'Congratulations' and a hearty handshake."

"So no kiss?" Kane joked, shaking the hand I had extended after speaking. "And you look so pretty."

"Ha, ha," I said sarcastically. "But that does remind me: I did have my own tux that I could have brought."

"I know, but they really didn't decide on a dress code until the last minute," Kane stated. "I didn't want you to bring something formal and then never take it off the hanger. Plus, it was just as easy to provide you with appropriate attire."

I was about to make a witty reply to that when a beefy fellow clapped a meaty hand on Kane's shoulder, saying, "Congratulations, Thuergist!"

"Hey, thanks," Kane uttered, shaking the man's hand. The fellow was obviously just passing by, because he moved on without making further comment, seemingly heading for a nearby buffet table.

"Thuergist?" I repeated, plainly curious.

"It's just a title," Kane explained. "It's what the Maximus was saying after my group received our medallions — that we were all theurgists now — but you probably couldn't hear him over the crowd. Anyway, it just denotes the level I'm at in terms of magical ability."

"He's being modest," Gossamer remarked. "For the Kroten Venefici, it's not the highest rank, but it's the most difficult one to attain and usually takes the longest."

"Just out of curiosity, how long are we talking about?" Ursula asked.

"About fifteen years on average," Kane replied, "although some might take twenty or more."

"But you did it in record time," I noted.

Kane merely shrugged, and empathically I detected that he was slightly embarrassed to be talking about himself in this complimentary fashion.

"So what's the deal on your cousin?" Ursula asked, staring across the room.

Following her gaze, I noticed that she was looking at Lamont. He was completely surrounded by what seemed to be an excited and enthusiastic mob, heartily slapping him on the back and offering their congratulations. From the way they crowded around him, you would have thought he was a movie star.

"Technically, he's my second cousin," Kane clarified. "His grandfather and my grandmother are brother and sister."

"Well, he certainly seems to be popular," Ursula commented.

"I think he's just enjoying his moment in the sun," Kane remarked.

I frowned. "What do you mean?"

"Mostly that this is a day that many people thought would never come," Kane stated. "Basically, Lamont never seem to have any real aptitude for magic. Thus, he was never expected to advance very far. However, he apparently decided to knuckle down awhile back, and this was the result."

"Good for him," Gossamer declared.

I nodded, finding myself of the same opinion. Like a lot of people, it seemed that Lamont had probably been plagued by an *attitude* problem rather than an *aptitude* problem. Kane looked as though he had more to say on the subject, but was cut off by someone calling his name.

"Hey, Kane!" shouted a feminine voice from across the room. I looked in the direction the voice had come from and saw a girl about our age who had been sitting in the luxury box with us.

Waving her hand in a come-hither gesture, she yelled, "Get over here!"

"Looks like your family's calling you," Gossamer noted. At that point, I realized that the girl who had shouted for Kane was with a large group of people, several of whom had been seated with us during the ceremony.

"Wow," Ursula muttered. "You've got a good-sized clan."

"Yeah," Kane acknowledged. "A lot more of them came out tonight than I anticipated."

"You should go see what they want," Gossamer continued.

"No way," Kane declared, shaking his head. "If I go over there, my evening's done. I'll be stuck all night listening to my family gab about nothing, like my Uncle Archie telling jokes that he's told a million times before, or my Great-Aunt Hannah talking about the ghostly green pants she saw riding a bike once."

"It'll be fine," Gossamer assured him. "I'll go with you. In fact, you can even pretend I'm your girlfriend to make all your cousins jealous."

Our entire table burst into laughter over Gossamer's comment, chuckling so loudly that several people nearby gave us odd looks.

After struggling to regain his composure, Kane said, "All right, I guess we can go over for a minute." He turned to me and Ursula. "Will you guys be okay on your own for a bit?"

"We'll be fine," I attested. "Plus, I wanted to explore the Templum a little bit anyway — assuming that's okay."

"It shouldn't be a problem," Kane confirmed. "Of course, you're both welcome to come with us, but I have to warn you: there are some real eccentrics in my family, and wizarding kooks are the worst kind."

"One magical kook's enough for me," I stated, cutting my eyes at Ursula (and getting an evil stare in return). "Why don't you and Gossamer go ahead, and we'll catch up with you later."

CONJURATION

"Sounds like a plan," he said. A moment later, he took Gossamer by the hand and began leading her towards his family.

CONJURATION

Chapter 29

Ursula and I took off almost immediately after Kane and Gossamer walked away. Truth be told, I'd been chomping at the bit to explore the Templum to some degree. As a teleporter, the utility of my power stems from the ability to instantly travel to different places. However, I generally can only teleport to a venue that I've actually been to. Thus, whenever I visit a new location, it's practically second nature for me to try to get the lay of the land.

In this instance, Ursula and I simply left the banquet hall and started walking. There were lots of people milling about for the most part, and from what I could gather, everyone present was free to roam wherever they liked. Presumably, if some area was off-limits, there would be wards or safeguards of some type in place. With that in mind, Ursula and I just wandered randomly through the Templum, going in whatever direction struck our fancy.

The first thing I realized was that the Templum was absolutely humongous. Of course, just based on everything I'd seen previously, I knew it was immense, but I hadn't fully appreciated the full size of it. There were rooms where we encountered vaulted ceilings several stories high, and in at least one instance we came across a stairwell which — although we didn't go down — appeared to extend well below ground.

"This place is huge," I remarked to Ursula as we passed through a large library.

"Actually, the Templum isn't a building as you understand it," Ursula stated.

I looked at her, plainly nonplussed. "What do you mean?"

"This place isn't actually a single piece of architecture. It's kind of a mishmash of various structures that have been mystically fused into one unit."

"Wait a minute," I said, frowning as I came to a halt. "Are you saying this whole building is basically just a bunch of rooms magically glued together?"

"That's a simple way of putting it, but yes."

I let her words roll around in my head for a second, then asked, "So how does that work? Every time they want to expand the Templum or add a new wing, they just bring over another building and apply some arcane paste to attach it?"

"Obviously I didn't explain that very well," Ursula admitted, giggling at my question. "The reason they need to be glued together, as you put it, is because the structures comprising the Templum are in disparate locations."

"Huh?" I murmured, trying to wrap my head around what I'd just been told. "All the rooms in this place are in separate geographic regions?"

"Not *all* of them," Ursula clarified. "Not every single room. Still, the whole in this instance is composed of many parts. Many *separate* parts."

"Clearly," I agreed, "although it still seems weird to me. If you need a temple the size of a city block, why not just build it the old-fashioned way — as one structure — rather than magically welding together a bunch of discrete suites, chambers, and cubicles?"

"Apparently someone's power set has made them elitist," Ursula smirked, looking at me in mock disdain. "Obviously you've forgotten what life's like for the average Joe."

I shook my head in confusion. "I have no idea what you're talking about."

"Okay," she droned. "Imagine for a second that you aren't a teleporter. You get up in the morning and get ready to go to work. But instead of getting in your car and driving, you just open a door, step through, and voilà — you're at the office. Or if you suddenly feel sick and need to go see a doctor, imagine just walking through a doorway and suddenly being at the hospital. Or—"

"All right, I get it," I interjected. "There's value in the way this place is put together."

"I'm sure the Kroten Venefici think so."

"And I'm not elitist," I added sullenly.

"Of course not," Ursula offered. "Who would think that of a guy called Kid Sensation?"

She then burst into laughter.

"That's it," I declared. "I'm not talking to you anymore."

I turned and started walking away. Still giggling, Ursula caught up to me and slipped her arm into mine, thereby making it clear that she either knew I wasn't really upset with her or didn't care.

"So," I began after a moment, "what do you think happens if you're standing in a doorway between two rooms that have been stuck together here and the magical glue comes apart?"

"I'd have thought that was obvious," Ursula replied without hesitation. "You get chopped in half."

Somehow my feet managed to keep shuffling forward, but my head swiveled towards her in shock.

"I'm kidding," she said with a wink. "Seriously though, from what I can tell, there are wards in place to prevent things like that. Basically, you'll get shoved into one room or the other."

"Hmmm," I droned, thinking. "So you can sense all the magic in the Templum and what it does?"

Ursula's brow creased for a moment as she appeared to ponder my question.

"The answer is a qualified 'Yes,'" she finally said. "I can home in on the major stuff pretty easily, like the magic holding together the various components of this place. Anything along those lines is like a beacon. However, there are a lot of minor enchantments as well."

"And those are harder to find?"

"Not really," she admitted, "but it's a lot like looking at the stars during daytime. You know they're there, but the sunlight obscures them and makes them more difficult to see. Likewise, with the lesser enchantments around here, I know they're present, but it's more work for me to examine them and figure out their purpose."

"But once you find them, you can figure out what they're supposed to do," I surmised.

"Okay, apparently I misspoke," Ursula stated. "I can ascertain what a spell is *capable* of doing, but I can't tell what it's *intended* to do."

I rubbed my chin, reflecting on her statement for a moment.

"I think I understand," I finally said. "It's like a guy who buys a motorcycle. He may have bought it to use for his daily commute to work, as a recreational vehicle on the weekends, or as a collector's item that he never intends to ride. You know what it *could* be used for, but not how it *will* be utilized in actuality."

"Exactly," Ursula stated with finality.

"Still, that's impressive," I acknowledged. And with that statement, another thought occurred to me, and I found myself considering something.

I spent a moment gathering my thoughts, and then said, "Let me see if I've got this straight. You can sense and perform magic, pretty much go anywhere you want, and also negate the powers of some of the most powerful wizards on the planet. And that's just the stuff I've seen."

"Well," she responded sheepishly, "I can't go *any*where. I mean, there are limits, but—"

"My point is this," I stated, cutting her off. "You said Endow wanted you to come here for a vacation of sorts, but she sent you off stuffed to the gills with power."

"You know Endow — she's super-protective when it comes to me."

"But to send you here packing this kind of firepower..." I continued. "Was she worried about something?"

"Well, if you must know, she *was* concerned," Ursula admitted, and I sensed a slight bit of nervousness as she spoke. "She was afraid that I might bump against one of the most potent, unrestrained, and unruly forces in the universe."

"What?" I asked anxiously. "Some kind of supervillain?"

"No," Ursula replied slyly. "Teenage boys."

CONJURATION

Chapter 30

We spent maybe another half-hour simply wandering through the Templum. At that juncture, we began heading back. In all honesty, however, I didn't get to see as much of the place as I would have on my own.

Ordinarily, when I'm exploring new environs, I usually phase and become invisible. Doing so allows me to move quickly and easily through a place without drawing unwanted attention. Needless to say, I hadn't felt comfortable following my normal routine with Ursula in tow. Moreover, it was actually fun meandering about the place with a friend. The end result was that I didn't become as familiar with the Templum as I should have, but I spent the time in a more enjoyable fashion.

We were maybe halfway back to the banquet hall when Ursula suggested that we stop by a room we had bypassed initially: a gallery full of paintings and other artwork. Being in no particular rush, I had no objection.

Frankly speaking, however, I don't really have a discerning eye when it comes to art. In essence, while I can acknowledge and appreciate the skill it takes to create true-to-life drawings, sculptures, and the like, I can't distinguish between great art and trash. In fact, I admitted as much to Ursula when she asked my thoughts about a mural painted on a wall depicting a coven of witches in a forest.

"It's well-drawn," I said of the mural, "and the images are certainly lifelike. But if you ask me about whether it properly contrasts light and shadow or whether the artist suitably incorporated shape and color, I'll be completely lost."

"It's fine," Ursula said with a smile. "Like beauty, I think the eye of the beholder determines good and bad art."

"Try telling that to art critics."

"Critics are just people who shout their opinions the loudest," she declared.

I snickered at her comment as we continued making our way through the gallery.

"Anyway," I droned as we walked, "I have to say that I'm a little surprised. I didn't think the artwork in here would be so…mundane."

"Mundane?" she repeated, raising an eyebrow. "You mean non-magical."

"I guess," I stated with an indifferent shrug.

Truth be told, however, she had hit the nail on the head. Considering what I'd previously observed in the Templum, I had expected to see something amazing in the gallery — maybe a canvas painting itself, or a statue that occasionally changed position.

"Unfortunately, it's my sad duty to inform you that nothing in here is magical," Ursula asserted.

"So, they're all just typical works of art," I noted, glancing around. "There's nothing particularly special in here."

"Well, I don't know if I'd say *that*."

There was a curious tone to Ursula's voice, and when I looked at her, I noticed that she was staring at a far corner of the room. She started walking, and I quickly fell in step behind her. A few moments later, we stood in front of the item that had drawn her attention: an oil painting that hung on the wall.

First and foremost, the painting was large — roughly three by five feet in size and set in an exotic wooden frame which, if I had to guess, I would have said was handcrafted. As to the painting itself, I had initially thought that it was some type of minimalist art. From across the room, the entire canvas had appeared red, like the artist had fallen completely in love with the color and used it with excess zeal and utter abandon. As we had come closer, however, I'd realized that it contained other features — specifically, people, and they were depicted in such minute and exact detail that one would have thought they had been miniaturized and grafted onto the canvas. Unfortunately, my appreciation of the artist's skill was overshadowed by one thing: all of the people shown were dead.

Basically, the painting depicted a death scene, with bodies all over the place. However, it was the *way* those depicted had died that was truly disturbing. At a glance, I saw decapitations, dismemberments, disembowelments, and more. Much, much more. As hard as it was to imagine, almost every horrid thing that could be done to a human body — almost every way in which a person could meet a vicious, violent end — was depicted somewhere on that canvas. (The ubiquitous red, I now realized, represented blood.)

Plainly speaking, it was one of the most grisly and ghastly images I'd ever seen depicted, including horror movies (which was saying quite a lot). Just looking at it, I found myself fervently hoping that the artist who had created it was living out the rest of his days in a padded room, wearing a straitjacket.

That said, as morbid as the painting was, it was also mesmerizing — an oil canvas train wreck I couldn't stop looking at. Thankfully, movement in my peripheral vision eventually drew my attention.

CONJURATION

It was Ursula, who had moved away from the painting without comment and now stood near a narrow, enclosed circular stairwell leading up. Walking over to join her, I recalled seeing the stairs earlier, but — based on their constricted design — I had assumed them to be some form of avant garde art. Now I realized that the stairwell was actually functional.

"Where do you suppose it goes?" Ursula asked, tilting her head to stare at the stairs winding above us.

"Up?" I deadpanned, causing her to give me a sideways look.

"You're hilarious," she said flatly. "Come on."

Without waiting for a response, she began going up the stairs.

With nothing better to do, I followed.

****

The stairwell didn't exit onto any floors directly above the gallery. It simply seemed to go up for what, in my estimation, amounted to several stories. Eventually it opened up onto a rotunda — a circular room about thirty feet in diameter with a domed ceiling.

Looking around, I saw a couple of couches and easy chairs nearby, as well as a few tables and a wet bar. I also noted a fireplace and a set of ornate bookcases against one wall. Finally, there was something I'd equate to an expensive Persian rug with an eye-catching floral design on the floor in the middle of the room. All in all, the panoply of furnishings and fixtures gave the place an incredibly cozy feel (although, in the back of my mind, I couldn't help imagining the rug as a flying carpet). However, the most prominent feature of the room was the outer wall, which consisted of floor-to-ceiling windows that offered a panoramic view of both the stars and the grounds of the Templum.

"Wow, this is nice," Ursula remarked, taking in the room as she walked towards the center of the rotunda.

"Yeah," I concurred with a nod. "I'd wager this is someone's retreat — a place they go to get away from it all."

"Well, you certainly can't beat the view," she averred as she continued striding forward, heading to the windows.

Following in her wake, I found myself agreeing with Ursula's comment. The rotunda windows offered a magnificent vista that touched both earth and sky. In fact, looking down, I saw people moving about the grounds of the Templum, their size giving me the impression that we were about five stories up. It also brought to mind a question that I had failed to ask earlier.

"Hey," I murmured, getting Ursula's attention. "Going back to the subject of this place being magically glued together, does that also apply to the terrain?"

"What do you mean?" Ursula asked.

"I mean, is the real estate the Templum sits on also located in various places around the globe?"

"No," she stressed, shaking her head. "As far as the grounds go, what you see is what you..."

Her voice trailed off as Ursula suddenly got a faraway look in her eyes. Her brow then creased as her face became a mask of concern, while empathically I sensed shock, anxiety, and dread swiftly rising in her.

"What is it?" I practically demanded, suddenly understanding that something was terribly wrong.

Ursula frowned in concentration as her eyes flitted back and forth, giving the impression that she was trying to solve some incredibly difficult mental problem. Her focus was so intense that I worried for a moment that she hadn't heard me. I was on the verge of asking my question again when she spoke.

"There's something bizarre going on here," she announced. And then she was gone.

CONJURATION

Chapter 31

I looked around wildly for a moment, plainly worried. I then felt relief wash over me as I realized that Ursula hadn't completely vanished — she was outside the rotunda, floating in the air. I immediately phased and flew through the window, joining her a second later and becoming substantial again.

As I had noted before, there were people on the ground below us, walking through what I assumed was the garden I'd visited with Razi. Although I couldn't make out the words, their voices drifted up through the night air. From what I could tell, none of them seemed to have noticed us. Or maybe they had and simply didn't find it significant. (After all, the Templum was full of wizards, witches, and so on. For all I knew, people floated through the air around here all the time.)

Like the garden, the rest of the estate surrounding the Templum appeared to be well-kept. Most of it appeared to consist of a meticulously maintained lawn that extended for about a hundred feet before gently sloping away from the building and eventually giving way to a lightly wooded area. Although it was night, the area was well-illuminated by what appeared to be lampposts placed randomly around the premises.

I turned my attention back to Ursula. She still had a look of deep concentration on her face, and you didn't need to be an empath to know that something was seriously bothering her. Assuming that there was little I could do, I merely stayed quiet, waiting for her to give some indication of what the problem was.

CONJURATION

After what seemed like forever but was probably no more than ten seconds, Ursula seemed to come back to herself.

"Got it!" she crowed triumphantly.

At the same time, I heard a high, tinny sound wafting through the air. The noise was slightly discordant, like a tenor trying to hold a musical note that was meant for a soprano. A moment later, I drew in a harsh breath as I suddenly recognized what I was hearing: someone screaming.

"Come on," Ursula said in a determined voice.

Based on her comment, I assumed Ursula was about to zip away, and I was prepared to follow her. Thus, I was a little taken aback when, rather than us moving, our locale appeared to shift. One moment, we were in the air outside the rotunda; the next, we were near the ground, in a small copse of trees about a hundred yards from the Templum. (This was, of course, the work of Ursula, who had taken us from our previous position to our current location.)

One of the lampposts I'd noticed from above was a few feet from us and provided more than adequate illumination. However, I almost did a double-take when, upon looking at it, I suddenly realized that it wasn't a lamppost at all. It was some type of oversized, luminescent flower.

A sound like a soft gasp drew my attention. Looking around, I saw several people nearby — a middle-aged couple and a young woman in her early twenties. All three of them looked horrified, but the young woman especially so. She was completely pale, practically shivering in fear, and so in shock that her mouth had dropped open. Just glancing at her, I suddenly had an idea of who I'd heard screaming. The question, of course, was what had she been screaming *at*, and I merely had to follow her shell-shocked gaze to figure it out.

Turning in that direction, I quickly understood what had unsettled the nearby trio. First and foremost, there was a body on the ground about twenty feet away — an elderly man with a white beard. A moment later, I recognized him as the Council member who had given Ursula such a hard time earlier.

It was painfully obvious that he was dead. The white tuxedo shirt he wore was soaked with blood, as was the ground all around him. And if that wasn't enough to confirm his demise, there was also the fact that he'd been torn to pieces.

CONJURATION

Chapter 32

I stood off to the side, maybe ten yards from where Ursula was currently engaged in a heated discussion with Razi, the Maximus, and a few other members of the Council. At the moment, we were still outside, not far from where the body of the bearded man had been found.

Immediately after sizing up the situation, I had told Ursula to stay put and teleported to the banquet hall, where Kane was still celebrating with his family and Gossamer. I was back less than a minute later with Razi, who had immediately taken charge of the situation.

First, she had reached towards her throat and snatched one of the wooden beads off her necklace. Rather than snapping, however, the necklace had somehow remained intact. Razi had then tossed the bead near the body.

As soon as it struck the ground, the bead had begun to rapidly expand, like a balloon quickly filling up with helium. At the same time, it turned opaque, taking on a dark, smoky color. Within seconds, it had become something akin to a giant black beach ball. More to the point, it had completely engulfed the area where the body was, effectively shielding it from sight.

And then, as quickly as it had expanded, the ball began to shrink. Moments later, it was back to its original size. However, it had continued shrinking, getting smaller and smaller until it essentially winked out of existence, thankfully taking the bearded man's body and all evidence of his passing. A few moments later, the Maximus and other Council members — having presumably been contacted in some manner by Razi — appeared out of nowhere and dragged Ursula off to the side for a discussion.

It had now been about ten minutes since the conference between Ursula and the Council had begun. I wasn't able to distinguish the words being said, but I was able to detect inflection and tone, among other things. More importantly, I was able to read them emotionally.

From Ursula, I detected a wide range of feelings, including anger, frustration, and annoyance. Surprisingly, I detected much the same from the members of the Council, along with a general mood of trepidation.

Eventually, I saw Ursula give a curt nod and mutter something. She then turned and practically stomped back towards me while the Council members seemed to huddle together for a moment.

"What did they say?" I asked when she drew near.

"Basically, don't leave town," she answered, looking agitated.

It took me a moment to grasp her meaning, at which point I gave her a dumbfounded look. "Are you kidding? They can't possibly think you had anything to do with this."

As I spoke, I glanced in the direction of the Council members, only to note that they were gone, having seemingly vanished as swiftly as they had appeared. In fact, there was almost no one around. Razi's removal of the body had meant that there was no spectacle for passersby and busybodies to gawk at, so the usual crowd that one might expect to see congregating around a crime scene had never formed. (Truth be told, based on the emotions that I picked up from a few people who came near while Ursula spoke with the Council, it didn't appear that word of the murder had gotten out yet.)

"If it's all right with you," Ursula said, bringing me back to myself, "I'd rather not talk here."

"Fine by me," I said.

Then, after confirming that she was ready, I teleported us to our suite.

CONJURATION

Chapter 33

We popped up in the great room, and Ursula immediately let out a deep sigh as she flopped down onto the sofa.

"First things first," she said. "I'm getting out of this dress."

I didn't notice her do anything, but all of a sudden the formal attire was gone and she was sporting a sleeveless black jumpsuit.

"That's better," she declared, becoming visibly more relaxed. Looking me over, she gestured towards the tux I was wearing. "Would you like me to…?"

She trailed off, but — knowing what she was suggesting — I shook my head. "No thanks. I'll change clothes later."

She shrugged. "Suit yourself."

"So," I droned, "what makes the Council think you killed that guy?"

"Malvern," she replied.

"Huh?" I muttered, blinking in confusion.

"Malvern," Ursula repeated. "Razi said that was the name of the man who was murdered."

"Got it," I declared. "Now, what makes them think you did him in?"

She appeared to reflect on this for a moment, then said, "You know how when you fire a gun, it leaves a distinctive smell in the air?"

I nodded. "Yeah — gun smoke."

"Well, something similar happens with certain types of magic. They leave distinctive traces. It's not something that *you'd* probably notice, but it would be

166

obvious to someone with the proper training in the arcane sciences."

"Okay, so they found some magical traces in the area where Malvern was killed. So what? Linking that to you is like the police finding a bullet at a crime scene and then suspecting me solely because I own a gun."

"You don't get it," Ursula informed me, shaking her head. "They got a taste of my power during that little witch trial they put me through earlier. That being the case, they have a very good idea of what it looks like, so to speak."

"And it's identical to whatever mystical elements they found at the murder scene."

"It's not an exact match, but close enough."

"But you have an alibi," I insisted. "You were with *me* all evening."

"I think you're overlooking the fact that this is magic we're talking about. You don't have to be physically present to make something happen."

"Still, I'd argue that any accusation against you is missing one critical detail: motive."

"Again, you seem to be forgetting my tête-à-tête with the Council earlier. It's a little hard to say I made any friends then."

"Maybe not, but I don't think there's any argument that you won that round. That being the case, why would you need to go after anybody?"

"Maybe I'm just spiteful and petty. After all, people have been killed for a lot less than simple arguments."

"But that's just it," I blurted out. "Not to be gruesome, but Malvern wasn't just killed — he was practically shredded."

CONJURATION

As I spoke, I couldn't stop the images of the scene from coming to mind: Malvern's arm ripped from its socket. A lower leg torn off just below the knee. His torso splayed open like a frog in Biology class...

"Basically," I continued, "it's hard to imagine someone orchestrating an attack along those lines over a disagreement — especially one that's been resolved."

Ursula didn't say anything in response — she just sat there with a brooding expression on her face. Emotionally, I could sense uneasiness and concern.

"Hey — it'll be okay," I assured her. "I doubt it'll take them long to figure out that you didn't do this."

"Thanks," she said, "but I'm not really worried about that."

"Oh?" I murmured, eyebrows rising in surprise. I know *I'd* be concerned if a powerful cadre of sorcerers thought I'd killed one of their colleagues. "Well, if the accusation of murder isn't bothering you, what is?"

She drummed her fingers on the arm of the sofa for a moment, apparently pondering her response.

"Do you recall," she finally began, "right before we found Malvern's body, that I was saying that there was something odd going on?"

I nodded. "Sure."

"Well, I was sensing some unusual magic then. Of course, now I know that it was related to whatever killed Malvern, but at the time I was struck by how similar it was to mine."

"Yeah, we already know about it resembling your power. It's the whole reason the Council suspects you."

"You're not seeing the big picture," Ursula asserted, sternly shaking her head. "As you noted earlier, the power I wield comes from the Incarnates —

specifically, from Endow. Now, assuming I'm not the killer, there's another source of that same type of power somewhere on the premises."

I spent a moment concentrating on what she'd said, trying to figure out the significance of her comment. And then the awful truth hit me, and my mouth almost dropped open in shock.

I leaped to my feet and practically screamed, "There's an Incarnate here?!"

CONJURATION

Chapter 34

The mere presence of an Incarnate, in and of itself, wasn't something that would normally cause me concern. As I'd tried to explain to Kane, they were just like regular people to a certain extent. However, based on what Ursula had just told me, an Incarnate was seemingly implicated in Malvern's death, and a *killer* Incarnate was another matter altogether. Moreover, having already had the pleasure of dealing with one in the recent past, I was in no rush to repeat the experience. (Basically, one murderous, nigh-omnipotent being per lifetime was my limit, and I'd already met my quota.)

All of this flitted through my mind as I stood there, trying to process exactly what this new revelation meant.

"I don't know that it's an Incarnate," Ursula admitted, breaking in on my thoughts. "Like I said, the power I detected — the *sivrrut* — is similar, but not exactly the same."

I let that roll around in my head for a second as I sat back down, recalling that *sivrrut* was a term Incarnates used to describe the power they wielded. "So could it be another person like you — an assistant to an Incarnate who's been given certain abilities?"

She shook her head. "No, I'd recognize the actual power of another Incarnate. As I keep saying, this was different. I guess one analogy would be to think of it like the difference between black and green tea — one comes from tea leaves that have undergone an oxidation process, and the other comes from tea leaves that haven't."

"Hmmm," I droned, thinking. "So you're saying this other magic you sensed is like an Incarnate's power that has been altered in some way."

"In essence, yes, although I can't say that's actually how it came about."

"Who would be capable of doing something like that?"

Ursula shrugged. "Outside of an Incarnate, I don't know. But it's not something they would do."

"Why not?" I asked, suddenly curious.

"Think about it," she said. "Incarnates are nigh-omnipotent. They're power personified. They already have the ability to do pretty much anything they want. Ergo, they've got no need to morph one form of power into another; it wouldn't make any sense. It would be like a chef who suddenly decided he'd rather cook with ice instead of fire."

"Okay," I intoned, reflecting on what Ursula had just said. "So it sounds like whoever did this isn't an Incarnate or anyone on their payroll."

"Agreed," Ursula said.

"Do you think you can find them using your ability to sense magic?"

She let out an exasperated sigh. "Believe me, I've tried. I've done almost everything I can think of and still can't get a bead on them."

I rubbed my temple in thought for a moment. "You said you've tried *almost* everything."

"Yeah," she confirmed with a nod. "There's one thing I haven't done which is probably a surefire method for finding the culprit."

"What's that?" I asked.

Ursula looked me in the eye and flatly stated, "Wait for them to strike again."

CONJURATION

Chapter 35

We sat in the great room for maybe another ten minutes discussing the situation. At that point, the door to the suite opened and Razi entered, followed by Kane and Gossamer. Both Ursula and I came to our feet and began expressing our condolences to Razi regarding Malvern (although presumably Ursula had also done so earlier).

"Thank you for your kind thoughts," Razi said before turning to me. "Jim, can I borrow you for a moment?"

"Uh, sure," I replied. "Did you want to go somewhere more private or—"

"No, this will do," Razi interjected, taking a seat in a nearby easy chair. She then looked expectedly at her grandson.

Taking his cue, Kane said, "Hey Ursula, why don't you take a walk with me and Gossamer? There's something we'd like to show you."

"Awesome," Ursula gushed, sounding more chipper than she probably felt.

I then watched as my three friends headed for the door. A moment later, it was just me and Razi in the suite.

"I suppose you know what I want to ask you," Razi stated without preamble.

"I think so," I responded, nodding. "I can confirm that Ursula was with me all evening, and no, I don't think she killed Malvern."

"But you have to agree that, given the known facts, it looks suspicious."

"I know you and the rest of the Council feel you have a smoking gun."

"Some do," she admitted. "But be that as it may, we'll still conduct a thorough investigation and try to figure out exactly what happened."

"Hmmm," I mused. "Does that mean you're trying to substantiate what *actually* occurred when Malvern was killed, or just looking for evidence that can link his murder to Ursula?"

Razi gave me an appraising glance and one corner of her mouth slid into a kind of sly half-smile. "Someone's got a suspicious nature."

"I just don't want to see my friend railroaded."

"I can understand that," Razi attested with a nod. "So let me just put this out there so you can have some peace of mind: I informed the Council that I felt Ursula was being sincere when she denied any wrongdoing."

"So you believe her?"

"Of course," she insisted. "I wouldn't let my grandson go off with her otherwise. That said, I'm still just one voice."

"But your voice carries weight," I noted.

"To some extent," she acknowledged. "But not enough to tip the scales against the rest of the Council. Not in *this* instance."

I nodded, understanding the limits of her influence. "So is Ursula your only suspect at this point?"

Razi gave me a sly look again. "You're asking if Malvern had any enemies."

"Did he?"

"I don't know if the term 'enemies' applies, but he definitely had people who didn't like him. Of course, the same could be said of just about anyone. We all have rivals, opponents, adversaries, what have you."

"But don't you think it's more likely he was killed by someone from his past than a girl he just met today?"

"It would certainly make more sense."

"Anyone from Malvern's hate list here tonight?"

"Some," Razi admitted. "We plan to check them out."

"That does raise the question: how many people know what happened to him?"

"Well, at this juncture, probably everybody. Why do you ask?"

"Just trying to figure out if we — or rather, Ursula — will be getting a bunch of weird stares from folks in the Templum going forward. That's what tends to happen when you're a murder suspect."

"The Council's general suspicions are confidential," Razi explained, much to my relief. "However, you do raise an interesting point: we don't have any misgivings where *you* are concerned. In essence, you can go home, if you like. In fact, given what's happened, it might even be advisable."

"No, thanks," I said. "Ursula's my friend, and I gather the impression she's going to need all the help she can get. I'd no more desert her than I would Kane if their positions were reversed."

Razi smiled, and I sensed that she was both impressed by and happy with my comment. "I told them you'd say that."

CONJURATION

Chapter 36

Razi left almost immediately after our conversation ended. My friends must have been standing by and watching closely, because she'd barely been gone a minute before they came back into the suite.

There followed an impromptu info session, in which it was established that Kane and Gossamer pretty much knew all the salient facts regarding Malvern's murder. Thankfully, although they'd essentially just met Ursula, both were willing to give her the benefit of the doubt (for which she was obviously grateful).

At that point, with nothing further to discuss, we decided to call it a night. Thus, after agreeing to huddle up again in the morning, we all headed to our respective rooms.

I couldn't speak for the others, but I couldn't wait to get to my room. In all honesty, it had been a long day, and I was mentally exhausted, if nothing else. That being the case, I was looking forward to a good night's sleep. However, I'd only been inside my room a few seconds before a gentle knock sounded at the door. Reaching out empathically, I immediately recognized who was outside. Letting out a tired sigh, I went back to the door, opened it, and stepped aside as Ursula came into my room.

"Just in case you need directions," I said, "your room's at the other end of the suite."

Ignoring my attempt at humor, she sat down on the edge of my bed, facing me.

"I didn't want to discuss it in front of Kane and Gossamer," she began, "but I wanted to know what Razi said to you — assuming it's something you can share."

"I don't think it's a state secret," I replied. "She essentially confirmed that you're the number-one suspect, but she doesn't believe you did it."

"Well, now I feel *much* better," she muttered sarcastically. It was a subtle reminder of the fact that she wasn't overly concerned about the Council's suspicions. "Anything else?"

"They're going to do a full investigation. Apparently Malvern had enemies and some were here tonight. Presumably, they'll figure this all out, find the real culprit, and clear you."

"Yeah, well, forgive me if I don't hold my breath," she uttered in a flippant tone.

I frowned. "You don't think they'll do a good job?"

"I think they're in over their heads," she immediately shot back. "If there really is an Incarnate-type power involved, they're not equipped to deal with it. I offered to help, but…"

"Let me guess," I chimed in as she trailed off. "They said it was bad form to let a murder suspect investigate the crime they're accused of committing."

"Something like that," she concurred.

Even without my empathic abilities, I could tell she was peeved to an extent.

"Look," I said, "I know it's a complicated situation, to put it mildly, but eventually the truth will come out."

"That's a nice sentiment," Ursula noted, "but I don't think this is a situation where we can afford to sit around and wait."

I frowned, sensing there was some context to her statement that I wasn't getting. In addition, I felt something like intent and resolve coming from her on an emotional level. I was about to ask her to expound on what she meant, but never got a chance.

"Well, goodnight," she said, coming to her feet. "I'll see you in the morning."

And then she was gone.

CONJURATION

Chapter 37

After Ursula left, I spent a moment letting our most recent conversation roll around in my head. I got the impression she was intending to take some kind of action, so my immediate thought was to seek her out and get clarity. However, it was late, and I highly doubted she'd do anything at the present hour. In short, any follow-up discussion could wait until morning.

With that decided, I headed to the bathroom and got ready for bed, which included taking a long, hot shower. As tired as I was, I would normally have zipped through everything at super speed. However, after the day I'd had, it was incredibly relaxing — almost therapeutic — to take things slow.

After exiting the shower, I got dressed and hung my tuxedo back in the closet before turning off the light and crawling into bed. I spent a minute or so reflecting on everything that had happened during the past day, then slowly drifted off to sleep.

****

I awoke in something of a mild panic. All of my instincts were going haywire, but it only took me a second to figure out why: someone was in the room with me.

There was a window on the wall near the bed. The blinds on it were currently closed, but no sunlight was filtering in so I immediately understood that it was still early. Empathically, I tried to get a read on my visitor — both their location, as well as their possible intent. At the same time, I reached out mentally, preparing to telekinetically switch the light on. However, I never even got started on that last task, as I suddenly heard a voice that I recognized.

"Great, you're awake," Ursula said softly. "Come on — we gotta go."

"Go where?" I asked as I followed through on telekinetically turning on the light and got out of bed.

"For our morning constitutional," she said sardonically. "Where do you think?"

"You're detecting the other Incarnate power," I concluded, ignoring her comment.

"Yes. Now let's go."

"Okay, give me a sec to freshen up."

"Fine — you're *fresh*," she declared with a wave of her hand.

Giving myself a once-over, I quickly realized that I was once again dressed in the cobalt uniform that had appeared on me the night before, while Ursula was in the superhero outfit she had previously sported. There was also a minty taste in my mouth, as well as a tingling sensation on my cheeks and nose, as if my face had just been thoroughly washed.

"You know, I'm old enough to handle my own hygiene," I informed her. "And can do it at super speed."

"Whatever," Ursula said dismissively, and then we vanished.

CONJURATION

Chapter 38

We appeared outside, maybe two hundred yards from the Templum. It was dark outside, confirming my previous assessment that it was still early, although a quick flash of lightning unexpectedly lit up the surrounding area.

"There!" Ursula said in an excited whisper, pointing.

I looked in the direction indicated — an area of hilly terrain a few hundred feet away. Some of the luminescent flowers were around, but nothing else in view seemed worthy of attention.

"I don't see anything," I admitted, even after telescoping my vision.

Ursula gave me an odd look, then appeared to mentally smack herself on the forehead. "That's right — it's not visible to you."

"Give me a minute," I said, and then began swiftly cycling my vision through the light spectrum in hopes of finding a wavelength that would allow me to observe what Ursula was seeing.

I had been at it for only a few seconds when a light, bold and bright, unexpectedly flared next to me. It came from where Ursula was standing, and for a moment I was worried that she had somehow caught fire, but then I looked at her and simply stared.

Once again, it seemed that Ursula had changed her attire. She now sported a magnificent golden headdress, inset with jewels and with angelic wings on both sides stretching up towards the heavens. From her ears hung lustrous, tassel earrings, and around her neck she wore a choker bib necklace made of precious metal and inlaid with gemstones. From there on down, she was similarly bedecked: there were armbands, bangles, a hand harness, ring chains, and more. Even her legs weren't spared, as they were covered by a dizzying array of thigh bands, leg chains, anklets, toe rings, and so on. Finally, an elaborate body chain hung from her shoulders and crisscrossed her torso in layers that almost obscured the short, white dress she wore.

All in all, she was adorned like a goddess, and it took me a second to find my tongue.

"What...?" I began. "What are you wearing?"

A befuddled expression settled on Ursula's face. "What are you talking about? You know what I'm—"

All of a sudden, she stopped speaking, as if she had unexpectedly gone mute. She glanced down at herself, then looked at me with a nigh-stunned expression.

"You can *see* me," she muttered, plainly surprised.

I nodded. "Yeah. Why are you—"

"Later," she stressed. Taking my head in her hands, she turned it in the direction she'd indicated earlier. "Do you see anything over there?"

"Not yet," I admitted, somewhat chagrinned at having allowed myself to be distracted (even if it was excusable). Picking up where I'd left off, I continued cycling through the light spectrum, noticing as I did so that Ursula's appearance shifted back; the glow vanished and she was once again attired in the superhero uniform. A few moments later, I finally obtained a wavelength that presumably allowed me to see what Ursula could.

Eyes wide in surprise, I blurted out, "What is *that*?"

CONJURATION

Chapter 39

It was hard to describe what I was seeing. It was some type of creature, but unlike anything I'd ever heard of.

It was about ten feet tall and maybe twenty feet long. It had an upper body that resembled a four-armed gorilla, albeit one with a mouth full of shark-like teeth and hands that ended in razor-sharp claws. This was attached to a lower body that resembled a giant scorpion, but with a reptilian tail rather than one equipped with a stinger. Finally, I noted that, depending on how the light seemed to strike it, the creature's skin would appear to change, such as appearing scaly one moment and crystalline the next.

I immediately understood that this thing was not the result of natural selection, mutation, or any other accepted evolutionary process, but was instead a magical construct. As it appeared to be composed of parts from different animals, it was technically a chimera. However, I viewed it as some sort of Frankenstein — the monstrous creation of what could only be a demented mind. Moreover, bearing in mind what had happened to Malvern, the thing was also murderous.

"That's our killer," Ursula said, both answering my previous question and concurring with my present line of thought. "Our rather, the person controlling it is."

"What's it doing?" I asked, highlighting the fact that the creature was moving oddly, like it was having a tug-of-war with an invisible opponent.

"I'd say it's trying to get out of the trap the Council set for it," Ursula replied nonchalantly.

"Hold on," I uttered. "It's caught in a trap?"

CONJURATION

"Not exactly," she replied. "I'll explain later. Right now, I'm trying to... Oh, crap!"

Ursula's outburst coincided with the creature suddenly turning in our direction and charging. It may have been caught in a trap before, but it certainly wasn't now, as it tore across the ground towards us. From the way it was built, I half expected the monster to be howling or roaring as it rushed at us. Surprisingly, it made no sound, which was somehow more disturbing.

I shifted into super speed and dashed at the creature. Time slowed as I raced across the Templum's grounds, meeting the thing halfway and slamming a shoulder into its left foreleg.

It was like striking a monolith, and I counted myself lucky not to have ricocheted off to the side. That said, I did rebound a few steps before zipping away and shifting back to normal speed.

As hoped, my blow had the effect of checking the creature's speed and also causing it to spin around to a small degree, much like what happens when someone bumps your shoulder when walking past you. However, that didn't stop it for long, and a moment later, it had resumed its charge, clearly heading for Ursula. Apparently, I wasn't even an afterthought.

Somewhat miffed at being ignored, I went at the creature at super speed a second time, performing the same maneuver (although this time I came at it from the back). Unsurprisingly, I got similar results as the first time, with my efforts essentially checking the monster's forward progress.

Having discovered what seemed to be a viable strategy, I went after the thing a third time. However, I either became overconfident or careless, because this time it was ready for me. Basically, as I approached at super speed, the monster had once again slowed down like the rest of the world around me. However, after I drew near, it suddenly whirled around, lashing out at me with its tail. The appendage struck me like a wrecking ball, solidly whacking me across the chest and sending me tumbling end over end through the air.

It took a few seconds for me to gain control of my momentum, stopping my impromptu flight. My chest was already starting to ache agonizingly, and I knew I'd probably have a nasty bruise later. For the nonce, however, I simply deadened my nerve endings to avoid feeling any pain.

Obviously, the creature had baited me by not immediately displaying its ability to match my super speed. Looking around, I espied the monster, which was still headed for Ursula. In fact, it was practically on top of her, and had drawn back an arm in preparation to strike at her. On her part, Ursula didn't seem to have moved since the time I'd first engaged with the creature.

In desperation, I phased Ursula, hoping the monster's claw would pass harmlessly through her insubstantial form. However, it turned out that I need not have bothered. The intended strike never came close enough to do harm, as the creature's hand seemed to be deflected in some way, bouncing back as though striking some invisible barrier. I immediately understood that to actually be the case; there was some sort of protective field around Ursula, which became all the more evident as the monster suddenly released a barrage of blows with all four arms. Not a single one of them came within a foot of Ursula, who never even flinched.

CONJURATION

I didn't know how long Ursula's barrier would hold, and I didn't really want to find out. Hoping to remove the immediate threat, I tried to teleport the creature. Nothing happened. As with my super speed, the monster had found a way to counter my teleportation power.

Now on the hunt for any advantage, I phased the ground under the feet on the left side of the thing's body. As expected, with the loss of solid footing on one side, its body lurched in that direction. In fact, it tipped over, landing on its back. It struggled for a moment trying to right itself, arms and legs wriggling madly, but had no luck. At that juncture, perhaps recognizing that it was helpless, the thing disappeared.

Still airborne, I let out a breath that I didn't know I'd been holding. Switching my vision back to normal and glancing around, I now realized that the blow from the creature's tail had knocked me in the direction where we had originally seen it. I also noticed something else that immediately drew my attention.

There was a body on the ground below me.

CONJURATION

Chapter 40

The victim turned out to be a woman this time. She appeared to be in her mid-forties, and — judging from her attire — had apparently been out for an early morning jog. It seemed like an odd activity to engage in considering that someone had just been killed on the premises the night before, or perhaps she simply hadn't heard about Malvern's death. (Or maybe, in an *it-can't-happen-to-me* frame of mind, she simply hadn't been concerned.)

Upon spying the body, which the hilly terrain had kept us from seeing at first, I had immediately called Ursula over. Then, while she stayed with the victim, I had teleported back to our suite to rouse Kane, who had in turn immediately gone to get his grandmother. The end result was that within five minutes, Razi was present and had used one of her beads to again remove the body (for which I was grateful since the victim this time had been decapitated).

Surprisingly, Razi didn't do much more than get basic information from me and Ursula: in essence, when we had arrived, what we had seen, and how we'd come across the body. I had expected more of an interrogation, but she had told us that was all she needed at the time. (She also didn't comment on the costumes we were wearing, which was a bit of a relief.) Now that we were effectively dismissed, I telepathically told Ursula that we needed to talk, then teleported us to my room.

Upon arrival, I noted that Ursula was no longer in her costume; she was now wearing a white blouse and turquoise palazzo pants. Likewise, I was back in the clothes I had slept in. Switching into super speed, I quickly got dressed, putting on a black T-shirt and a pair of jeans. I

186

then switched back to normal speed, at which point Ursula once again took a seat on the edge of my bed while I pulled up a nearby chair.

"So where would you like to start?" she asked.

"I don't know," I admitted. "I have so many questions bubbling over in my brain that it's hard to know where to begin. I suppose that outfit you played dress-up in is as good a place as any."

I then gave her an overview of how she had appeared to me when I was cycling my vision through the light spectrum.

"That's easy enough to explain," she said. "Basically, you were right when you said Endow sent me here with a fair amount of power. However, as you know, there's a limited amount of *sivrrut* that the human body can hold."

I nodded in understanding. Human beings could only house so much power from an Incarnate; beyond a certain threshold, it would burn you to a cinder — like wiring with too much electrical current running through it. In fact, both Ursula and I had seen it happen.

"The workaround," Ursula continued, "is for an Incarnate to imbue any excess power they want someone to have in an object."

"So all that stuff I saw on you," I remarked, "the headdress, bracelets, toe rings, and so on — they're all relics infused with *sivrrut*."

"Yes."

"So I was right before: you're uber-powerful."

A sly smile crept onto her face. "Let's just say I can hold my own."

"Well, bearing in mind all the things you can probably do, is there any particular reason you didn't just destroy that creature we saw outside?"

Ursula nodded. "That thing's obviously a product of magic. I needed it alive, so to speak, in order to find out who's actually controlling it."

"So how does that work, exactly?"

She paused for a moment, clearly weighing how to answer my question. "It's a little hard to explain. I suppose you could compare it to a cop finding a gun at a crime scene. He doesn't destroy it; instead, he dusts it for prints, does ballistics tests, etcetera."

"Got it," I said. "So that creature is basically the smoking gun that you're going to use in some way to identify the culprit."

"Exactly."

I thought about that for a moment. "So why didn't you simply trap it the way the Council did?"

"Okay, first of all," Ursula began with a bit of umbrage, "what the Council did wasn't really a trap — not for this thing, anyway. As I said before, they're in over their heads. They constructed something that they thought would be like a cage to hold it, but in actuality it was more like a pebble that someone stepped on barefooted."

"In other words, they just hobbled it for a second; they didn't really stop or contain it."

"Now you get it," Ursula declared.

"Any idea how they knew where it would be?"

Ursula looked at me in confusion. "What do you mean?"

"I'm curious as to how the Council knew where to set their trap."

"You're thinking about this all wrong," Ursula admonished. "You're imagining the trap as something like a snare set in a particular location. Keep in mind that this was a mystical deadfall. Thus, it was more like a net that could be dropped from overhead on any area."

"In other words, it would trigger wherever that thing happened to show up. That still doesn't explain why you didn't lay your own trap after it escaped from the Council's."

"Because this is a more delicate operation than it appears at first blush," she explained. "Trapping this thing is very much like catching an egg being dropped off a skyscraper without breaking it. I have to find the sweet spot that will allow me to capture it without killing it, for lack of a better term."

"Well, I may not be much help," I stated. "This thing seems able to match or counter my powers."

Ursula merely nodded at my admission, although it shouldn't have come as a surprise. The last time I'd gone up against someone with the power of an Incarnate, they'd been able to thwart me in the same way. (Left unsaid was the fact that Ursula could probably do the same.)

"That does remind me of something," I remarked. "Although I was the one attacking that thing outside, it pretty much ignored me and went after you. Any idea why?"

"Who knows?" Ursula said with a shrug. "Maybe it simply saw me as the bigger threat."

Her comment wasn't braggadocio, just simple fact. Moreover, it seemed like the most plausible explanation, and I was about to comment to that effect when a knock sounded at the door.

CONJURATION

Reaching out empathically, I identified who had come calling. I then telekinetically unlocked the door and called out, "Come in — it's open."

A moment later, Gossamer poked her head inside.

"Don't know if you guys have eaten yet," she said, "but we've got breakfast out here."

CONJURATION

Chapter 41

Frankly speaking, I was happy to head to breakfast. Using super speed typically shifts my metabolism into high gear, resulting in a need to replace burned calories with food (and lots of it). Ergo, after following Gossamer to the dining room, I was happy to see an ample amount and variety of food laid out on the table, including muffins, breakfast burritos, cereal, and more.

"Dig in," ordered Kane with a smile. He was already at the table (where four places had been set), but had graciously waited for the rest of us to arrive before eating.

"Happy to oblige," I said with a grin.

A moment later, we were all busy putting food on our plates.

****

Conversation during breakfast remained rather lighthearted, with us basically discussing the fun we'd had in the Wish Room and the previous night's ceremony. We all studiously avoided the elephant in the room, as it was a gruesome topic and not suitable discourse during the consumption of a meal.

After we were done, I offered to wash up, but Kane insisted that it would be taken care of (presumably by magic). Taking him at his word, I retreated to the great room with everyone else. At that point, the discussion became serious, with Kane asking us for an overview of the morning's events.

"Sounds like a rough way to start the day," Gossamer noted when we were done.

"Yeah," I agreed before turning to Kane. "So I'm going to make a wild guess and say this kind of thing isn't common here."

"What, murder?" Kane uttered in surprise. "Absolutely not."

"So everyone here must be freaking out," Ursula surmised.

"Yes and no," Kane answered with a shrug. "They're concerned by the fact that people have been killed, but most are reasonably certain their own magic can keep them safe."

"That's the thing about stuff like magic," Gossamer chimed in. "It can make you overconfident."

"Is that how that woman happened to be out this morning?" asked Ursula. "The one we found?"

"You mean Agatha?" Kane asked.

Ursula and I exchanged a glance. "I don't think we ever got her name," I admitted.

"Agatha," Kane confirmed. "I can't swear as to her mindset, but she was an accomplished mage. That being the case, it wouldn't surprise anyone if she felt secure in her ability to defend herself and didn't see a need to change her routine."

"That's a problem," Ursula asserted. "This isn't the type of magic you people are used to dealing with. It's beyond the scope of your abilities. If precautions aren't taken, more people will die."

"What type of precautions?" Gossamer asked. "Like staying indoors?"

"I see what you're getting at," Ursula said. "Both murders were committed outside. Truth be told, however, I don't know if that means anything."

"Hmmm," Kane murmured. "So you didn't see anything noteworthy outside?"

"No," Ursula answered, and I concurred.

"Well, did you see any*one* out there?" Kane inquired.

I shook my head. "Nope. Just Agatha."

"So there's no one else who would have seen this monster that was out there," Kane concluded.

"Even if there had been, you couldn't see it with normal vision," I explained. "At best, anyone catching sight of us would have probably thought Ursula was being a mime and I was playing charades."

"Well, an invisible fiend would definitely explain why Malvern and Agatha didn't appear to defend themselves," Gossamer noted. "They never saw it coming."

"Or heard it," Kane added, "if it was as silent as you said. Tell me again what it looked like."

Ursula and I then gave another quick rundown of what the creature had looked like, making sure we didn't miss any details. When we were done, Kane sat there for a moment, brow knitted in thought.

"Unfortunately," he noted, "it doesn't sound like anything I've ever seen."

"You see chimeras on a regular basis?" I asked, raising an eyebrow in curiosity. "You guys have a menagerie of monsters around here or something?"

Kane didn't immediately respond; instead, he and his girlfriend shared a knowing glance.

"Show them," Gossamer said.

CONJURATION

Chapter 42

"What are those things?" I asked, staring in open surprise.

"Mage-beasts," Kane replied. "Magical monsters created for war."

I merely nodded in acknowledgment, tacitly agreeing that the creatures I was seeing were clearly built for battle.

We were currently in something akin to an underground bunker deep beneath the Templum. After his girlfriend's comment that he "show us" something, Kane had led our little troop out of the suite. He had then guided us through the Templum for about five minutes before ushering us to an obscure stairwell located in a small room off a minor corridor.

From there, we had gone down several flights of stairs before finally reaching what appeared to be the final floor. However, the area contained nothing but seven red doors on the far wall, each of which was marked with a unique, bizarre symbol. Kane had selected the second door from the left, which opened onto a long, narrow hallway.

At the end of the hallway was an elevator, which we had entered. The elevator had only one direction — down — and, after descending for a few minutes, the doors had opened onto our current location: a square-shaped area about fifty feet in both length and width, with multiple windows evenly spaced on each wall. It was after looking through a couple of these (and noting what was on the other side) that I had asked my question about what I was seeing.

Basically, each window offered a view into what could only be described as a prison cell, and in each was a monster of some sort. These were the things Kane had described as "mage-beasts," and each in its own way was fascinating to behold.

For instance, one of them resembled a bipedal moose carved from marble, with the mouth of a crocodile and paws of a bear. Another appeared to be a centaur with an antlered skull in place of its head and daggers instead of hands. Yet a third looked like a furry, ambulatory oak tree with a huge gaping maw in its trunk, man-sized butterfly wings, and branches that moved like the arms of a squid (and which terminated in spear tips). All in all, there were about a dozen of these mage-beasts locked up.

"Okay, I admit it," Ursula said, drawing everyone's attention. "This was worth the wait."

Her remark alluded to the fact that, while leading us here, Kane had sidestepped any inquiries from me and Ursula about where we were going. (Instead, he had continued questioning the two of us about our early morning escapades, which we had answered as best we could.) Eyeing the things in the cells, I found myself agreeing that we'd received an adequate payoff for being kept in suspense.

"You come down here a lot?" I suddenly asked Kane.

"Every now and then," he answered. "Not *too* often."

"Don't believe him," Gossamer chimed in. "He loves this place. He brought me here the first time we went out as a couple."

Ursula gave Kane a look of playful disdain. "Kind of an unusual first date, don't you think?"

"She wanted to go to the zoo," Kane shot back. "I thought this was better."

CONJURATION

"And it just happened to be one of his favorite hangout spots," Gossamer added with a grin.

Kane shook his head in derision. "If you must know, this is one of the most spelled, enchanted, and warded places on the planet. I come here to study *those* things, not gawk at these monstrosities."

"Hmmm," I intoned. "All of that, coupled with the fact that they're locked up, would seem to imply that these things are dangerous."

"Very," Kane conceded with a nod.

"Are they alive?" I asked.

"No," Kane stressed, shaking his head. "However, they've been animated by magic, usually through the use of some potent relic or artifact."

"Good to know," I said. "Still, it feels like this one is looking at me." I tilted my head towards the cell of the tree-monster as I spoke.

Kane chuckled slightly. "Even if it had eyes, it couldn't see you. None of them can. All that's visible inside each cell is four bare walls."

"But this is it," I determined as certain facts became clear. "These monsters are the reason for your ban against non-living things."

"You nailed it," Kane confirmed. "But whatever animates them mimics true life just well enough to avoid triggering the appropriate enchantments."

"Can they sense us?" Ursula inquired.

"Some probably can," Kane admitted.

"I don't think I've asked this before," Gossamer remarked, "but any particular reason they all look like the failed experiments of a mad scientist?"

"They're intended to wreak havoc on the battlefield," her boyfriend replied. "Ergo, they were

196

specifically designed to look grotesque in order to terrify the enemy — as if killing everything in sight wasn't enough."

I rubbed my chin in thought for a moment. "So if they're all nothing but killer creations, why not destroy them?"

"It's not that easy," Kane declared. "Creating these things is like building a nuclear bomb in your basement. It takes a certain level of knowledge, skill, ability, and resources. Even then, you make the slightest mistake and it's all over. In fact, that's happened before — a couple of these things went haywire during construction and killed their creators before going on a murderous rampage."

I nodded as he spoke, noting that Kane's narrative jibed neatly with my previous invocation of Frankenstein's monster.

"Likewise," he continued, "dismantling these walking atrocities is just as difficult. They're animated by relics of incredible power, and removing them isn't as simple as popping a battery out of a toy. Using the bomb analogy again, you do it wrong, and things go kaboom. In addition, some mage-beasts have singular talents that are intended for self-preservation, so to speak."

"In other words," Ursula summed up, "they have unique — and presumably lethal — abilities that are only triggered if you try to shut them down or destroy them."

"Bingo," Kane uttered with a nod. "And unfortunately, we had to find that out the hard way."

"So the solution is to just warehouse them until their batteries run dry?" I asked.

"Pretty much," Kane confirmed, "although they do still serve a purpose. Basically, they're used as examples of what can happen when power is misused, misapplied, or allowed to run amok. In essence, every member of the Kroten Venefici is required to come here at least once and view the mage-beasts, so they can personally see how certain actions can have terrible, long-lasting consequences."

"Long-lasting?" I repeated, slightly confused.

"Yes," Kane said. "Most of the mage-beasts are hundreds of years old — if not older — and the horrors they committed on the battlefield occurred centuries ago. However, since it's difficult to get people to appreciate how dangerous they are in the abstract, those who are obliged to come here are usually shown a couple of images that reveal just how savage a mage-beast can be in the theater of war."

As he finished, Kane twirled his right index finger and something like a box formed on a nearby wall. It was roughly three by five feet in size, and encompassed what appeared to be a red, hazy image that slowly began coming into focus. However, before it coalesced into anything recognizable, Gossamer grabbed her boyfriend's wrist.

"Uh, babe," she began, "we just had breakfast. Now, I don't know what kind of constitutions Jim and Ursula have, but I'm sure they'd like to keep that meal in their stomachs."

"Sorry," Kane muttered sheepishly. "Guess I just got carried away."

At that juncture, the square he'd formed on the wall disappeared. The image within it vanished as well, and — although it had never really come into focus — it had seemed incredibly familiar. A moment later, it came to me: the bloody portrait Ursula and I had seen in the gallery.

"Anyway," Kane continued, "thanks to you, we now know it was a mage-beast that killed Malvern and Agatha."

Suddenly curious, I asked, "What were you previously thinking it might be?"

"Assuming you mean the Council, I don't think they had a firm idea," Kane remarked. "In truth, there's a fair amount of wizardry that can rattle someone to pieces, pop their head like a grape, or do all kinds of other nasty stuff. Knowing what they're dealing with is incredibly helpful."

"Except you basically said they're trying to punch above their weight," Gossamer recalled, turning to Ursula. "Is there anything you can do to help, like maybe track this thing?"

"I wish I could," Ursula answered, "but I think it's retreated to another form."

"Excuse me?" I uttered, looking at Ursula in surprise. "What does *that* mean?"

"Exactly what I said," Ursula replied. "Just like water has three different states — solid, liquid, and gas — the mage-beast we saw has more than one form."

I continued looking at Ursula in befuddlement. I understood the reference to the three states of water, but wasn't quite making the connection.

"Maybe I can explain it," Gossamer offered, plainly seeing my confusion. "Basically, if you're going to attack a specific person with a mage-beast, you don't do it directly. They'd see it coming a mile off."

I nodded. "Okay, I'm following you so far."

"Good," Gossamer said with a smile. "Now, to really get someone with one of these monsters, you need to get it close to them in an undetected fashion. In order to do that, you'd disguise the mage-beast as something else — something innocuous, like a toy, a book, or maybe even a hat. And then, when it's in position…"

"You spring it like a booby trap," I concluded as she trailed off.

"Precisely," Gossamer declared, giving me a high five.

I turned to Ursula. "So the mage-beast can shift at will between its two forms?"

"I'd say it probably shifts between them at the behest of whoever is controlling it," she corrected. "The problem is that, when it's in its non-threatening form, it's shielded in some way that prevents me from locating it."

I spent a moment mulling over what I'd just heard. I then made a gesture encompassing the mage-beast cells and asked Kane, "Is it possible one of these things is the mage-beast we saw?"

"I don't see how," Kane answered.

"Well, this form-changing they can do sounds something like shapeshifting," I noted. "Could one of them have gotten out, changed into the creature we saw, and then killed Malvern and Agatha?"

"No way," Kane insisted, "and for three reasons. First, I didn't exaggerate when I mentioned how much sorcery is employed to hold the mage-beasts here. They can't get out, and if they did, we'd immediately know about it. Second, not all have an innocuous mode, but for those that do, it's the only other form they can assume. And none of that even considers the fact that the thing you guys ran into this morning can't be seen with the naked eye."

"All right," I said, nodding as I took all this in. "So — sidestepping the invisibility issue for now — what's the third reason why it couldn't be one of the mage-beasts in these cells?"

"Because if any of these got out and started killing people," Kane stated matter-of-factly, "it wouldn't stop at just one."

CONJURATION

Chapter 43

We left the mage-beast area a short time later. Ursula and I had obviously learned some things, but it didn't feel like any of it had really helped us advance the ball in terms of finding the creature we'd seen that morning (or figuring out who was controlling it). I had really thought I was onto something with the shapeshifting line of questioning, but apparently that was a dead end.

Or was it? I thought as something new occurred to me.

We were in the elevator at the time, having just begun ascending from the floor the mage-beasts were on.

Turning to Kane, I asked, "Can you cast a glamour on a mage-beast?"

"Huh?" he murmured in confusion.

"I know you said that none of the mage-beasts in the cells can shapeshift into the one we saw this morning," I said, "but could you cast a glamour on one — like Gossamer did with the snowcat — to make it look physically identical to the creature we're after?"

He seemed to ponder the question for a moment, then replied with, "I suppose, but what would be the point? One monster with a terrifying appearance is just as good as another, and in this case the mage-beast was actually invisible. That means a glamour makes even less sense. Plus, how would you control it?"

"Good question," I conceded, mentally kicking myself for overlooking the invisibility issue again. "But let me spin it and send it back to you: how were *any* of the mage-beasts in the cells ever controlled?"

"Some never were," he answered, "like the ones I mentioned that went bananas while being constructed.

202

Others were never *meant* to be controlled; the intent was to drop them behind any lines and let them cause as much death and destruction as possible. However, there were a few that were subject to control techniques and devices, but nobody alive today knows what those were or how they worked."

"But what if someone could come up with a way to control them?" I countered. "What's to keep him from sneaking down to the cells and attempting to get a mage-beast to do his bidding?"

Kane seemed to reflect for a moment. "Well, considering all the safeguards in place to keep the mage-beasts incarcerated, I don't think he'd be able to get one out. But let's leave that aside for the moment. Just getting down to the cells is going to present an issue because the current enchantments prevent translocation spells from working there. That's to keep some idiot from accidentally popping up in a cell with one of those things, as well as stop any maniac from taking one out."

"Makes sense," Ursula stated with a nod.

"So the only way in is the route we took," Kane continued. "Basically, on foot and via *this* elevator. However, while it probably hasn't been evident to you, access to those areas — the red door, the elevator, the mage-beast area — requires a key."

As he finished speaking, he held up his left hand, and the ring on his middle finger began to glow with a soft blue light. It brought to mind the fact that Kane wore rings on every digit. In fact, I'd never seen him without them, but I'd become so accustomed to seeing them on his person that their presence barely registered with me anymore. The current display was a reminder that the bands he wore on each finger were not really accessories but actually served a purpose.

"So that ring acts as an access card of sorts," I surmised.

"Correct," Kane said as he lowered his hand and the glow faded. "Moreover, there are a limited number of 'access cards,' as you put it, and they only work for the person to whom they're assigned."

"They give those out to a lot of teenagers?" Ursula asked impishly.

Kane laughed. "No — I freely admit that my grandmother pulled some strings to get me one so I could study the wards and enchantments in the mage-beasts area."

"Yeah, my baby's a spoiled brat," Gossamer teased, pinching her boyfriend's cheek.

"Look who's talking," Kane shot back with a grin.

"So what's next?" I interjected, attempting to keep the conversation on track.

"For *us*, nothing," Kane said. "But the Council can narrow their focus now, since they only need to speak with people capable of conjuring a mage-beast."

"Excluding us, right?" Ursula pleaded. "I mean, we've already told *you* everything we know."

And that's when it happened.

CONJURATION

Chapter 44

Following Ursula's statement, there was an immediate and simultaneous shift in three different arenas.

First, the atmosphere in the elevator changed as an incredibly awkward silence took hold. It had a stark and chilling effect that was impossible to miss or ignore.

At the same time, Kane's emotional state seemed to go through a wild battery of sensations. I picked up on strong feelings of regret, obligation, compassion, concern, and many, many more.

Finally, Kane's face became an open book of what he was feeling. I didn't need empathy, telepathy, or anything along those lines to know what was going on in his mind. Even worse, it was obvious that he knew that I knew.

"I'm sorry," he muttered softly, eyes downcast.

"Don't be sorry," I grumbled, probably more harshly than necessary. "Just explain."

He sighed. "Bearing in mind Ursula's demeanor the last time she spoke with the Council, it was felt she might be less guarded if someone in her circle asked her questions about what happened this morning."

"And you were elected," I concluded, to which Kane merely shrugged in response.

"Are you kidding?" Ursula groused angrily. "You've been pumping us for information?"

"No," Kane insisted defensively. "Not really. I asked the same questions and expressed the same interest I would have under any other circumstances."

"Except that things we thought we were telling you in confidence will get reported to the Kroten Council," I noted.

"Look," Gossamer interjected, "it's not like he *wanted* to do this. He didn't volunteer."

"But he didn't turn them down, either," Ursula countered.

"You talk like he had a choice," Gossamer shot back.

"Didn't he?" Ursula demanded.

Gossamer glared at the two of us. "So neither of you has ever had an assignment you didn't like?"

I frowned. Gossamer certainly had a point, but I didn't want to admit it — didn't want to cede the moral high ground.

Looking at Kane, I asked, "So when are you supposed to report in?"

"My grandmother's coming by the suite when we get back," he replied.

"Wow," Ursula intoned. "For a guy who allegedly hated this assignment, you sure are hustling to get brownie points for it."

This earned her another evil glance from Gossamer, who looked as though she wanted to skewer Ursula with one of her daggers.

CONJURATION

Chapter 45

Unsurprisingly, nothing more was said as we made our way back to the suite. Everyone seemed to be preoccupied with their own thoughts, and I was no exception.

Plainly speaking, I was pretty annoyed with Kane. Not angry, because I'd felt he was being sincere when he apologized, but definitely irritated. His behavior just wasn't what I'd expected from a friend.

When we finally reached our suite, I headed straight to my room without a word to anyone. After a few seconds, I realized that Ursula was right behind me, at which point I found myself feeling rather ambivalent about having visitors. On the one hand, I wanted some time alone to think; on the other hand, she was someone I could easily commiserate with, if necessary.

As we reached the door to my room, I heard Kane shout something in our direction about lunch later. I made a noncommittal grunt in response, which he may or may not have heard.

"We'll let you know," Ursula blurted out in his direction just before we went in.

Once inside, I went over to the bed and practically collapsed onto it. Closing my eyes, I reached up with a hand and began massaging my temples, at the same time letting out a deep breath. Mentally, this trip was really starting to take a toll on me.

A moment later, I felt Ursula take her usual position on the edge of the bed. However, she just sat there, with neither of us speaking for a couple of minutes.

"Do you think we were too hard on him?" she finally asked.

I shrugged, still keeping my eyes closed. "I don't know. This visit has just gone completely off the rails since the moment we got here. It makes it hard to evaluate things by normal standards."

"I'm sorry. Part of that's my fault for just tagging along."

"It's fine," I assured her as I crossed my arms. "Given what's going on with this mage-beast situation, it's actually a good thing you're here."

"I'm not sure the Council feels that way."

"They'll get over it — especially after we figure out who's behind all this."

"We?" she echoed curiously.

"Yeah," I said. "If the Council really is outside their weight class on this thing, we — or rather, *you* — are probably the only one who can do anything about it."

"I appreciate that, but—"

I frowned, noting that Ursula hadn't trailed off but had abruptly stopped speaking. Finally opening my eyes, I saw that she was turned towards me but had a look of fierce concentration on her face.

Automatically realizing that something was wrong, I sat up and asked, "What is it?"

"It's here!" Ursula exclaimed.

Not needing to ask what "it" was, I simply blurted out, "Where?"

"*Here!*" she yelled.

At the same time, I heard commotion from somewhere in the suite, accompanied by a couple of loud thumps that were reminiscent of a horse trying to kick its way out of a stall.

A moment later, we vanished.

CONJURATION

Chapter 46

We reappeared in the great room, courtesy of Ursula. It was a scene of bedlam, and I instinctively phased while trying to get my bearings.

First, much of the furniture was strewn about, haphazardly tossed around the room with abandon. Moreover, the sofa was overturned and at least one table had been smashed.

Standing off to one side and facing the center of the room was Razi. There was a look of intense concentration on her face as she held up one clenched fist that had a whirlwind of sparks encasing it. Maybe twenty feet from her and facing the same direction as his grandmother was Kane. He stood with one leg bent in front of him and arms extended, giving the impression that he was pushing a giant invisible box. (I also noted that his fingers were spread out and his rings were glowing brightly.)

I didn't immediately see Gossamer, but decided to focus on the threat in the room: the mage-beast. Cycling my vision so I could see it, I found the creature — as expected — in the center of the room, where it was seemingly under attack from Razi and Kane. At the moment, the thing was struggling mightily to get to the latter, but moved as if it was shackled in some way. I was suddenly reminded of what Ursula had said about the Council setting traps that would ultimately prove inadequate, so it was not a total surprise when the fiend suddenly seemed to regain its full range of motion.

Razi flicked her hand towards the floor as the mage-beast drew back to strike at Kane. I saw something round fly from her hand — one of her wooden necklace beads. It landed near the feet of the creature, and hot, glowing sparks suddenly erupted from the floor like a geyser.

The mage-beast brought two of its hands up to shield its face as its mouth dropped open in what looked like a howl. But, as when we'd encountered it outside, the monster made no sound, despite the fact that the sparks appeared to burn it.

Suddenly the creature lurched forward, ignoring the sparks and reaching for Kane. I phased him, and the mage-beast grabbed empty air. At the same time, I caught movement with my peripheral vision.

Wary of some sort of sneak attack, I turned in that direction and saw the overturned sofa move. A second later, Gossamer crawled out from under it. She looked slightly disoriented; her hair was mussed, and I saw that she was bleeding from a spot near her hairline.

Assuming she was more or less okay, I turned back to the mage-beast and almost swore. During the time I'd been distracted by Gossamer, the thing had managed to grab Kane, who now looked groggy and had a bruise on his cheek. In essence, it had negated my phasing power and currently held my friend dangling in the air with his right wrist gripped in a meaty paw.

I attempted to teleport Kane, but nothing happened. Again, the creature had thwarted me; mentally I screamed in frustration, but didn't have time to dwell on the issue as the mage-beast suddenly pulled my friend in close. However, before it could take any further action, Ursula was there, thrusting her hand palm-first at the thing's face, emitting a powerful burst of light from it that shined right in the monster's eyes. At the same time, Gossamer — belting out a wild battle cry — leaped onto the creature's back and began stabbing it with her daggers, while Razi threw another bead that hit the floor and rolled under the thing's body.

The mage-beast turned its head to the side and brought up an arm to shield its face from Ursula's light. It may not have been alive in the normal sense, but whatever Ursula was doing seemed to be distressing it.

Without warning, the monster reached down and grabbed the leg from a smashed wooden table. Swinging the table leg like a club, it tried to bat Ursula aside. However, in a repeat of the morning's escapades, some sort of field around her deflected the blow. In fact, the monster's arm not only rebounded backwards, but it also lost its grip on its makeshift club, which would have been something of a minor victory if not for one thing: the broken table leg was flying straight at Razi like a javelin.

Shifting into super speed, I dashed towards Razi. Thankfully, I managed to reach her before the projectile, gently grabbing and moving her out of harm's way. I then shifted back to normal speed, watching as the table leg zipped through the spot where she'd been standing a moment earlier before embedding itself in the wall. Realizing what had almost happened, Razi let out a small gasp.

A yelp drew my attention. My head snapped in the direction of the sound, which had come from the mage-beast's back, and I saw that the monster's tail had wrapped itself around Gossamer's waist. The appendage then snapped forcefully to the side, cracking the air like a whip as it flung the elf away like a torpedo from a launch tube.

At the speed she was going, it was plainly obvious that if Gossamer hit anything more substantial than a soft white cloud, she was going to break a lot of bones. With that in mind, I was about to grab her telekinetically but never got a chance. Instead, Ursula appeared, somehow catching Gossamer as well as arresting the elf's momentum without hurting her.

At that moment, I felt movement and realized that I still had a grip on Razi.

"Forget me!" she ordered. "Help Kane!"

Nodding, I used my super speed to dash to the wall and then pulled out the embedded table leg. Now with a weapon, I floated up a few feet and then flew at the mage-beast, which had never released its hold on my friend's wrist. I struck it solidly on the cheek as I zipped by, making its head snap to the side. I immediately turned and flew at it again, preparing to land a second blow.

Apparently, however, I had learned little from my encounter with the monster that morning. Obviously ready for me, it phased and my follow-up blow connected with nothing. In fact, the miss threw me off-balance, and I went tumbling away for a second or two.

I quickly regained control and turned back towards the creature just in time to see its head jerk towards Kane's captured hand in a manner reminiscent of a snapping turtle. Although still looking dazed, Kane let out an ear-piercing scream as blood suddenly shot from his imprisoned hand.

The mage-beast dropped Kane, who fell to the floor in a heap, moaning and cradling his right hand. Its face covered with blood, the monster shook its head once or twice as if to clear its vision, and then it vanished.

CONJURATION

Chapter 47

Razi and Gossamer both raced towards Kane, as did Ursula and I a moment later. His grandmother reached him first and dropped to the floor next to him. Kane was still moaning and holding his wounded hand as Razi cradled his head in her lap.

Taking a look at his injuries, I feared for a moment that his entire hand was gone. Fortunately, that wasn't the case, but the actual truth was almost as grim: only the index finger and thumb remained on his right hand, which was gushing blood. The mage-beast had bitten the others clean off.

Still holding Kane's head in her lap, I saw Razi reach for something on the floor nearby. I fought to hide my shock when I realized what it was: one of her grandson's fingers.

Understanding that something might still be done for my friend, I shifted into super speed and made a quick inspection of the surrounding area. A moment later, I returned to Razi with Kane's other two missing digits.

"Thank you," she said flatly.

I mumbled something in response, but didn't recall what it was. Frankly speaking, my mind was racing as I contemplated what to do.

In truth, I had developed a healing power in the recent past that could probably help my friend. The problem was that it worked sporadically, and there was no guarantee that I could do anything for him. That said, the decision was taken out of my hands by Razi, who — to my surprise — was broadcasting a vibe that encompassed calm resolve, determination, and hope.

CONJURATION

Ignoring Kane's groans of pain, she placed her grandson's severed fingers in the palm of his right hand. Next, she plucked one of the beads from her necklace, put it in his injured hand as well, and then covered it with her own. A moment later, their hands became enveloped by a soft glowing light with an amber hue. It persisted for about thirty seconds; at that point, Razi removed her hand, and I was almost shocked to see Kane's fingers once again attached. They were wan and pale, but nevertheless back in place on his hand.

"Help me get him up," Razi said.

Gossamer and I both promptly offered our assistance, and a moment later we had Kane on his feet. That said, he still looked like he was in a fugue state or something.

"He's going into shock," his grandmother said. "Lost too much blood. We need to get him to the infirmary."

As she spoke, she draped one of Kane's arms over her shoulder to help keep him up. I was on the verge of taking the other, but Gossamer beat me to it, which left me feeling unchivalrous and loutish.

I didn't witness anyone do anything, but suddenly the very air seemed to part in front of Kane, Razi, and Gossamer. I could see a room through the opening that had appeared, but not much else. Razi and the others walked through. I was about to follow them when I felt a tug on my sleeve.

It was Ursula, of course. She didn't say anything, but simply shook her head. Her meaning, of course, was easily understood: *Don't go with them.*

I didn't say anything, but merely glanced back at the magical opening that the others had gone through.

CONJURATION

Moments later, it closed, leaving me and Ursula alone in the wrecked suite.

CONJURATION

Chapter 48

"I'm sorry," Ursula began. "I know you wanted to go with your friend and make sure he's okay, but I needed to talk to you."

"Don't worry about it," I said. "So what's going on?"

"Basically, we need a plan for dealing with this mage-beast."

"I thought we *had* a plan," I shot back. "We find it, then you shut it down."

She paused for a moment, thinking. "Do you recall what Kane said about some mage-beasts having lethal abilities that are triggered if you try to turn them off or destroy them?"

"Yeah," I said with a nod. "But I can't believe that would be a problem for you."

"You're right — I can shut down those that we saw in the cells without breaking a sweat. But this one's different."

"In what way?"

"During that little battle we just had with the mage-beast, I was able to see that it's not only animated by the weird *sivrrut* I detected before, but if I try to shut it down or destroy it, that power will be released."

"So?" I asked.

"It will be released *explosively*," she clarified. "It will permeate anything and everything close by. And human beings can't withstand that much Incarnate-level power."

"So that's why you didn't just shut it down when it attacked a few minutes ago. Doing that would have killed everybody."

"Well, probably not *me*, but you guys for sure."

I spent a few moments chewing on that, then asked, "So how do we deal with this?"

"Based on what I've seen, I don't think the *sivrrut*'s active when the mage-beast is in its innocuous state. Presumably, it's not just shielded in some way but also dormant during those times."

"So our best bet is to find that monster when it's in its other form."

"Yes. *That's* what we need to come up with a plan for."

I frowned, thinking. "And you're sure you can't just destroy it and shield us from the effects of any *sivrrut* it releases?"

"As I mentioned, the Incarnate power I keep sensing is different than what I'm accustomed to. I couldn't make any promises. It would take someone with more power than I'm sporting right now to guarantee everyone's safety."

"Great," I muttered sarcastically. "Where's an Incarnate when you need one?"

It was a rhetorical question, but it suddenly brought something to mind that I had overlooked up to that point.

Giving Ursula an inquisitive look, I asked, "Where's Endow?"

"Huh?" Ursula muttered. She then shrugged, saying, "Who knows? She's an Incarnate. She could be anywhere."

"No, I mean why isn't she *here*?"

Ursula frowned. "I don't think I understand the question."

"Then let me clarify. Where you're concerned, Endow's like a mother grizzly protecting her cub. Now you've battled that mage-beast twice so far. Even though you weren't hurt either time, there's no way Endow would let that happen even once and not intervene."

"I think you're wildly overestimating Endow's need to keep an eye me."

"Maybe she doesn't *need* to, but I'm betting she does. And with the Cosmos Corridor, she can see any part of the universe. Bearing all that in mind, I don't think she'd overlook you going toe-to-toe with a magical monster."

"Assuming that's true, she probably thought I could handle it," Ursula suggested.

"Except you just admitted that your handling of the situation might put everyone in danger," I reminded her. "Both of us even acknowledged that we need an Incarnate to safely get rid of the mage-beast. Which again raises the question of why Endow isn't here."

"Going with your theory for a second, perhaps not showing up is her way of sending a message," Ursula stated, sounding a little irritated.

Plainly curious, I asked, "What type of message?"

"That maybe I shouldn't get involved," she grumbled.

I stared at her for a moment, not sure I'd heard her right, then muttered, "You can't believe that."

"You obviously don't know Endow — or *me* — as well as you think," she snapped.

"I know she wouldn't want you in danger, but there's no way Endow would condone you completely turning your back in this situation."

"Ha!" Ursula barked. "That just shows how much *you* know."

"So you're saying that Endow would be okay telling you to stand down — and you'd do it — even though there's a mystical Grendel out there killing people."

"Absolutely," she uttered with finality.

I looked at her in disbelief. "How can you say that?"

"Because I'm not Beowulf!" she blurted out in frustration. "And dealing with monsters isn't my mission!"

I blinked several times, trying to process what she'd just said.

"Your mission?" I repeated in confusion. "What mission?"

"Forget it," Ursula said. "I misspoke."

Except she hadn't. I'd been reading her empathically as we talked, and had a pretty good sense of her emotional state in terms of veracity. For instance, I had felt her irritation and frustration building as we conversed; it had ultimately resulted in the outburst about her "mission," which I perceived as being truthful. In contrast, the statement about misspeaking felt disingenuous.

"What kind of mission do you have?" I asked.

"I don't," she insisted. "As I said, I misspoke."

I ignored her denials. "Why are you here?"

"Will you just drop it?" she pleaded, her voice making it plain that she didn't care for my questions.

"You said this was a bit of a vacation and you wanted to hang out," I recalled. "That's why you've been on my heels almost everywhere, practically tailgating—"

I stopped mid-sentence as the truth didn't just hit me, but clubbed me like a baseball bat to the temple. At the same time, Ursula lowered her eyes self consciously while emotionally I felt dread, remorse, and embarrassment flaring within her.

"It's me," I concluded. "*I'm* the mission."

CONJURATION

Chapter 49

"It's not what you think," Ursula said.

"Oh, really?" I uttered acidly. "Seems like I've been getting that a lot lately. First Kane, now you. But I believe I'd give you the edge in the spying-on-friends department."

"That's hurtful, Jim," she declared.

"But it's the truth, right? Isn't that why you're here — to spy on me?"

"Not *spy*," she insisted, shaking her head. "Just keep an eye on things. You have to understand — you shouldn't exist."

I gave her an incredulous look. "What do you mean, I shouldn't exist?"

"I don't mean that you as a *person* shouldn't exist. I'm talking about you as…whatever you are."

I frowned, but had an idea of what she was alluding to.

"You're talking about my Incarnate status," I deduced. "Or rather, my *non*-Incarnate status."

"Yes," she confirmed. "You can do some of the things they can, but you're not one of them."

"And that's a problem?"

"Who knows?" she said with a shrug. "No one's ever seen anything like you — not even Incarnates. That makes you a bit of a wild card. I'm just here to see what we can learn from boots on the ground."

"Incarnates can see the entire universe via the Cosmos Corridor," I noted. "Why send you?"

"Because of what I just said," she replied. "And also because none of them can see you anymore."

I looked at her with a dumbfounded expression on my face. "What are you talking about? Thanks to the Cosmos Corridor, they can see *everything*."

"Maybe before, but not now," she corrected, shaking her head. "Not with respect to you. All they can see as far as you're concerned is an ambient blackness that obscures you and everything you do."

"Hold up," I almost screeched. "Are you saying there's some kind of black cloud around me?"

"Something along those lines, but that's just what it looks like in the Cosmos Corridor. Here, of course, I don't see anything like that."

"But it's present."

"Undoubtedly."

I contemplated for a moment, then asked, "And no one has any idea what it means?"

"I'd say the immediate takeaway is obvious," she answered. "There's something cosmic going on with you, Jim, and the fact that it's making Incarnates nervous tells you all you need to know."

It went without saying that everything I was hearing was far beyond anything I'd ever expected, and just wrapping my head around it was a task in itself.

"Okay," I said after a few moments, "if Endow can't see you, that means you're reporting in. What have you told her?"

"Nothing," she replied. "Because messages aren't getting through."

"What?" I uttered in surprise.

"Do you recall when I first put us in costume?" she asked.

I nodded. "Yeah. You created the illusion of us being outside and bombs exploding overhead, among other things."

"It was actually only half-illusion," she stated. "But my point is that the explosions were really an attempt to pierce this dark field surrounding you, but I couldn't get through."

I thought about that for a moment. "Does proximity have anything to do with it?"

She looked at me with a nonplussed expression. "What do you mean?"

"Your message-sending capability," I explained. "Will you have better luck if you're away from me?"

"Wait a minute. I thought you were upset about me allegedly spying on you, but are you saying that you actually *want* me to report back to Endow about what I've observed?"

"No," I declared, shaking my head emphatically. "What I want you to do is send a message to Beowulf, asking him to come kill Grendel."

"Oh," she murmured softly, now understanding what I'd been hoping for.

"So, will distancing yourself from me help?"

"Unfortunately, no," she answered.

"Why not?"

Ursula contemplated her answer for a moment before responding. "Do you remember when I told you how the Templum was put together? That it's not just one structure but a bunch of them magically welded together and that they're actually spread out all over?"

"Yeah," I stated with a nod.

"Well, I think that same sorcery has caused the darkness around you to become spread out as well."

"Meaning what?" I inquired. "That every separate room and chamber here now has a piece of this darkness you mentioned in it?"

"That theory seems to suggest that the dark field we're talking about got broken up, with a piece in each different location. In truth, it's more like it got stretched out and now covers a much larger area."

"But isn't that a good thing?" I asked. "I mean, if this dark energy around me has suddenly grown, isn't that going to make Endow or some other Incarnate come running?"

Ursula shrugged. "It depends on what they're seeing, and there's no guarantee that the Cosmos Corridor is displaying anything here as we perceive it."

"So it might appear to be something more benign than it actually is," I concluded. "What happens if it comes across as something worse?"

Ursula gave me a frank stare. "As I said, the situation with this dark field is already getting some Incarnates out of sorts. If they start viewing it as an issue, they may take action."

"Meaning what?" I asked, noting that there was a gravity to Ursula's tone that she rarely exhibited.

"Incarnates usually take one of two approaches to things they perceive as a serious concern," she sternly declared. "They either eliminate the problem, or eliminate the source."

CONJURATION

Chapter 50

Following Ursula's last statement, I suddenly found myself needing some air. She tried to offer assurances that the Incarnates were unlikely to do anything drastic, but I wasn't in the mood to hear it and teleported.

I popped up outside the Templum, not far from the pond. Probably not the wisest decision, considering there was a killer monster on the loose (and that it had found a couple of its victims outdoors), but I needed time to think and wanted to do it away from other people.

That said, I saw no need to be a complete idiot about the situation. Therefore, I immediately phased and became invisible, then zoomed up into the air. I didn't go far, however — just up to the height of the Templum's roof. At that point, although the possibility of a mage-beast attack had been diminished, I cycled my vision to the appropriate part of the light spectrum so I could at least see the thing if it decided to come after me. Now satisfied that I was fairly safe, I turned my mind to everything I'd recently learned.

The issue about the dark field around me was obviously disturbing. I, of course, had never noticed anything along the lines of what Ursula had suggested. That said, I had been reading her empathically and noted that she hadn't been lying. More importantly, there was nothing I could do about it. Sure, I could (and probably would) continue to ask questions on the issue, but I had no clue when — or if — I'd receive satisfactory answers. My mentor Mouse might be able to help (he was pretty much the smartest guy on the planet), but did I really want to get him caught up in the middle of something involving nigh-omnipotent beings?

CONJURATION

Probably not, I thought.

Ergo, the dark field situation most likely involved a wait-and-see approach. It wasn't ideal, but I really didn't have a lot of options.

The other item causing me concern was the spying situation. Basically, two people that I considered to be friends had admittedly engaged in what I'd label as espionage. It really shined a spotlight on my judgment, or possible lack thereof.

In all honesty, I'd really been a loner for most of my life. It was only during the past year that I'd really started cultivating friendships and relationships with people outside my family. I thought I'd done a good job of choosing the people to be in my inner circle, but recent events made me feel like my judgment in that arena was suspect.

Was that it? I wondered. Had I, on some subconscious level, been so desperate for friends that I'd failed to properly vet those around me?

In all honesty, it seemed unlikely. The people I'd become close to — like Kane, Gossamer, and Ursula — were folks who were willing to go to the mat for me. Had put themselves in harm's way at my request. Had helped me save the world, and more. (And it went without saying that I'd do the same for them.) Weighed against all that, their recent actions that I'd taken issue with seemed like small potatoes.

In addition, my empathic abilities told me that both Ursula and Kane had been sincere in their apologies. More than that, I'd always sensed that they were people who actually cared about me and my well-being. And I, of course, felt the same way about them. In fact, after Kane's injury, I had suddenly realized that I didn't really care what he'd done; all I'd wanted was for my friend to be okay. The only thing that really put his actions back on my radar was finding out what Ursula had done. It was that double-whammy — the feeling of being figuratively shanked twice in the same day — which now had me reassessing and reexamining my relationships with people. That said, I was pretty confident at this point of how I felt.

In essence, Kane and Ursula had done some stuff I wasn't wild about, but that didn't mean that the bonds we'd forged should be shattered. It simply meant that friendships, like other relationships, were dynamic and complex. More to the point, good friends were hard to come by and were worth the occasional conflict.

With that in mind, I spent a little more time simply floating in the air, enjoying the peace and solitude, and then teleported back to the suite.

CONJURATION

Chapter 51

I popped up in the great room, becoming visible and substantial, as well as switching my vision back to normal. Much to my surprise, the place was back to its regular appearance. All of the furnishings that had been smashed or tossed about were now repaired and back in place. (And thankfully, there was no sign of blood anywhere.)

I had been hoping to find Ursula here — hoping for a chance to finish our talk. It was important for me to let her know that we were still friends. After all, her experience with other people (aside from Incarnates) was extremely limited, and I didn't want her taking things too hard.

Unfortunately, Ursula wasn't there, but someone else was: Razi. Although I appeared behind her, she must have sensed my presence because a few seconds later she turned around. One would have thought she'd be wary in a place where a magical attack had occurred just a short time earlier, but she seemed rather calm.

"Excellent — you're back," she said, skipping over any pleasantries. "And your friend?"

I shrugged. "I don't know. I needed a minute to think, so I took off. Apparently she did as well, but I'm sure I can find her if you—"

"No, no, no," she stressed, shaking her head. "It's just that Kane's awake now if you'd like to go visit him."

"He is?" I muttered in surprise.

"Yes," she said with a smile. "I know — you're thinking that was pretty quick, but the right set of healing spells can do wonders."

I merely nodded, but she had pretty much nailed what I was thinking. How long had it been since the attack? Counting the time I'd spent chatting with Ursula and then alone with my thoughts (not to mention when I was simply floating and relaxing), it had been what — maybe an hour? Certainly not more than two.

"That's great," I finally said after a few moments. "I appreciate you coming to tell me."

"Well, I also had another motive," she admitted, glancing around. "I was looking for something that apparently became lost when we were fighting the mage-beast."

"One of your beads?" I implied. "Maybe Ursula picked it up."

"It's not important," Razi suddenly declared with a dismissive wave of her hand. "If you're ready, we can go see Kane now."

"Sure," I said.

As before, I didn't see what Razi did, but the air parted and we walked through the gap that appeared.

CONJURATION

Chapter 52

We emerged in a broad hallway that extended maybe fifty feet in either direction before intersecting with other corridors. The floor, I noticed, was covered by a thick carpet, and ceiling fans were geometrically spaced above us. On the walls hung bright, cheery paintings: children on a playground; a gorgeous sunset on a beautiful beach; a couple holding hands, strolling through a field of flowers.

All in all, although we were presumably in the infirmary, the place didn't have the cold, antiseptic feel that is commonplace in hospitals. It felt much more like a warm, cozy room where one could fall asleep reading a book in front of the fireplace.

There were doors on either side of the hallway, and Razi walked towards one of them. A second later, she opened it and we walked in. At that point, I found myself staring in surprise, because Kane's hospital room was far different than what I expected.

First of all, it was large — at least four hundred square feet in size. I caught sight of a sitting area with a couch and a pair of recliners, as well as a small breakfast area consisting of a table and a couple of chairs. The most prominent feature of the room was a queen-sized bed that was currently occupied by Kane, who was sitting up. Surrounding his bed were his parents, sister, and other family members, as well as Gossamer. They all turned in the direction of the door as Razi and I entered.

"Hey," Razi said to her grandson. "I brought you a visitor."

"Awesome," Kane intoned with a smile. He looked a little pale, but otherwise none the worse for wear.

CONJURATION

I gave a quick wave and uttered an all-encompassing "Hello" to everyone in the room, getting the same in return from those present.

"Uh, could you guys give us a moment?" Kane said, addressing everyone generally. "I need to talk to Jim about something."

His family willingly acquiesced, and — after a smattering of well-wishes — they filed out the door, including Razi. Roughly a minute later, Kane and I were alone, except for Gossamer.

Kane looked at his girlfriend. "Hey babe, could you—"

"Don't even," she warned, cutting him off as she sat down on the bed next to him. "I'm staying."

For a moment, it appeared as though Kane was going to insist, but one look at Gossamer's face and he knew this was an argument he couldn't win. Letting out a sigh, he turned to me.

"Look, dude," he began, "I just want to say again how sorry—"

"Water under the bridge," I interjected. "Don't give it another thought."

"Thanks," he replied with a grateful smile. "But I wanted you to know that Gossamer wasn't—"

"Doesn't matter," I cut in, again not letting him finish his thought. "Look, we're going to have disagreements, but you guys are my friends. I don't know if that will always be the case, but I know it'll take more than what's happened *here* to change that."

Kane and Gossamer shared a glance, with the latter smiling and saying, "See, I *told* you..."

"Anyway," I droned, drawing their attention back to me, "I'm glad to see you're doing better."

"Thanks," Kane said.

"Also," I continued, "I've yet to get the full story of what happened back in the suite."

"That's easy," Kane declared. "My grandmother showed up about a minute after you and Ursula went to your room. We were, uh, discussing what you guys had told us about the attack this morning when the mage-beast suddenly appeared out of nowhere."

"How'd you know it was there?" I asked. "I mean, it's invisible."

"The Council had laid a trap for it," Gossamer chimed in, reminding me of something I shouldn't have forgotten. "That didn't stop it completely — it still knocked around furniture and stuff — but it was enough to give us fair warning and provide a chance to mount a defense."

"Did you see my girl go after that thing?" Kane asked, brimming with pride. "She's absolutely fearless!"

Gossamer blushed slightly, but that brought up a question I had for her.

"When you jumped on that thing's back," I began, "how'd you know where it was?"

"Elf eyes are different than a human's," she explained. "Going off something you said before, I was able to cast a glamour that let me see it to a certain extent, but it wouldn't have helped you guys."

"Well, I'm just glad we were all able to walk away in one piece," I said, and then realized how callous my comment may have seemed. Looking at Kane, I muttered, "Sorry, that came out wrong."

"It's cool," he assured me. "See?"

CONJURATION

He held up his right hand — the one the mage-beast had bit. As I'd seen before he was taken to the infirmary, his fingers were again attached.

"Good as new," Kane continued, wriggling his fingers. I also noted that each digit was once again adorned with a ring — all except, ironically, his ring finger.

"That's amazing," I remarked.

"Yeah, my grandmother's bead did a good job," Kane said, "although not quite as good as my health stone would have."

"Excuse me?" I uttered, frowning. "Health stone?"

"Yeah, it's one of my rings," Kane explained. "It basically heals wounds, keeps you healthy, and all that jazz. Unfortunately, it was on one of the fingers that our friendly neighborhood monster bit off. We found the others, but not that one."

As he spoke, he tapped his bare ring finger with the thumb of that same hand. At the same time, my brow wrinkled in thought as I recalled Razi saying she was looking for something in our suite.

"So your ring would have done a better job than Razi's bead?" I asked. Frankly speaking, I'd been pretty impressed by what the bead had done.

Kane nodded. "The bead reattached my fingers, but it took additional spellwork to make them hale and hearty again, with full functionality — not to mention healing the bruise on my cheek."

"But your health stone would have done all that on its own," I surmised.

"Oh yeah," Kane confirmed. "It's a pretty cool accessory."

"So does every member of the Kroten Venefici get one of those?" I asked.

"No — not enough of them to go around," Kane answered. "In fact, there are only…"

He trailed off and a faraway look came into his eyes. His brow crinkled, and I could tell that he was thinking furiously about something.

After about ten seconds, he seemed to come back to himself.

"Get my grandmother," Kane practically ordered. "I know what the mage-beast was after."

CONJURATION

Chapter 53

Fortunately, when Kane had told his family to give us a minute, his grandmother hadn't gone far. In fact, when he asked us to get her, she was actually waiting out in the hallway. Moments later, she was inside with the rest of us, at which point Kane laid out his theory.

"It's trying to get the Salubrious Gem," Kane stated.

"The Salubrious Gem?" Razi repeated skeptically.

"Yes," Kane affirmed, nodding.

"It doesn't exist anymore," Razi said. "Not in its original form, anyway."

"Regardless, that's what it's after," Kane stated emphatically, although his grandmother frowned as though she found this incredulous.

"I'm a little lost here, and I'm sure Jim is as well," Gossamer pointed out. "What's the Salubrious Gem?"

"I can explain," Razi replied, "but it requires giving a little history lesson."

"That's fine," I assured her.

"Well, according to legend," Razi began, "the founder of the Kroten Venefici had a lot of powerful artifacts. One of these was a jewel that gave long life and health to its owner."

"The Salubrious Gem," Gossamer offered.

"Yes," Razi confirmed. "At some point, it allegedly passed from our founder to three of his pupils. Unfortunately, they couldn't decide who should have it, so they split it into three pieces — three separate health stones, which have been passed down from generation to generation in the families of those pupils."

"And your family has one of them," I concluded.

Razi nodded. "Somewhere in the past, our stone got fashioned into a ring, which was in my possession for the past few decades. However, given some of his recent escapades, I gave it to Kane not long ago."

Chuckling, Kane looked at me. "She was worried that hanging out with you would get me killed."

"That's an exaggeration," Razi insisted. "But I did think he needed extra protection."

"So the other two stones," Gossamer chimed in. "I'm guessing Malvern and Agatha had them."

"Correct," Razi said. "Agatha usually wore hers on a pendant around her neck."

"And Malvern?" I asked.

An odd look settled on Razi's face. "Malvern was actually very old and very sick. The health stone was probably the only thing keeping him alive. In essence, he fused it with a kind of mystical pacemaker that he used."

"Wait a minute," I blurted out incredulously. "The stone was inside him?"

Razi nodded. "As I said, he was very sick."

I frowned, as a lot that had happened was suddenly making sense.

"So," Kane intoned, "were Malvern and Agatha's health stones recovered with their bodies?"

Razi shook her head, saying, "No, but that just means someone in their respective families might have them."

"No, the mage-beast took them," I declared as my thoughts crystallized. "It sliced off Agatha's head to get her pendent, and it tore Malvern apart to find the stone inside him. Kane's lucky it didn't take off his entire hand."

No one said anything for a moment. They all simply stared at me, digesting what I'd said.

CONJURATION

"If what you're saying is true," Gossamer finally remarked, "then whoever controls the mage-beast now has all three stones, but we're no closer to figuring out their identity."

"Sure we are," I countered, then looked at Kane and Razi. "Any idea what would happen if all three stones were brought together?"

"The original gem was supposed to be the most powerful relic of its kind in the world," Kane responded. "Presumably, if the stones were somehow merged or simply brought together, the health effects would be notably — maybe *exponentially* — amplified."

"And there's our answer," I said. "Or rather, we know the right question: who's powerful enough to create a mage-beast, and sick enough to need the Salubrious Gem?"

"Or has someone close to them who's deathly ill," Kane added.

"Good point," I noted. "Regardless, it has to be a short list."

I looked at Razi, who simply said, "I can make some inquiries. But to be clear, you think Kane's right — that whoever's behind the mage-beast is after the Salubrious Gem?"

"I just know that monster attacked three people who all have a distinct, identifiable connection," I said. "And in situations like this, once is random. Twice is a coincidence. Three times is a pattern."

"Except it actually attacked *four* people," Gossamer noted. "You're forgetting Ursula, this morning."

I frowned as Gossamer finished speaking. Of course, she was right, and for a moment the whole health gem theory was on the verge of blowing up. And then I remembered something.

"We need Ursula," I announced.

CONJURATION

Chapter 54

Locating Ursula actually turned out to be fairly easy. I had assumed that I'd have to zip through the Templum at super speed (or something along those lines) in order to find her, but it turned out that there was a simpler method.

"We've been keeping tabs on her since our meeting in the Council chambers," Razi revealed after my statement about needing Ursula to join us. "She went wandering around for a while earlier, but at the moment, she's in her room."

After thanking Razi for the info, I teleported outside Ursula's door in our suite. I then knocked firmly.

"Come in," I heard Ursula call out in a lackluster tone.

I tried the knob and, finding the door unlocked, went in as invited. Ursula was lying on her bed, eyes closed. Empathically, I picked up on a vibe of melancholy and sadness.

"Hey, you," I said, trying to sound cheerful.

"Hi," she glumly replied. "You still mad at me?"

I chuckled softly. "Do I sound mad?"

"No," she admitted, "but you're the kind of guy who can pull the wool over a girl's eyes — especially a gullible young thing like myself."

I laughed. "You're a lot of things, but gullible isn't one of them."

She opened her eyes and propped herself up on her elbows. "So if you're not mad, to what do I owe the pleasure?"

"We need your help with something," I said, and then gave a brief overview of the theory about the health gems. "Basically, I need you to corroborate some info. Are you okay with that?"

"Of course," she replied, coming to her feet. "And I'm sorry about what I said before. You were right."

"About what?" I asked, curious.

"When you said that Endow wouldn't want me to walk away and that I wouldn't turn my back if I could help. Me saying that I would was just a knee-jerk response. I don't know why, but everyone's been pushing my buttons lately. First Razi, then you…"

"Razi?" I echoed as she trailed off.

"Yeah," Ursula asserted with a nod. "After we found Malvern's body, she was asking most of the questions when the Council was quizzing me, and she just really managed to get under my skin."

"Hmmm," I droned, thinking. "Anyway, if you're ready?"

"Of course," she said. "Let's go."

CONJURATION

Chapter 55

Only Kane and Gossamer were present when I teleported back with Ursula. Razi had left to make the inquiries we'd talked about, and — not knowing when she'd return — the rest of us decided not to wait. Ergo, I asked the question I had for Ursula, which was pretty straightforward.

"Do you have any kind of charm or relic that's related to health or well-being?" I asked. "Something that will keep you from getting sick, heal you when you're injured, and stuff like that?"

"Of course," Ursula replied matter-of-factly.

"How powerful is it?" I inquired.

Ursula reflected for a moment. "I don't think you have a scale for it."

Kane gave her a skeptical look. "But would it be more powerful than the Salubrious Gem?"

"Frankly speaking, there's no comparison," Ursula told him.

"Hold on," Gossamer demanded, looking at Ursula. "How do you know that?"

Ursula looked at her in befuddlement. "Know what?"

"How do you know you've got a relic more powerful than one you've never seen?" Gossamer asked.

Ursula sighed. "When the mage-beast attacked me this morning, it had a health stone. I didn't realize the significance of it at the time and just thought the stone was part of its normal makeup. Now I know better, thanks to what Jim told me. That said, you could collect *ten* of those stones, and it still wouldn't match what I have."

CONJURATION

Ursula's comment caused an unexpected silence to take hold as everyone contemplated what she'd said. Before things became awkward, I decided to speak up.

"Okay," I chimed in, "here's what I think happened. I believe the mage-beast was sent after the most powerful health stones its creator was aware of. However, after killing Agatha, it somehow sensed what Ursula had and got distracted. Ursula's health relic was more powerful than anything it had come across, so it came after her."

"Okay, if that's the theory," Gossamer said, "why didn't it go after her in the suite?"

I shrugged. "Who knows? Maybe it realized it was overreaching with Ursula, or that her relics weren't compatible with the other stones."

"Or it simply couldn't detect my power," Ursula offered, prompting us all to look at her. "When we encountered it this morning, the mage-beast basically ignored Jim and came after me. I thought it was because it identified me as the greater threat. So when it showed up in the suite, I kind of lowered my output — like turning a dial down in order to make the light in a room dimmer. I had hoped that, if it couldn't detect my power on any level, I could sneak up on it, so to speak."

"Well, I'd say that puts the Salubrious Gem theory back in play," Kane said.

"Yeah," Gossamer intoned, "but the pattern's not exactly the same for all the victims. For instance, the mage-beast attacked the first two outside, but the last one indoors."

"Before we attach significance to any of that," I remarked, "do we know why Malvern was outside in the first place? Agatha, we know, was jogging."

"According to my grandmother," Kane related, "Malvern said it was stuffy inside — too many people — so he decided to get some air. At least, that's what his family told her. They also said it wasn't uncommon for him to do that."

"Okay," Ursula chimed in, "nothing unusual there. Any particular reason Agatha was out jogging?"

"For health, maybe?" Gossamer suggested sarcastically. "I'm not sure I understand the question."

"I mean, why was she jogging when she has a health stone?" Ursula clarified.

"Because it's a *health* stone," Kane stressed. "It'll prevent your arteries from getting clogged with cholesterol and keep you from getting high blood pressure, but it won't give you washboard abs or stop you from gaining five hundred pounds if you pig out at every meal."

"So it's a *health* stone, not a *fitness* stone," I concluded. "Got it."

For a moment, it appeared as though Ursula wanted to say more, but then Razi strode through the door.

"All right, I asked around," she informed us as she walked in. "Unfortunately, there's nobody who fits the bill."

"Really?" Kane queried in a disbelieving tone.

"Really," his grandmother attested. "I checked not only our own people but other sects as well. There's no one with the ability to create a mage-beast who's also very sick, nor do any of them have someone close to them with a debilitating illness."

Kane let out a groan of frustration, which probably expressed everyone's sentiments. It had really felt like we were on to something.

"I can't believe we're wrong on that," Kane finally admitted after a few seconds. "After all, there's not much else you'd take those stones for."

I gave him a curious look, his words having given me a new train of thought.

"So what other use does the Salubrious Gem have?" I asked.

"Huh?" Kane muttered.

"Assuming we're right about the mage-beast being after the health stones, seems like we're wrong about the reason why," I explained. "If that's the case, it suggests that there's another use for the Salubrious Gem. The question is, what is it?"

Kane shook his head, plainly indicating that he didn't have an answer. He then turned to his grandmother, as did the rest of us.

Obviously feeling the weight of our scrutiny, Razi said, "In all honesty, I don't know if there's another use for the health stones or the gem. I've certainly never heard of one, but that doesn't mean there isn't."

"Is there a way to find out?" Gossamer asked.

Razi appeared to contemplate for a moment, then said, "There might be something in the archives."

"Great," Ursula said. "Where can we find them?"

"It'll take you forever to locate anything in there," Razi noted. "I'll send Lamont. As my famulus, he's become completely familiar with the archives."

"Famulus?" I repeated.

"It refers to someone who's an assistant," Razi explained. "Anyway, I'm not sure where Lamont is at the moment, so it may take a little time to find him."

"I saw him earlier," Ursula noted. "I needed some time to myself, so I went for a walk in the woods and saw him and his spectral girlfriend."

"Excuse me?" Razi intoned, looking at Ursula with a baffled expression.

"Well, I don't *know* that she was his girlfriend," Ursula confessed. "And she was actually in astral form, as opposed to being spectral."

"What are you talking about?" Kane demanded, with an expression that mirrored his grandmother's.

"The girl Lamont was with," Ursula said. "She was an astral projection. I assume she couldn't get an invite because of the restricted guest list, but still wanted to be here to support him."

At that moment, her head swiveled back and forth between Razi and Kane, as she suddenly realized that they were both giving her incredulous stares.

"I'm sorry," Ursula unexpectedly blurted out. "Is that going to get him in trouble? I mean, I wasn't trying to rat him out or any—"

"You must be mistaken," Razi interjected. "Astral projection isn't allowed here."

"Yeah, right," Ursula snickered sarcastically — and then she noticed that Razi wasn't joking. "Wait, are you serious?"

"*Completely* serious," Razi told her. "The Council conducts its most important business and confidential discussions in the Templum. That being the case, we can't have people wandering around in astral form, hiding in the walls, eavesdropping on conversations, and so on."

"We even have a ton of wards in place to prevent it," Kane added.

CONJURATION

"Well, I'm not sure what to tell you," Ursula said, "but the woman with Lamont was definitely astral, although I don't think they realized I could see her. Also, not to be flip, but your wards are far from perfect."

"As if we didn't have enough on our plates already," Razi grumbled, almost to herself. "Now we've got to deal with *this* situation — this blatant flaunting of the rules."

"Can you describe what the woman looked like?" Kane asked.

Ursula smiled. "I can do better than that."

She pointed towards a blank area on a nearby wall and then traced a rectangle in the air. A similar rectangle, but much larger in size, appeared on the wall in question. Then, akin to what Kane had done in the mage-beast cells, images began to form within the rectangle.

At first they were vague and blurry, and it was hard to make anything out. However, the images quickly began to take on recognizable forms: trees, grass, shrubs...even people. I quickly understood that this was the place in the woods where Ursula had seen Lamont, which was confirmed when a hazy mass condensed into the form of Lamont himself. At that point, we could also see his "girlfriend," as Ursula put it.

She was a little older than Lamont — perhaps mid-thirties — with long, dark tresses and gorgeous, runway-model looks. At about five-nine, she was taller than average, and dressed in something like a dark maxi dress. And, as Ursula had indicated, she was indeed spectral in that her body didn't appear to be solid, allowing one to see through it.

I stared at her in near shock, and had to consciously fight to keep my mouth from dropping open — not because of her ghostly appearance, but because I recognized her. In fact, so did everyone in the room except Ursula.

"That's not his girlfriend!" Kane finally belted out. "That's Gloriana Mano!"

CONJURATION

Chapter 56

In the annals of history, there are some people — some *faces* — that are immediately recognized by everyone. The *Mona Lisa*, for instance. Essentially everyone on the planet knows her face, her smile. Likewise with Napoleon; in his uniform and bicorne hat, he is immediately identifiable. In a similar vein, everyone in the world knew the face of Gloriana Mano, also known as the Hand of Glory.

She had been a powerful sorceress — quite possibly the strongest on the planet — and initially a tireless force for good. Aligned with one of the major superhero teams, she had helped save countless lives during the early years of her career. And then, it all changed.

While battling a dark force from another dimension, something in Gloriana's mind became unhinged. Afterwards, she saw humanity — *all* life, in fact — as some sort of blight. Since then, her only aim had been the complete destruction of the planet.

Fortunately, Gloriana never got an opportunity to fulfill her ambition. She was incredibly smart and cunning, but utter destruction of the planet is rarely something that can be accomplished in subtle fashion. More to the point, subtlety was not her style; she was completely open about her intentions, and as a result gained worldwide infamy and notoriety. Eventually, she was captured, but since ordinary means of incarceration were inadequate for someone with her abilities, she was placed into a medically (and magically) induced coma. She had been in that state for years, and it was assumed she would remain that way for life.

CONJURATION

We explained all this to Ursula, whom Kane still couldn't believe had never heard of the Hand of Glory.

"Where've you been?" he practically demanded. "An alien planet?"

His assessment actually wasn't that far off base, but this wasn't the time to enlighten him. What we really needed to do, among other things, was figure out why Lamont was hanging out with the astral projection of one of the most dangerous psychotics on the planet. (There was also the question of how any of this connected to the mage-beast. Maybe it didn't, but that would seem to be one heck of a coincidence.)

"I prefer the direct approach," Razi stated when we discussed how to deal with him. Since she had the most experience with Lamont, the rest of us acquiesced.

CONJURATION

Chapter 57

It was something of an ambush. Razi got word to Lamont that she wanted to see him immediately in her study, and when he showed up a few minutes later, we were all waiting.

Showing that she did indeed prefer being direct, Razi skipped the pleasantries and barked, "Why are you hanging out with Gloriana Mano?"

Shockingly, Lamont didn't deny it. He simply seemed to wither under her gaze, collapsing into himself before slumping into a nearby chair.

"Thank heavens," he murmured in relief, which I also felt echo from him emotionally.

His reaction seemed to take everyone by surprise. We had been expecting denial, flight, or maybe even a fight. (In fact, I think everyone was geared up to go on the attack, if necessary.) This calm, peaceful surrender of sorts hadn't even been considered a possibility.

Unwilling to be lulled into a false sense of security, Razi marched over, leaned in close to his face, and ordered, "Talk!"

****

"She came to me about a year ago," Lamont confessed, looking downcast. "Not here — when I was away from the Templum, after I had failed the provisos for advancement. Again."

"What happened?" I asked.

"She offered to help me," Lamont replied. "She said she'd been watching me, saw how hard I was trying.

249

She told me she could help me advance through the rankings of the Venefici."

Kane gave him a look of incredulity. "Everybody on the planet knows what kind of monster she is. Why would you even talk to her instead of reporting it to somebody?"

"I didn't know who she was at first," he argued.

"You've got to be kidding," I chimed in. "Everybody on the planet knows the Hand of Glory. Newborns in the hospital can identify her." It was obviously an exaggeration, but not by much.

"She kept her features hazy at first," Lamont explained. "All I could really tell was that she was an astral projection. She didn't reveal her face until later — after she'd helped me achieve some success with my magic."

"And at that point you were hooked," Razi concluded. "Like some junkie on drugs."

"You don't know what it was like," Lamont protested. "To always have people — members of your own family — constantly looking down on you. Thinking you're pathetic. Treating you like a loser. And all because you're not good with magic."

"But Gloriana was different," Gossamer remarked.

Lamont nodded. "She treated me like a person. Like I had value. Like I mattered."

"So she gave you a hug and a cookie," Kane stated disdainfully. "And that was enough for you to overlook the fact that she's a confirmed psycho who wants to destroy the world."

"She said she'd changed," Lamont declared. "That her time locked away in a coma had given her mind time to heal. She knew that she'd never be released physically, but she thought — in astral form — she could do some good to make up for her past misdeeds."

"And you bought that," Razi muttered, shaking her head in disgust.

"Again, she was helping me with my magic," Lamont offered. "I didn't think she'd do that if she was still evil."

"Your ambition blinded you," Razi shot back. "But at least now I understand how you suddenly became adept at the arcane. It was never *you* — it was *her*."

"The Templum has spells and incantations against astral projection," Kane noted. "How'd you get Gloriana in here?"

Lamont snorted slightly in derision. "The Templum's protections are nowhere near perfect, and you have no idea how good she is at magic. It was nothing for her to identify the chinks in this place's armor."

I shot a glance at Ursula, recalling that she had said something similar.

"After that," Lamont continued, "it was just a matter of casting the right spell to give her access."

"And you helped," I surmised. "You basically held the door open for her to walk in."

Lamont shrugged. "I needed her. Continued advancement up the Venefici hierarchy necessitated that I complete some of the requirements *here*. Needless to say, at that point, I couldn't do it without her."

"Tell us about the mage-beast," Ursula urged.

Her statement was actually a leap-of-logic, as we hadn't established a connection between Lamont's actions and the monster — didn't even know if there was one. However, Lamont simply lowered his head and nodded, while on an emotional level I sensed him accepting our knowledge as being factual rather than a hypothesis.

"That wasn't what it was supposed to be," he revealed. "It was intended to be a small magical construct about *so* big." He held up his right hand as he spoke, stretching out his thumb and forefinger to encompass an area of about six inches.

Gossamer frowned. "What was that going to do?"

"If I could animate something within the Templum — even a small construct — despite the ban on non-living things, it would establish my reputation as a formidable mage. My future would be assured."

"So what happened?" Razi demanded.

"Gloriana repurposed it without my knowledge," he confessed. "She altered its structure, giving it a dual configuration."

"Two forms," I noted.

Lamont nodded. "One was the original figure, and the other was…"

He trailed off, seemingly unable to finish.

"The other was a monster," Gossamer stated.

"Honestly, I didn't know what she was planning," Lamont stressed. "It didn't become clear until after Malvern was killed."

"But you knew *after* that, didn't you?" Kane chided, almost in disgust. "You knew, and you didn't say anything to anybody."

"I didn't have any proof!" Lamont shot back. "Someone had been killed by a mage-beast that, for all intents and purposes, appeared to be *my* creation. Who would believe me if I blamed it on an astral projection that isn't even supposed to be able to appear here? And Gloriana wasn't going to step up and confess."

"Did you know what Gloriana sent the mage-beast after?" I asked. "The health stones?"

"Not initially," Lamont admitted. "But after Malvern, Gloriana couldn't stop crowing about it. She was practically euphoric. That's when I understood."

"So you knew and just sat on your hands," Kane admonished. "Just zipped your lip, even though you knew that thing was going to try to kill Agatha. That it would try to kill *me*."

"No!" Lamont practically screamed. "Not *you*! Never you! In fact, I made Gloriana promise that it wouldn't kill you, or I'd confess everything, no matter the consequences."

"How kind of you," Kane declared brusquely. "I guess I should be thanking you that your pet only bit off my hand."

"It's not *my* pet," Lamont corrected. "Gloriana controls it."

"That brings up another question," noted Gossamer. "What exactly can she do?"

Lamont ruminated on the question for a moment. "She's nowhere near as powerful as she would be in the flesh, but she still has all of her mystical knowledge. She also has some magical skill, including the ability to manipulate arcane objects and relics. And, of course, she has dominion over the mage-beast."

Razi seemed to reflect for a moment. "When she sent it after Malvern, how did Gloriana know he'd be outside alone?"

"She didn't," Lamont replied. "It was just a crime of opportunity."

"But if she's been hanging around the Templum for a while with you," Razi continued, "she must have had other chances to get his health stone, as well as the other two. Why all of this frenzied activity now?"

"Because she finally got a power source that could properly animate the mage-beast."

"What source?" asked Ursula, her interest suddenly piqued.

"*You*," Lamont told her. "You showed up bursting at the seams with power, like sweat gushing from every pore. Gloriana could sense it, and knew she could use it."

"How?" Ursula inquired.

"There are innumerable antiques and antiquities in the archives," Lamont stated, "and nobody knows what they all do. Gloriana identified one that could harness some of your power and use it for her purposes. All we had to do was get it close to you."

"Where's that artifact now?" queried Razi.

"In my quarters," Lamont responded.

"And the mage-beast?" his great-aunt continued.

Lamont sighed, then gently brought his hands together in front of him, as though he were trying to clap without making a sound. A moment later, he pulled them apart to a width of about half a foot. And there, between his hands, was something like a figurine about six inches in length. My eyebrows rose in surprise as I realized that it was an exact replica of the mage-beast.

"I'll take that," Kane declared, reaching out and snatching the figurine.

"Go ahead," Lamont said. "Gloriana doesn't need it anymore. She doesn't need *me* anymore."

"Meaning what?" Kane asked as he brought his hands together, making the figurine disappear.

"Meaning that she has what she was after," Lamont explained. "The Salubrious Gem."

"So what's she going to do with it?" quizzed Gossamer.

Lamont frowned. "What do you mean?"

"How's she planning to use the Salubrious Gem?" Gossamer clarified.

Lamont gave her a look of confusion. "Isn't it obvious? She's going to use it to wake herself up. And after that…"

"After that, all bets are off," I said.

CONJURATION

Chapter 58

Following our conversation with Lamont, Razi tossed one of her beads at his feet. Golden strands of rope immediately shot up and encircled him, effectively binding him to the chair (as well as gagging him).

"So what now?" Kane asked his grandmother.

"I need to tell the rest of the Council what we learned," she replied.

Kane merely nodded at this. Under normal circumstances, the members of the Council would have all been present when Lamont was questioned. However, with Gloriana Mano running amok, having the leadership of the Kroten Venefici all together in one place had seemed like a bad idea.

"Anything in particular *we* should do?" queried Gossamer.

Razi shook her head. "No, the four of you have—"

She abruptly stopped mid-sentence, as if she had suddenly been robbed of the power of speech. At the same time, her brow crinkled, and I got the distinct impression that she was either hearing or seeing something that was imperceptible to the rest of us.

Correction: it was imperceptible to everyone else except Ursula, who had an expression similar to Razi's on her face.

Picking up feelings of surprise and alarm from both of them, I asked, "What's wrong?"

"One of the traps we set for the mage-beast," Razi responded. "It's been triggered."

"That's not possible," Kane stressed. "The mage-beast is still in its non-threatening form, with me."

As proof, he mimicked the silent clap that Lamont had done, allowing us to see that he still had the figurine. A moment later, he made it disappear again.

"Well, something triggered it," Ursula declared. "Jim and I will check it out."

"The three of us will," Kane asserted adamantly.

"Make that four," Gossamer added.

For a moment, Ursula looked as though she might push back on everybody going. Then she simply shrugged and we vanished.

CONJURATION

Chapter 59

We reappeared outside the Templum. There was no one around, but that wasn't surprising given the general belief that there was a killer on the loose. Ursula took a quick look around, then seemed to fixate on a spot about fifty feet away.

"There," she said, pointing to an object on the ground.

We all began walking in the direction indicated, with me noting that the object we were approaching looked like a palm-sized ball that was red-orange in color. However, we'd taken no more than a dozen steps before the ball began to glow, as well as expand in size.

I suddenly sensed dread, shock, and alarm flare up in both Kane and Ursula. Before I could say anything, the latter flicked her hand towards the rest of us and we disappeared.

****

Kane, Gossamer, and I reappeared in the Templum — specifically, in what I recognized as Ursula's room. Ursula herself was not with us, and I felt apprehension so profound coming from Kane that it bordered on terror. I was about to ask him what was going on when the entire room began to shake, accompanied by a noise that seemed to combine the sound of a giant redwood being uprooted, a skyscraper collapsing, and the roar of a tornado.

I immediately phased the three of us, a move that offered some level of protection in case the roof collapsed or the walls fell in. Fortunately, the tremors and the noise only lasted about ten seconds.

"Okay," I said after making us substantial again, "what just happened?"

"Finis-sphere," Kane replied.

I frowned. "You mean that ball we saw outside?"

He nodded. "It's the magical equivalent of a nuclear bomb."

"So that's what triggered the trap?" I asked.

"It was a trap, all right," Gossamer chimed in. "But one for *us*, not a mage-beast."

Of course, I thought. Gloriana Mano had gotten us to go investigate, then tried to blow us to bits (or whatever a magic bomb does to a person). Which suddenly brought to mind...

"Ursula?" I queried anxiously.

"Don't know," Kane said with a shake of his head as he walked towards the door. "But I do know this: we're not in Kansas anymore."

As he spoke, he opened the door. Outside I saw what appeared to be a lush tropical rainforest filled with exotic trees and plants. The call of birds filled the air, along with the drone of insects and the cries of wild animals.

Seeing that, I immediately understood what had happened — what had caused the room to shake wildly a short time before.

The magical glue holding the Templum together had come undone.

CONJURATION

Chapter 60

"I should explain," Kane said as he closed the door. "The Templum isn't just a single building. It's —"

"I know," I interjected, cutting him off. "It's a bunch of sections mystically welded together. But now it's come undone."

"The Hand of Glory did that?" Gossamer asked.

Kane shook his head. "I don't think so. If I had to bet, I'd say it was Ursula."

"Ursula?" I repeated. "Why would she break the Templum into its constituent pieces?"

"Because," he replied, "in the event of a threat, that's what it's designed to do."

I blinked for a second, mulling that over, and then it became clear. The Templum's design wasn't just for convenience; it basically served as a lifeboat (or rather, life*boats*). If the Kroten Venefici ever faced an overwhelming threat, the individual sections of the Templum could immediately whisk people to safety all over the world, and a mystical nuke probably checked all the requisite threat-level boxes.

"Ursula," I muttered, as those thoughts raced through my mind. "I need to check on her."

"Don't," Kane warned me. "A finis-sphere has arcane aftereffects that rival radiation from an actual nuke. You'd only be putting yourself in danger, even in phased form."

"He's right, Jim," Gossamer added. "You can't do anything for her."

I scowled, not wanting to accept this, and then groaned aloud in frustration. It felt like we'd been beaten without even putting up much of a fight. And Gloriana

Mano had barely gotten started, hadn't even physically awakened yet. And with that came a new thought.

"How close does the Salubrious Gem have to be in order to work?" I asked.

"How close to a *person?*" Kane said, obviously thinking aloud. "If the individual stones are any indication, I'd say pretty close."

"So Gloriana Mano would need it near her body if she wants to wake herself up."

"I'd argue that's a given," offered Gossamer.

"But her body's locked up in an undisclosed location," I argued, "presumably under armed guard. How would she get the Salubrious Gem close enough to be effective?"

Kane gave me a confounded stare. "You're asking *us?*"

"You're the magic-wielders," I shot back. "Who better to ask?"

Gossamer chewed her lower lip in concentration. "She's got a mage-beast. She could use that to clear the way."

"Except *I* still have it," Kane protested.

"Plus, I don't think she'd use it," I added. "Would she really want her pet monster battling armed guards near her comatose body? There would be bullets flying, grenades being tossed, and so on."

"So what are her other options?" Gossamer asked.

"I'm not sure," I admitted, shaking my head. I turned to Kane again. "Are you sure there's no way she can use the gem from afar?"

"She wishes…" Kane muttered dismissively.

I didn't have any counterargument to offer, but his statement triggered something at the back of my mind, and

CONJURATION

I found myself struggling to bring it to the fore. A few seconds later, I had it, and I turned to my friends with a stunned expression.

"The Wish Room!" I exclaimed.

CONJURATION

Chapter 61

We took a calculated risk with me teleporting us to the hallway outside the Wish Room. Basically, we didn't know what parts of the Templum — if any — might have been affected by the finis-sphere before the magical glue came undone. Therefore, we popped up phased, but from what I could tell, the place appeared unaffected (aside from ending in a wall, that is, as opposed to being connected to the rest of the suite).

I made us substantial again, and Kane wasted no time activating the globe; a moment later, we rushed into the Wish Room. I'd had no idea what to expect, but the scene was far different than anything I had imagined.

We were in the desert, with sand dunes in every direction, as far as the eye could see. The sun beat down from overhead, hot and oppressive, and I felt myself already starting to sweat. All in all, it looked like a scene ripped from the pages of an *Arabian Nights* storybook except for one out-of-place feature: a hospital bed.

It was located about twenty feet from where we stood and had a woman lying on it. She was dressed in a patient gown, with three objects resting on her torso: a large ring that was emerald in color and two gemstones of the same hue. A quick glance at her face revealed that the woman was the spitting image of the spectral image Ursula had shown us. In fact, her astral form stood next to the bed with its back to us.

The astral Gloriana looked back at us over her shoulder and a sly smile formed on her face as she announced, "You're too late."

The astral projection vanished. At the same time, the eyes of the woman on the bed popped open. She immediately sat up, then swung her feet to the side of the bed and stood. A moment later, she let out a scream.

At first I thought it was a shout of pain — that the hot sand had perhaps burned her feet. Then I realized that this was a shout of victory. A shout of celebration. A shout of freedom.

Gloriana raised a hand to the heavens, and a bright flash of lightning seemed to strike her out of the clear blue sky. It was accompanied by an earsplitting thunderclap, and kicked up a cloud of sand that obscured her from vision.

A moment later, the dust cleared, and I saw that the hospital bed was gone. Gloriana was now sporting the same black maxi dress her astral form had worn. In addition, she gripped something like a staff in one hand, while the other held a square cube with gilded edges that radiated a soft fuchsia color. Finally, she wore a necklace that held a half-globe pendant, inside of which were the ring and stones I'd seen on her torso earlier, although they now seemed to exude a pulsing jade glow.

Hit by a sudden inspiration, I tried to teleport the necklace into my hand. It didn't work. In fact, I had assumed it wouldn't, but still had to try. In essence, things on her person were apparently protected, but that was to be expected. She wouldn't have gone through all the trouble of getting the stones if someone like me could just take them away.

"Leave now," Gloriana said in a clear voice, "and you may live another day."

None of us said anything; instead, we simply attacked.

I dashed at her at super speed, slamming a shoulder into her midsection. She flew through the air about twenty feet, then hit the ground and went tumbling for twenty more.

Hoping that had knocked some fight out of her, I stood there watching as Gloriana slowly came to her feet. As she stood up, I saw that she'd endured more injuries than I'd intended. The sand — apparently abrasive (especially when bouncing across it at high speed) — had left her with bloody elbows and a severely scratched cheek. As I watched, however, the wounds began to heal.

The Salubrious Gem, I realized, staring at the objects in the half-globe.

Hoping to catch her off-balance, I dashed at her again. This time, however, when I drew close, my speed unexpectedly diminished. In fact, it dropped back to normal just as I reached her, causing me to stop dead in my tracks.

"Surprised?" Gloriana jeered, giving me an evil look and gripping the cube (which now glowed more brightly) in a meaningful fashion.

I immediately understood that it was the reason I was suddenly moving no faster than normal.

Having lost the advantage of speed, I teleported just as Gloriana swung her staff at me. Connecting with nothing, she spun around slightly off-balance as I reappeared a dozen yards away.

A crimson line suddenly appeared behind Gloriana, splitting the air vertically. A second later, daggers in hand, Gossamer stepped through the slit. She made slicing motions with the blades, and Gloriana howled, arching her back in pain.

Understanding that there was danger behind, Gloriana suddenly dropped down low and, in one fluid motion, spun around with her staff outstretched. The move took Gossamer's legs out from under her, and she hit the ground hard, banging her head.

There were now twin lines on Gloriana's back weeping blood. But, as with her earlier wounds, they began to heal as she stepped towards Gossamer, who was still on the ground. However, before Gloriana could do anything further, I teleported Gossamer a safe distance away.

Apparently understanding what I'd just done, Gloriana screeched, at the same time pointing her staff at me. I phased — just before a bolt of lightning flew from the walking stick and struck the exact spot where I was standing, sending up a geyser of sand.

Scowling at me, Gloriana sent another bolt my way. This time, however, it rebounded almost immediately after leaving the staff, as if it had struck a wall. It went flying back at Gloriana, hitting her in the abdomen.

I glanced at Kane, noting that he had his hands up and was frowning in concentration. Presumably he had put some barrier around Gloriana, for which I was grateful. Turning back to our adversary, I saw her doubled over in pain, and I thought I saw blood dripping from the spot where the lightning had struck.

Without warning, Gloriana vanished. I glanced around wildly, trying to locate her.

"Look out!" shouted Gossamer, who had apparently rejoined the fray, but it was clear that her warning wasn't directed at me.

Spinning towards Kane, I saw that Gloriana had reappeared behind him, swinging her staff with a speed that was not just uncanny, but unnatural. It whacked him across the shoulders with a sound that seemed to echo across the dunes, and he bellowed in pain before dropping down on all fours. She then raised the staff above her, clearly intending to impale him.

I phased Kane, and the staff passed harmlessly through him, striking the sand. Howling in frustration, Gloriana struck at him a few more times before realizing the futility of her actions. She had obviously recovered from the lightning strike and was intent on punishing Kane, who — either dazed or in pain — was still on his hands and knees.

Suddenly, Gloriana focused on the cube she held, and I knew with certainty what was next. The rosy light within it glowed for a moment, and then she turned to Kane and kicked him, landing a solid blow that sent him somersaulting through the air. Our antagonist had apparently negated another of my powers.

I put that out of my mind as I reached out telekinetically and caught Kane, then teleported him next to me.

"Thanks," he muttered as I slung his arm over my shoulder in an effort to help him stay standing. Judging from the kick he'd received, I'd be shocked if he didn't have any broken ribs. Then, wary of letting the enemy out of my sight for too long, I turned back towards Gloriana to find Gossamer engaging with her.

I had seen Gossamer go on the attack with her daggers before, and she was an excellent combatant. Much to my surprise, Gloriana was just as good, going toe-to-toe with my elfin friend while wielding the staff with only one hand.

Thinking I could give Gossamer an advantage, I tried to teleport our adversary's staff. As with the necklace, however, nothing happened. Even worse, I saw the cube glow again and had the sinking feeling that another of my abilities had been shut down. And if that wasn't bad enough, Gloriana suddenly got an opening and slammed her staff into Gossamer's midsection, causing her to stagger back a few steps before flopping onto her rear.

As Gloriana advanced on her, Gossamer suddenly extended her arm, throwing her dagger directly at her opponent's heart. To my shock and dismay, the blade passed harmlessly through her as if she were phased.

Gloriana glanced at me and winked, as if saying, *Thanks for the tip.* She then turned back towards Gossamer, whose arm was still extended from throwing her blade. Then, Gloriana's back arched wildly and she wailed as Gossamer's dagger, magically recalled by its owner, returned to her hand — passing through Gloriana along the way.

With her dagger back in hand, Gossamer scrambled away, heading for me and Kane as Gloriana dropped down to one knee. She had received what should have been a mortal wound, but based on past experience, there was no doubt she would heal in record time. Even worse, I felt a white-hot anger building in her, and I understood that she was through playing around.

As soon as Gossamer was close, I turned all three of us invisible, and my vision cycled over to the infrared. Being concealed in this fashion wouldn't fool Gloriana for long, but it would buy us some time.

Opening a telepathic channel between the three of us, I said, <We're getting creamed. Any ideas?>

<Nothing's coming to mind,> Gossamer answered. <She's too strong.>

"Where are you?!" Gloriana suddenly demanded. Looking in her direction, I saw that she had apparently recovered from being skewered with Gossamer's dagger.

CONJURATION

"Where are you?!" she shouted again, looking around. "Answer me!"

I looked at the ground, suddenly worried that footprints in the sand might give away our position. Thankfully, there were enough of them from our running back and forth that tracking us that way would be difficult.

"Fine," Gloriana said in a way I didn't like. "You can hide from *me*, but you can't hide from *this*!"

I didn't see her do anything in particular, but suddenly the wind started picking up. Within a few seconds, it was blowing sand through the air. Within ten seconds, the sand was hitting us with a bit of force, feeling uncomfortable against the skin. Within thirty seconds, the sand striking us was painful, and the wind was shrieking wildly.

The truth was plainly evident: Gloriana had created a powerful sandstorm that would strip the flesh from our bones.

Gossamer suddenly crossed her daggers, and a moment later the sand stopped buffeting us, although the sandstorm continued to rage. She had, in effect, placed a protective barrier around us.

<I can't hold this for long,> she confessed, <so we need to come up with something quick.>

I nodded, but was really out of ideas. Dealing with magic was not my bailiwick, with Exhibit A being how my powers were being whittled down. Kane could probably help if he wasn't injured. To that end, it was possible my healing power could help him, but I didn't know if we had time for me to try it. It would be a lot easier if we could get one of the healing stones from Gloriana Mano. In fact, it would be helpful if we could just get the stones *from* her.

And with that, the rudiments of a plan formed. I quickly shared it with my friends. Although Gossamer was on board, Kane seemed shocked.

<You...you know what will happen if this works, right?> he asked.

I nodded. <I do, but we're running out of options.> As I spoke, the sandstorm appeared to roar even louder.

Kane gulped. <All right, let's do it.>

I removed his arm from my shoulder and stood in front of him, ready to catch him if necessary. Kane concentrated, then performed the silent clap I'd seen before, and the mage-beast figurine appeared. Kane took it in his hand and seemed to stare at it for a moment, and I felt some sort of resolve harden in him.

"Ready," he announced with a nod.

I reached out telepathically, looking for the only other mind in the vicinity. It didn't take long to find it.

<Hey,> I said to Gloriana, <this is nice. Thanks for whipping up this breeze for us. It was getting a bit warm.>

<Where are you?!> she bellowed.

<Right over here,> I said, sending a mental ping to indicate our location.

Emotionally, I felt Gloriana's anger. It was so intense and overwhelming that she somehow never considered the fact that she could be walking into a trap. (Unless she simply didn't care or wasn't worried about it.)

Within moments, it seemed, I could see her coming towards us through the storm, apparently protected by a barrier similar to ours. Thankfully, she gave no indication that she could see us.

CONJURATION

I looked at Kane, who closed his eyes in concentration. A few seconds later, the figurine he held vanished, and I draped his arm across my shoulder once more.

After that, we all just stood silently in the barrier, waiting, with the sandstorm still raging around us. Suddenly, there was a sound — a noise like a scream of terror, so loud that we heard it above the storm. It was followed by another, and then wails of anguish, fright, and pain. They only lasted a few minutes and were drowned out by the sandstorm to a large extent, but what reached our ears was actually unnerving.

When the noises stopped, the sandstorm had passed. I turned us all visible again and, much to my delight, discovered that all my powers were back. Then, we walked towards the area where I had last seen Gloriana Mano.

As expected, she was still there, but one thing was distinctly different: she had been torn to pieces.

And on the ground, not too far away from her remains, were the health stones, the fuchsia cube, and the mage-beast figurine.

CONJURATION

Chapter 62

Nobody wanted to stay in the Wish Room with the remains of Gloriana Mano, so we left and returned to Ursula's room. We did, of course, take the health stones, cube, and figurine with us. (In fact, after putting his ring back on, Kane was fully recovered within minutes.)

We then waited around for the inevitable: the separate parts of the Templum being brought back together. According to Kane, that's what constituted the "all clear" signal, and he insisted we all stay put until it happened.

Fortunately, it only took a few hours. However, as soon as the Templum was once again a single structure, so to speak, Kane took off to check on his family, with Gossamer in tow. I realized then that he must have been under tremendous strain during that time. Most — if not all — of his family had been in the Templum when the finis-sphere had activated. And despite being unaware of their fate, he had still managed to take on one of the most notorious supervillains on the planet. In retrospect, his calm and poise had been nothing short of remarkable.

Much like Kane with his family, I was anxious about Ursula. It had been all I could do to simply wait while the Templum was being glued back together, but now I really needed to make sure she was okay. The problem was, I didn't know where to start.

While mulling over what to do next, I recalled that the suite had a well-stocked pantry that I had neglected thus far. Needing to load up on calories again, I went there and found a fair amount of items to my liking, including nuts, cereal, muffins, and more. I grabbed a bunch of them and took them to the dining room, at which point I dumped them on the table and began eating. I was actually on my second bag of family-sized chips when Ursula unexpectedly walked into the room.

"Hey," she said cheerfully as she took a seat. "Hope you saved some for me."

"Help yourself," I replied.

Needing no more of an invitation, she grabbed a bag of pretzels and began munching on a few. We then sat there snacking in silence for several minutes.

"Okay," I finally droned. "You want to go first or me?"

She shrugged. "Doesn't matter."

"Well, let's start with the trap Gloriana Mano set."

"Yeah," Ursula murmured in chagrin. "I can't believe I fell for that."

"So I take it that it was you who broke up the Templum, after sending me, Gossamer, and Kane to your room."

"Guilty as charged. Right before the finis-sphere detonated, I figured out what it was and got rid of you guys."

"What happened after that?"

"Fortunately, I was able to contain it — nobody got hurt."

"And afterwards?"

"I went to Razi and explained that I was the one who had separated the Templum. I also told her why. Believe it or not, she was very understanding."

"I would hope so. You clearly saved a bunch of lives."

"She seemed to think so as well," Ursula added. "Guess I'm growing on these people."

"Don't get your hopes up," I advised, causing her to chuckle.

"Anyway, I also went to talk to Lamont again."

"Oh?" I droned. "About what?"

"Curiosity about why the mage-beast came after me. You'll be happy to know he confirmed your theory."

My eyebrows went up in surprise. "Really?"

"Yeah, but don't let it give you a big head," Ursula teased.

"That reminds me," I remarked. "I'll be back in a sec."

Without waiting for a response, I teleported to Ursula's room and returned a few seconds later with a couple of items: the fuchsia cube and the figurine.

"Here," I said, putting them in front of her. "You're probably better equipped to deal with these than anyone else."

She looked at the figurine first. "Just to be clear, I'm going to destroy this."

"Can you?" I asked. "I seem to recall something about it releasing *sivrrut* explosively."

"That was in its mage-beast form. Like this, getting rid of it is a piece of cake. But are you sure these people don't want it for their little collection?"

"I can't speak for everyone, but I know Kane doesn't ever care to see it again."

"Oh?" droned Ursula, raising an eyebrow.

"Yeah — he had to use it to kill Gloriana Mano."

I then explained about the plan I'd come up with in the Wish Room of using the mage-beast as a weapon. Of course, Kane was the person who had studied those monsters the most, so he was the one most capable of getting it to do what we needed.

"Gloriana never shut the mage-beast down," I said. "More importantly, she never changed its directives. Ergo, when active, it was still driven to collect the health stones, and to kill in order to get them."

"So she was a victim of her own machinations," Ursula noted.

"Yes. I had been a little concerned because Lamont had said Gloriana controlled the mage-beast, so there was a possibility that she could make it stand down. But Kane understood that it really obeyed the person who activated it, so to speak."

"And Kane was the one who turned it on in the Wish Room."

"Exactly," I confirmed. "And he did it with that cube."

"Actually, Kane didn't really have to do anything with the cube," Ursula corrected, picking up the object in question. "I mean, it's what powered the mage-beast, but as long as it was within a certain proximity, the monster could draw on it and become active. Kane merely needed to flip the magic switch, as it were, that would trigger the monster's change into its other form."

"So the cube's the artifact Lamont mentioned."

"Yes."

"Hmmm," I murmured. "He told us it was in his quarters, but Gloriana actually had it."

"I think we all know by now that Lamont was wrong about a lot of things — particularly where the Hand of Glory was concerned."

"Well, something else just occurred to me," I said. "Both Gloriana and the mage-beast drew on the power of the cube. Why did the monster come out victorious when they fought, and not her?"

275

CONJURATION

"Remember our discussion about how there's a limited amount of *sivrrut* that human beings can handle?" Ursula asked, to which I nodded in the affirmative. "I think this was simply a case where the mage-beast could utilize more of it than Gloriana. In other words, it was stronger than her."

I stared at the cube for a moment. "So did that thing really siphon some of your power?"

"You know, Lamont really is a terrible mage, because he got that wrong as well," Ursula stated. "What actually happened was a little different."

"Go on," I urged.

She held up the cube, saying, "This thing actually was infused with an Incarnate's power at some point, but from what I can tell, it ran dry long ago. Much like the way one brand of car battery can be used to jump start another, they used my power to recharge it, in a sense. But what they got was kind of a corrupted form of *sivrrut*."

"That's why you said it seemed weird to you."

"Yeah," she agreed with a nod. "That said, it was still a potent form of power that could be used to do incredible things."

Like matching or negating my powers, I thought, but kept that to myself.

"What will you do with it?" I asked.

"Well, I can't leave it lying around here," she declared. "I'll probably drain it of power and then stick it someplace where it can't do any harm."

She didn't expound, but I recalled that the Incarnates had a special Relic Room that was full of powerful artifacts. It wouldn't surprise me if the cube ended up there.

"So what happens now?" she asked.

CONJURATION

"Well, I can't speak for you, but I'm exhausted," I admitted. "I was thinking of staying here another night and then going home tomorrow. Considering everything that's happened, anything longer than that might be overstaying our welcome."

"And after?"

I gave her a confused look. "I'm not sure what you mean."

She looked down for a moment, then said, "Do you want me to leave?"

"Huh?" I muttered. "No. I told you, I'm not mad anymore."

"You said that when you needed something from me. Things might be different now."

"I'll tell you like I told Kane and Gossamer: we're going to butt heads on occasion, but I don't foresee it stopping us from being friends."

"Thanks," she said with a smile.

"The real question is this: with this dark field or whatever around me, how long will it be before momma grizzly makes an appearance?"

She snickered at my comment. "Endow and I actually talked about that. Truth be told, she actually *wants* me where she can't see me. It'll help her learn to let go."

"Hmmm," I droned. "You know, I really like Endow, but I don't see her holding that position for long."

CONJURATION

Chapter 63

The rest of the visit was blissfully uneventful. Ursula and I had dinner that evening with Kane's family, then spent the rest of the night simply hanging out with Kane and Gossamer. It didn't sound like much to write home about, but after everything we'd gone through, it was more than enough excitement.

The next morning was more of the same to a certain extent. Ursula and I had breakfast with our friends, and then they showed us a couple of places in the Templum we had previously overlooked, including a greenhouse with singing flowers and a magnificent butterfly pavilion. It was actually a lot of fun, and before we knew it, afternoon had arrived and it was time to go.

With only an overnight bag, I was able to pack rather quickly. Ursula, as usual, carried no visible luggage. However, we had a last-minute change of plans: Razi asked to see me before we left.

****

We met in her study, and I was surprised to see her in a rather chipper mood.

"Thanks for coming by before you left," she said with a smile.

"No problem," I assured her, "although I was certain you guys wanted me and Ursula shipped home asap."

"Nonsense," she declared, pooh-poohing my concerns. "Nothing that happened was the fault of either of you. And you saved not just us here in the Templum, but the world."

I frowned. "What do you mean?"

"I was one of the people who went to retrieve Gloriana Mano's body," she said. "You probably know this already, but that room where you fought her really wasn't designed to show live locations."

I nodded. "Kane mentioned that before. Obviously Gloriana warped the enchantments around the Wish Room to provide access to her hospital bed."

"She did far more than that. She actually corrupted the wards so that she could bring weapons into the, uh, Wish Room, as you put it. Incredibly destructive weapons."

I frowned and was on the verge of asking what kind of weapons, but found that I already knew the answer. "Finis-spheres."

"Correct," Razi said. "An entire stack of them — enough to blast the planet to a cinder."

"Let me guess: she was going to use the Wish Room to place them all over the world."

"That's the assumption, but there's no way to know for sure."

I scratched my temple, pondering. "How could she build so many of those things so quickly?"

"Well, she had access to a powerful relic, so that could have helped. They could also have been a hoard she had stockpiled before she got captured. Or…"

She trailed off, looking away, clearly unable to finish.

"Or Lamont may have given her a hand," I stated, finishing her thought.

Razi nodded. "He's apparently enough of an idiot that he may have done it without realizing what they were."

"Could he have been ensorcelled?" I asked. "Not acting of his own free will?"

"He was obviously manipulated, but I don't think anyone forced him to do anything. It was unbridled ambition that led him astray, plain and simple."

"What will happen to him?"

She shrugged. "Hard to say. It probably depends on how much of this fiasco is determined to be his fault. Or maybe I should bear some of the blame. After all, he was *my* famulus. I had hoped that by giving him something constructive to do — by providing another path for him — he'd come to realize that he could make meaningful contributions to our sect without the need for magic."

"You can't blame yourself," I told her.

"But I was with him almost every day. I should have seen what was happening."

"Why? Because you're an empath?"

Razi suddenly looked at me in shock, as if seeing me for the first time. "How'd you know that?"

I shrugged. "Some of the things you say. The way you ask questions."

"For example?"

I reflected for a moment. "When you first met Ursula, you made the comment that she didn't *seem* evil. When we initially talked, it seemed like you were paying attention to more than just my verbal responses. Also, Ursula said you pushed her buttons during a recent Q&A, which implies that you knew what questions would trigger an emotional response."

She sighed. "The utility of being an empath is inversely proportional to the number of people who know you have that ability."

"The fewer people who know, the better," I translated.

"Exactly," she said with a smile. "If they know that you can tell when they're lying, they're more guarded." She then gave me a sly look. "But you already know that, don't you?"

I shrugged, not saying anything.

"Anyway," Razi continued, "the main reason I wanted to talk to you was to clarify my grandson's comment."

"Excuse me?" I blurted out, not sure what she was talking about.

"I don't believe you're going to get him killed."

"Oh," I muttered, then found myself trying not to grin.

"You'll put him in *danger*, but I don't believe you'll be the death of him," she said, smiling. "But my point is that I don't want you to leave here thinking that I consider you a bad influence or don't want you to be his friend. In all honesty, I think he needs more friends like you, and I told him that."

"You did?" I asked in surprise.

"Of course," she stated in a matter-of-fact tone. "In fact, it's exactly what my grandfather told me about some of my teammates over forty years ago. Right before he gave me the health stone ring."

CONJURATION

Chapter 64

Not long after my conversation with Razi ended, Kane transported me and Ursula home. It had obviously been an unusual visit, but he and I both sincerely mentioned how we looked forward to hanging out again. And then he was gone.

Reaching out empathically, I quickly found that no one was home and relayed that to Ursula. I then teleported to my room to put away my things. Afterwards, I checked my cell phone (which I had left on my nightstand) and found a couple of texts.

One was from Mouse, asking if I could meet him early in the evening to help with a project. The other was from Smokey, indicating that he and Myshtal were out running errands and planned to catch a movie later with friends. I then tried calling Electra to see if she'd like to have dinner later, but got no answer. Most of my friends, it seemed, were too busy for me.

Going back downstairs, I found Ursula in the living room, reading a book.

Looking up as I came into the room, she asked, "So, where are our housemates?"

"Out running errands," I replied. A moment later, my brow furrowed as her question brought something to mind. "Oddly enough, though, they didn't mention you."

"Well, I'm the new girl, so maybe I don't merit a mention yet."

"No," I said, shaking my head. "What I mean is that you were supposed to be staying here while I visited Kane. Instead, you tagged along with me."

"So?" she muttered. "We already know all that."

CONJURATION

"Well, from Smokey and Myshtal's perspective, you probably just disappeared. But there's no text to me saying anything like 'Where's Ursula,' 'We can't find her,' or 'That weird new chick is missing.'"

"Cool!" she blurted out excitedly. "They think I'm weird?"

"My point is that they should be asking about you, but they're not."

"Oh, *that*," she droned dismissively. "I left a note for them to find after I tagged along with you and Kane. It was in your handwriting, basically saying you decided to take me with you."

I looked at her in surprise. "You left a note from *me*?"

"Of course. If it had been from *me* they might have just thought I'd run away or something — especially since you'd already said I couldn't go with you. But a note from *you* has an air of legitimacy, like maybe you changed your mind."

"There's faulty logic in there somewhere, but I'm not going to worry about it right now," I decided. "Since we're on our own, I thought you might want to go to the mall and grab some lunch — my treat."

She gave me a coy smile. "Any chance you could take a girl shopping, too, while you're at it?"

I laughed. "Not a problem."

⋆⋏⋇⟊⟊⟊⟊⟊⟊⟊⟊⟊⟊⟊⟊⟊⟊⟊⟊⟊⟊⟊⟊⟊⟊⟊⟊⟊⟊⟊⟊⟊⟊⟊⟊⟊⟊⟊

We ate a quick lunch at the mall's food court, with me getting tacos and Ursula trying a kabob. We then went shopping, which turned out to be a lot of fun — more so because of the company than the spending of money.

283

CONJURATION

Ursula was just such a vivacious and fun person that it was almost impossible *not* to have a blast when she was around.

By the time we finished at the mall and made it home, it was close to the time for me to go meet Mouse. After confirming with Ursula that she'd be okay, I teleported.

CONJURATION

Chapter 65

I popped up in Mouse's lab. My mentor was nearby at a worktable, fiddling with some sort of electrical device.

"Hey," he called out. "Right on time."

I smiled. "I aim to please."

"So how was the trip?"

"Kind of a mixed bag," I admitted.

I then gave him a quick overview of everything that had happened (sans a few details related to Incarnates, dark fields, and such). By the time I finished, he had put aside the item he'd been working on and was giving me his undivided attention.

"Well, as you might imagine," he said, "we got word about Gloriana Mano disappearing. That put superhero teams all across the globe on high alert. The next thing we knew, reports were coming in that she was dead. No one mentioned your involvement, though."

"Fine by me," I insisted. "I wasn't angling for any accolades. I'm just glad it's over and nobody else died."

"Unfortunately, you're going to have to settle for at least *one* accolade," he declared. Then, clapping me on the shoulder, he smiled and said, "Good job."

"Thanks," I replied. "So what's this project you need help with?"

"Just some logistical support," he stated as he began tapping on the computer tablet he always kept on hand. "See that box over there?"

Still typing on his tablet, he tilted his head towards a nearby wall without looking up. Glancing in the direction indicated, I saw an oversized cardboard box that was about three feet wide and four feet tall.

"What's going on with that?" I asked.

CONJURATION

"Your old man's asked me to install some new equipment in his place," Mouse explained as he finally stopped typing and looked up.

"You mean the mansion?"

"Yeah."

I merely nodded in response. My dad was Alpha Prime — universally hailed as the world's greatest superhero — and his main residence these days was a palatial estate that made most castles look like hovels. Plainly, Mouse wanted me to teleport the box there. I had been hoping for something more engaging, but I was always happy to help my mentor out.

"So is it just the one box?" I asked.

"And *me*," Mouse chided. "Did you think the equipment would install itself?"

"I'm actually thinking you could have driven it there by now instead of waiting all day for me."

Mouse sighed. "Just take us to your dad's foyer, smart guy."

I chuckled and then teleported the two of us, along with the box; we immediately popped up in my dad's foyer, as requested.

When we arrived, I suddenly went on alert as I realized that there were a ton of people present. More to the point, their level of emotional excitement was sky high. And then they all shouted.

"Surprise! Happy Birthday!"

CONJURATION

Chapter 66

As unbelievable as it might sound, with everything that had happened recently, I had indeed forgotten my own birthday. Or rather, I just hadn't thought about it in terms of being notable.

In the past, I had generally only celebrated my birthday with my family — specifically, my mother and grandfather. With them currently off-planet, the day simply didn't seem to have any particular significance.

Bearing that in mind, I was indeed shocked to see what appeared to be a massive turnout. It was all my friends, other teens from the Alpha League, acquaintances, and more.

My immediate thought upon realizing what was happening was to turn to Mouse and say, "Did you do this? Did you plan this?"

"Not me," he insisted, grinning. "Talk to your friends."

I had then found myself being surrounded by throngs of people, all wishing me a happy birthday. Caught completely by surprise by the entire event, I could do little more than express my sincere thanks in each instance. In short, I spent something like the next two hours essentially being congratulated, shaking hands, and receiving hugs.

Eventually those in attendance spread out and started socializing, giving me a chance to catch my breath. To be honest, being the guest of honor was exhausting, but it was great to see everyone. Not only were the people from my inner circle there (like Smokey, Myshtal, and Li), but so were those I rarely got to spend time with, like my friends Vestibule and Cat from the West Coast. Also present were my cousins — Avis, Vela, and Monique — whom I didn't get to see nearly enough. Just the fact that they had all made this effort for me was very telling, and I was grateful.

At some point, I heard what sounded like live music and recognized a hit single being belted out by what I assumed was a cover band. Impressed, I followed the music to the ballroom and got my next surprise.

It wasn't a cover band on stage. It was the *actual* band — the actual *platinum-selling* band — singing their own song. Somewhat stunned, I looked around and realized I had overlooked some of the signature features of my own party: ice sculptures, multi-layered cakes, servers dashing about with trays of *hors d'oeuvres...*

My party was kind of swank.

More curious than ever about it, I started seeking out my friends, trying to find out who had orchestrated all this. After talking to Smokey, Vestibule, and others, the guilty party became obvious: Electra.

Honestly, it was a little surprising to find that my ex had pulled all this together. After our previous discussion about doing things that would involve just the two of us, a giant blowout birthday party seemed to send the wrong message. I also realized all of a sudden that I really hadn't seen her all night. It was possible she was avoiding me, but that wasn't really her style.

It took about thirty minutes of effort, but I eventually tracked her down by the pool out back. She was chatting animatedly with a group of friends, and I was suddenly reluctant to approach her — didn't want to come off as the stalkerish ex-boyfriend. Instead, I tried a more subtle approach.

Reaching out telepathically, I gently pinged her to get her attention and said, <Hey. Any chance we can talk?>

<Sure,> she replied. <Meet me in our spot in thirty minutes.>

I frowned, not really sure of where or what "our spot" was. I was about to ask for clarity when a familiar hand fell on my shoulder.

"Enjoying your party?" asked Mouse.

"Yeah," I answered. "I didn't realize I knew this many people."

Mouse laughed. "That's always the case. Your popularity goes through the roof when you're having a party."

"I'll try to remember that."

"Anyway, it's time for me to give you your present. Can you take us back to my lab?"

"Uh, sure," I said.

A moment later, we were back in the lab at League HQ. Mouse immediately began typing on his tablet.

"Up there," he said a few moments later, pointing to one of the large monitors that hung around the room. I simply watched the screen, which was initially blank, and then got a bigger shock than the surprise party when an image suddenly came into view.

"Happy Birthday!" shouted my mother, grandfather, and grandmother.

This time, my mouth actually did fall open.

"Mom!" I yelled excitedly. "Gramps! *Sxahnin!*"

They all beamed back at me.

"Where are you guys?" I asked excitedly.

"Some backwater galaxy," my grandfather said dismissively. "This touring-the-stars thing isn't all it's cracked up to be."

"Ignore him," my grandmother chimed in. "He's loving it. You'll have to try it one day, too."

"Yes, *Sxahnin*," I replied, addressing her with a grandmotherly term of affection that was common among Caelesians.

"Well, how have you been?" asked my mother.

"Please, Geneva," chided my grandfather. "It's an intergalactic call. Don't burn time asking the boy if he's had a cough."

"As you can see, your grandfather's as gruff as ever," Mom said. "If you were on fire, he'd just say 'Rub some dirt on it.' So again, how have you been?"

"Fine, Mom," I assured her, laughing. "I've been just fine."

CONJURATION

Chapter 67

I spent maybe twenty minutes talking to my family. It wasn't a lot of time, but enough for me to hear some anecdotes about their trip, and tell them a few of mine. I also passed along Razi's hello, at which point my grandfather grinned broadly and said to send her his warmest regards. My grandmother said the same, but there was a steely glint in her eye and a flatness to her tone that suggested her regards were of a slightly cooler temperature than her husband's.

After breaking the connection, I turned to Mouse and said, "Thanks. That had to be the best birthday present ever."

"No problem," he assured me.

"How hard was it to set it up?"

"It was a little tricky," he admitted, "but you know me: I love a thorny problem."

We both laughed at that, following which we chatted for another minute or two, and then I teleported back to the party.

****

Talking to my grandparents had reminded me of a few things. Specifically, I had recalled the party thrown in their honor before they left the planet. It had also been at my father's estate, and during that party Electra and I had had a small tiff. We had ultimately made up, but had spent much of the night on a high veranda facing the rear of my father's mansion.

I popped up there after leaving Mouse's lab. As before, the veranda offered a spectacular view of the

291

grounds and surrounding area. I was a few minutes early, but Electra was already there, standing at a stone railing and looking out.

"I was wondering if you'd remember," she teased.

"Of course I did," I replied, walking over to join her. "It was great being up here last time, away from everyone and just spending time together."

She gave me a brief smile. "I thought so, too."

"Anyway, I understand you're the person who put this little shindig together for me."

"Well, Alpha Prime paid for everything and provided the venue, but I guess you can say I did the planning. Do you like it?"

"I think it's great."

"Well, soak it up, because it's probably not happening again."

"Huh?" I muttered in confusion.

"Do you know how hard it was keeping all this from you?" she asked. "You're an empath, so nobody who knew could be around you today — at least not towards the evening. There was too much of a chance that they'd start getting excited about the party the closer we got to kickoff. And if you started sensing a bunch of people being excited about something on your birthday…well, you're not stupid."

"Okay," I intoned. "So how does that lead to no more surprise parties?"

"Because if your next birthday rolls around and everybody's avoiding you, how suspicious will you be?"

"Point taken," I said. "But you wrangled my mentor into your scheme, and he never gave anything away."

"We needed someone to get you here, and Mouse seemed the least likely to drop any hints, either verbally or emotionally."

"I can't argue with that," I said.

"I'm sorry," she apologized. "I didn't even ask yet: how was your trip?"

I sighed. "It's a long story; I'll tell you later." Then I winced as a thought occurred to me. "Gossamer and Kane…when they hear about the party, they'll think they got snubbed."

"Relax," Electra said with a grin. "I told them about the party before you even went on your little visit."

"So they're here?"

"Yes. They even scooped up your little friend."

My brow crinkled as I tried to figure out who she meant, and then I almost laughed. "Ursula."

"Yeah, that one," Electra replied, sounding indifferent. "Anyway, I got something for you."

She turned and walked to a nearby table. I saw her reach for something, and when she turned around, she held a large cupcake with frosting on it.

"Happy birthday," she said coyly.

"Thanks," I replied, taking the cupcake from her.

Knowing what was expected of me, I took a bite. I hadn't known what to anticipate in terms of taste, but it was actually pretty good.

"How is it?" Electra asked.

"Great," I answered truthfully. "I really like it."

"You'd better," she shot back. "I made it from scratch."

She then leaned forward, staring at my lips.

"Hold on," she softly muttered, eyes narrowed. "You've got something on the corner of your mouth."

CONJURATION

Before I knew what she was doing, Electra had stepped in close and put her arms around my neck. At the same time, she brought her face close to mine and I felt her tongue lightly touch the corner of my mouth. Next, she gingerly kissed the same spot, and a moment later moved her lips over to mine.

She kissed me then, deeply and passionately, with a fervor that made my head swim. Somewhere along the way, I realized that I had dropped the cupcake and wrapped my arms around her.

Eventually, she ended the kiss, but didn't pull away. Instead, she placed her cheek next to mine.

Then, with her lips near my ear, she said in a breathy, enticing whisper, "Tell your little friend that's how it's done."

With that, she stepped back, turned, and began walking from the veranda.

"Enjoy the rest of your party," she said indifferently, like someone giving the time to a stranger on the street.

Empathically, I felt her roiling with mirth and glee. It was as if she knew that — following *that* kiss — no matter how many platinum bands played, how many ice sculptures there were, or how much swag I received, the party was going to be a very dull affair.

THE END

CONJURATION

SPECIAL 'THANK YOU' TO PATRONS

I wanted to offer a special thanks to my Patrons below who have graciously extended their kind words and support to my writing efforts. I am both humbled by and deeply grateful for everything you've done and hope my work continues to entertain.

Alexander Rodriguez
Amanda
Benjamin Dahl
Christopher Stewart
Howard
Jacob Shaw
JJ Samuel
Kage Uzumaki
Phil Jordan
Ricardo
Ryxis Ackher
Stephen Caperton

CONJURATION

Thank you for purchasing this book! If you enjoyed it, please feel free to leave a review on the site from which it was purchased.

Also, if you would like to be notified when I release new books, please subscribe to my mailing list via the following link: http://eepurl.com/C5a45

Finally, for those who may be interested in following me, I have included my website and social media info:

Website: http://www.kevinhardmanauthor.com/

BookBub: https://www.bookbub.com/authors/kevin-hardman?follow=true

Amazon Author Page: https://www.amazon.com/Kevin-Hardman/e/B00CLTY3YM

Facebook: www.facebook.com/kevin.hardman.967

Twitter: https://twitter.com/kevindhardman

Goodreads: https://www.goodreads.com/author/show/7075077.Kevin_Hardman

And if you like my work, please consider supporting me on Patreon: https://www.patreon.com/kevinhardman

Made in the USA
Coppell, TX
06 February 2021